"If Levi marries before me, he'll get the ranch. I've worked hard all my life on this spread. My blood, sweat and tears are in the soil. Hannah, I can't let Levi have it."

"And I can't marry you right now, Daniel."

"Because you want love?"

"Yes. I want to fall in love. I want to be the center of my husband's world. I won't settle for less." Having love jerked from her before had hurt her too deeply to take the chance it would happen again.

Hannah sighed. Where was she going to go? It was obvious she wouldn't be staying here. Daniel wanted only the land; he didn't really want a wife.

"We have time, Miss Young. Levi's mail-order bride didn't arrive today. Until she does, I am willing to court you. I can't promise you love, but maybe we can become friends. I've heard that friends have been known to fall in love and marry. Who's to say it won't happen with us?"

Books by Rhonda Gibson

Love Inspired Historical

The Marshal's Promise
Groom by Arrangement
Taming the Texas Rancher

RHONDA GIBSON

lives in New Mexico with her husband, James. She has two children and three beautiful grandchildren. Reading is something she has enjoyed her whole life, and writing stemmed from that love. When she isn't writing or reading, she enjoys gardening, beading and playing with her dog, Sheba. You can visit her at www.rhondagibson.net, where she enjoys chatting with readers and friends online. Rhonda hopes her writing will entertain, encourage and bring others closer to God.

Taming the Texas Rancher

RHONDA GIBSON

HARLEQUIN® LOVE INSPIRED® HISTORICAL

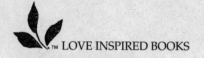 LOVE INSPIRED BOOKS

ISBN-13: 978-0-373-82985-9

TAMING THE TEXAS RANCHER

Copyright © 2013 by Rhonda Gibson

This edition published by arrangement with Love Inspired Books.

® and TM are trademarks of Love Inspired Books, used under license. Trademarks indicated with ® are registered in the United States Patent and Trademark Office, the Canadian Trade Marks Office and in other countries.

www.LoveInspiredBooks.com

Printed in U.S.A.

When my father and my mother forsake me,
then the Lord will take me up.
—*Psalms* 27:10

To the Bards of Faith, my life hasn't been the same
since you kidnapped me at an ACFW conference.
It has been much richer and blessed.
Thank you for taking a misfit into your group
and making her your friend. I love you all!

To James Gibson, my dream of writing books
would never have come true without your love
and support. Thank you.

To my Lord and Savior:
Who is the true author of my books.
Without Whom I'd never meet a deadline.

Chapter One

Granite, Texas
Spring 1886

"What are you doing here?" Daniel Westland scowled at his younger brother, Levi. He'd been running late, and seeing his brother standing there, looking freshly cleaned and pressed, was not what he'd expected. The wildflowers in Levi's hands spun daintily in the breeze that swished about them as the stagecoach pulled to a stop.

Dust filled the air, and both men shaded their eyes against the grit. As soon as the horses came to a complete halt and the dust settled, Levi answered, "I imagine I'm here for the same reason you are, big brother."

Levi grinned. His green eyes sparkled with mischief. Daniel's scowl deepened. Surely Levi hadn't sent off for a mail-order bride, also? But then again, maybe he had. Daniel pulled his hat farther down on his forehead to shade his eyes from both his brother and the sun.

While they waited for the driver to leap down and open the carriage door, Daniel thought of the woman within the stagecoach. She was a schoolteacher and had written that she felt it was time to have children of her own. The letter promised she had all her teeth, that she was twenty-eight years old and believed in God.

Daniel's jaw tightened. Once more he wanted to scream that he didn't have time for this, he had a ranch to run! Why his mother, Bonnie Westland, felt the need for grandchildren now was beyond his comprehension.

Truth be told, he wasn't ready for a wife or children, but his mother was feeling the pinch of old age. At Christmas she'd decided that her sons needed wives and she needed grandchildren. She'd proclaimed over dinner that the first son to marry and produce a grandchild would inherit the ranch.

Daniel swept his hat off and ran a weary hand through his hair. His mood darkened as he again noticed the fresh bouquet of wildflowers in Levi's tan hand. Why hadn't he thought to pick Miss Hannah Young flowers?

The two men's gazes met and clashed. Levi winked at him and then continued to watch the door expectantly. Why did Daniel let his younger brother get under his skin so? He shook his head to clear his thoughts.

Unlike Levi, he didn't have time to stop and smell the flowers, or in this case pick them for a stranger. He slapped at the dirt on his pant legs. He'd been more concerned about fixing the west fence on the ranch before he had to meet the stagecoach and his mail-order bride than he had sprucing up for her.

The driver set a wooden box in front of the coach door and then reached for the handle.

Daniel quickly did a self-inventory. His tan shirt hid most of the day's sweat and grime. Thankfully, he was wearing dark brown pants or he'd really look shabby to his new bride. His work boots were covered in a fine layer of dirt and mire. He knocked a chunk of dried mud off the hem of his trouser leg.

The sound of Levi's low, appreciative whistle brought Daniel's head up.

A vision of loveliness stood in the doorway of the coach. As she stepped down onto the wooden box, her blue travel dress floated about her, much how he would imagine ocean waves would look. Silky black ringlets framed her heart-shaped face. Stormy blue eyes scanned the small town and then alighted on him.

She held his gaze for several long minutes, and during that time Daniel felt as if his heart were being squeezed and his lungs had lost all means of holding air. He hadn't expected Hannah Young to be so beautiful.

Levi stepped forward and clasped her hand in his. "I'm Levi Westland." He helped her step down from the box until her feet touched the ground. "Are you Millicent Summer?"

Her voice sounded soft and almost musical. "I'm sorry, Mr. Westland. I'm Hannah Young." Confusion laced her pretty blue eyes. "I am here to meet Daniel Westland. Did he send you to pick me up?"

"No, ma'am. I'm his brother, Levi."

Daniel stepped forward. "I'm Daniel Westland." His words squeaked out, making him sound much like an adolescent instead of the thirty-three-year-old man he was. He cleared his throat and stepped forward, extending his hand.

She smiled and placed her small gloved fingers in his. "Nice to meet you, Mr. Westland."

The coach driver set two large bags down beside

her. "Here is your luggage, ma'am." He picked up the wooden box and replaced it inside the carriage.

Hannah released Daniel's hand and thanked the driver.

Levi looked inside the vehicle. Disappointment laced his voice. "Weren't there other passengers?"

The driver grunted as he climbed back aboard the stage. "Not this trip." He slapped the reins over the horses' backs, heading to the livery at a fast pace.

Levi stood watching them go. The dejected look on his face said it all: he had hoped to have a bride today, as well. Was Levi disappointed because he was behind in the game? Or had he somehow learned to care about Millicent Summers through her letters?

The look on his younger brother's face bothered Daniel. He squashed the feelings. He couldn't let them affect him now. Thanks to his mother's challenge, the ownership of the family ranch was at stake.

He returned his attention to Hannah Young and offered what he hoped was his best smile. "It's nice to meet you, too. Are you ready?" At her slight nod, he pressed on. "I thought we'd head on over to the preacher's house, and then enjoy an early supper before going out to the ranch." Now that the time to actually get married was here, Daniel felt as if someone had tied a big stone around his neck and was about to toss him into the river.

Would he ever feel right about marrying a woman who he wasn't sure he'd be able to protect and love? After the death of his sister and his inability to protect her on the ranch, what made him think he could take care of a complete stranger? If only his mother hadn't interfered in his life, he'd never have to find out.

He picked up her bags and looked again in Levi's direction. His brother stood off to the side with the flowers still clutched in his hand. Confusion furrowed his brow.

A featherlight hand landed on Daniel's forearm. "I'm sorry, Mr. Westland, but am I correct in my assumption that you are planning on our wedding being today?"

"Of course." He turned toward the buckboard, which waited in front of the general store. The sooner they got this over with, the better.

Her hand slipped from his arm. He'd taken several steps before he realized Hannah was no longer by his side. Daniel looked over his shoulder and saw that she stood where he'd left her, her arms crossed and a stern look upon her face.

He walked back to her. "Is something amiss, Miss Young?"

A new sharpness filled her voice as she informed him, "Mr. Westland, I don't believe that is what we agreed upon. Per my letter, we will not be married until I am properly courted, and only if we find there is love in our hearts for one another."

Daniel dropped the bags. He didn't like the firmness in her voice when she spoke to him. He wasn't one of her students, and they had to get married today.

Anger caused his next words to come out swift and full of emotion. "Madam, getting married today isn't something I relish, either. But it is what happens when a man places a mail-order bride ad and a lady accepts the offer. I did not agree to any other terms. I have a ranch to run, and the sooner we get this…" for a moment he faltered for words "…this marriage thing over with, the better. Now come along." He reached for her arm, figuring the tone he'd just used with her had scared more than one cowpoke into doing what he ordered.

She stepped back out of his reach. Determination laced her blue eyes and she responded in a stern manner of her own. "I don't think so, Mr. Westland. I sent a letter and told you my stipulations. By sending me tickets to come here, you agreed to those terms."

Daniel spread his legs and planted his fists on his waist. He ignored the grinning Levi, who'd taken a sudden interest in them. His sibling no longer resembled a dejected hound dog.

He turned his gaze from his little brother and focused on her. "Miss Young, I did not receive your letter and would never have agreed to your demands. Did you or did you not answer my mail-order bride ad?"

She offered him a sweet smile. Her blue eyes sparkled in the morning sunlight, much like a woman's jewels. Daniel felt sure she was about to say that it was all right and she'd be happy to marry him on the spot.

Instead, Hannah said, "Yes, I did. And I only did so because I thought you agreed to my terms. I'm sorry to hear that you didn't get my letter, but the terms still stand. I am not trying to be a demanding woman, Mr. Westland. But I will not be forced into a quick marriage."

Sweetness dripped from her lips, but determination filled her eyes. He could tell this woman was giving no quarter in their disagreement. He also realized they were gathering more attention than a bucking bull on Main Street.

He ground his teeth and scowled at his brother, who grinned back at him. This was not working out as Daniel had planned. "Come along. We'll discuss this over lunch." He walked back to her luggage and jerked it up.

Leave it to him to pick a bride who wanted to marry, but only for love. Why hadn't he gotten the missing letter? In the last one he'd received she'd said yes, that she'd like to come to Granite and meet him. Had she mentioned a long engagement? No, he felt sure he'd have remembered it if she had.

Upon reflection, he realized she'd said "meet" him, not marry him. His assumption that all mail-order brides had to get married might have cost him his ranch.

Hannah followed behind Daniel Westland. His straight shoulders and tight jaw screamed of his anger and confusion. She believed him when he'd said he hadn't gotten her letter, but Hannah held fast to the dream of marrying for love.

She'd already been left at the altar once because the young man didn't love her. It was too bad he'd decided to tell her so in front of all their friends and family. It was a hard lesson, but she'd learned it well. Now Hannah refused to marry a man until she was sure of his love and she heard him proclaim the words *I love you* with his own lips. Hannah didn't think it was too much to ask.

"Miss Young?"

She turned to see a smiling Levi Westland strolling beside her. He looked a lot like his older brother, with the same green eyes, even white teeth and sandy-brown hair. Only where Daniel's was short, Levi's touched his collar, and twin dimples winked from his cheeks. He was shorter than his brother by a few inches. "Yes?"

He cleared his throat and spoke in a louder-than-necessary voice. "If my brother isn't willing to agree to court you, I will. I'll even wait until you fall in love with me before we marry." Levi held out the wildflowers he'd been holding tightly, and offered her a bright smile.

If the situation had been different, Hannah would have laughed at the comical way he'd gallantly made his announcement. Levi seemed very sure that he could make her fall head over heels in love with him. Her gaze moved to Daniel as he lifted both her bags into the buckboard. What did he think of his brother's declaration?

Hannah took the flowers Levi offered and smiled sweetly at both men. "Thank you, Mr. Westland. I'll keep that in mind."

A low growl came from Daniel as he turned from the buckboard. Hard green eyes swept over his younger brother.

"Levi, leave Miss Young alone."

Mischief danced in Levi's face. His dimples deepened as he grinned. "Why, big brother? Have you changed your mind already?"

Daniel ignored him and came to stand in front of Hannah. "Would you like to eat at the hotel dining room? Or The Eating House?"

She squared her shoulders and asked, "Which is more private and offers a pot of hot tea?" Had Daniel changed his mind? She didn't think so. From the set of his jaw and the fire in his eyes, she'd almost bet that he hadn't.

"Probably The Eating House," he said, stepping to her side and cupping her elbow in his callused hand.

She marveled at the gentleness of his touch. Even though he was mad enough to spit nails, Daniel's hand betrayed none of the anger Hannah was sure he was feeling.

Levi moved to the other side. "I think pot roast and fresh bread are the special today," he offered as he grinned across at Daniel.

Hannah felt small as she walked between the brothers. She straightened to her full height of four feet eleven inches and was still almost a foot shorter than Levi. Daniel towered a few inches over his brother, making her feel even smaller.

Aware of the limp she'd attained as a child, she tried to keep her footsteps strong and even with theirs. So far neither Daniel nor Levi had mentioned her slight hobble; perhaps it wasn't as important to them as she had feared it would be.

Normally Hannah would have relished the silence among the three of them, but when she'd made the decision to start a new life, she'd also decided to become more sociable. Talk more, express more, live more.

So to break the tension-filled stillness she asked, "Mr. Westland, who is Millicent Summer?" She turned her gaze on Levi.

He cleared his throat and looked away. "She's the woman who answered my mail-order bride advertisement. It seems I'm not the only one who had that idea." Levi cut his eyes toward his brother once more.

Hannah followed his gaze. Daniel continued walking, but his jaw worked and his lips had thinned. Confusion warred within her. "But why did you both send for a mail-order bride?" She looked about the small town. Maybe there just weren't enough women to go around here in Granite, Texas.

"Let's get a pot of tea in front of you and I'll tell you everything," Levi answered.

Hannah nodded. A sick quiver churned her already unsettled stomach. She prayed it was simply because she hadn't eaten since the early hours of the morning, but knew it was her normal reaction to forthcoming bad news.

Daniel growled between gritted teeth. "Don't you think I should be the one to tell her?"

They walked toward a large building with the name The Eating House painted over the door. The fragrance of fresh bread drifted from an open window, which sported red-and-white curtains. Hannah's stomach growled.

Levi followed them and chuckled. "You should, but I didn't think you would."

Daniel ignored his brother. He released her arm and yanked the door to the restaurant open. His green eyes blazed in Levi's direction.

Hannah entered in front of the men. The rich fragrances of coffee and roasted meat filled her nostrils, but she ignored them. Her mind circled the question: What secret was Daniel Westland withholding from her?

Once more he took her arm, and began to direct her to the back of the room. They passed wooden tables and chairs. Salt and pepper shakers were the only objects on the tables. She was happy to see that the tabletops looked clean.

Why wouldn't Daniel tell her? What had he been keeping from her in his letters? She'd thought him an honest and hardworking man. The letters had hinted at long hours and a busy life. Hannah had been looking forward to working by his side.

Now dread caused her hands to shake. Daniel stopped at the last table and held out a chair for her. She laid the flowers down, slid into her seat and then clutched her hands together in her lap.

What did she really know of the Westlands? Had she allowed her romantic thoughts to put her in a mess of hot water? A new knot developed in the pit of her stomach as Hannah realized her friend Eliza might have been right. Becoming a mail-order bride might have been a bad idea.

Chapter Two

Daniel noticed Hannah's limp for the first time as he guided her to the back of the room. The sweet scent of honeysuckle drifted from her as he pulled out a chair and waited until she was seated before gently pushing it forward. Hannah Young was not what he'd expected. He knew from her letters that she was a schoolteacher, but he hadn't expected her to be a stubborn woman or to have a limp. Maybe he should put her back on the stagecoach and send her home to New Mexico. Ranch life was too hard on a healthy person, let alone someone with a disability. He wondered if it caused her pain, and realized that, come winter, she might suffer in her joints.

Levi hurried around the table and sat with his back to the wall, opposite Hannah. His knowing grin forced Daniel to reconsider his earlier thought. If he sent Hannah home, then he'd have to start his hunt for a bride all over again, giving Levi time to marry and have the first child.

Daniel thought about the conversation they'd had earlier in the week. He regretted taunting his brother and telling him he could always work on the ranch once he won it. The realization that Levi could still win and that the tables could easily be turned, and he'd be the one staying on and working for his brother, caused Daniel to frown. Would he be able to do such a thing?

The owner of The Eating House, Bertha Steward, hurried to their table. "Well, I declare. Daniel and Levi Westland, and who is this lovely young woman?"

Daniel made the introductions. "Mrs. Steward, this is Miss Hannah Young."

Bertha handed each of them a menu. "Nice to meet you, Miss Young." She wiped her hand on a flour-covered apron, and then extended it for Hannah to shake.

"Please, call me Hannah." She took Bertha's hand and smiled. "I'm not a big fan of formality."

The older woman laughed. "I like her, boys." Then she turned her attention back to Hannah. "You must call me Bertha. What would you like to drink?"

Hannah laid the menu to the side. "I'd like a cup of hot tea, if it's not too much trouble."

"No trouble at all. Boys?" Bertha tucked a graying strand of light brown hair behind her ear.

Daniel felt a grin ease onto his face. All his life Bertha had called him a boy. Even though he was now thirty-three, she still saw him as the six-year-old who used to beg her for cookies. "Coffee, black, please."

"Levi?"

"I'll have the same as Daniel."

"I'll be right back." Bertha hurried away to fill their drink orders.

Hannah studied the list of foods. "If everyone is as nice as her, I'm going to like it here." She lowered the menu and grinned at Daniel.

He noticed the paper menu shook slightly. Was Hannah Young nervous? Scared?

"They are." Levi laid his menu down and grinned across at him. "Well, are you going to tell her? Or shall I?"

The teasing in his brother's eyes irritated Daniel. "Don't you have someplace else to be?" He hoped his brother understood he wanted him to leave, without him actually coming out and saying it in front of Hannah.

Levi's dimples winked. "No. Since I haven't eaten today, I'll stay here and have lunch with you two." He smiled at Hannah and sat up straighter in his chair.

Daniel gave him his most irritated look. There were times when he wanted to strangle his little brother, and one of them was now.

Bertha arrived with the drinks and took their orders of roast beef stew and fresh bread. Daniel was aware of Hannah's gaze upon his face. He felt heat enter his neck and cheeks.

"I'll have your food right out." Bertha gave them all a big, toothy smile, took the menus and headed back toward the kitchen.

Daniel gulped his coffee, scorching his tongue in the process. He sputtered and grabbed for his napkin. More heat filled his face and neck. Could this day get any worse?

"Since my big brother seems to be having a hard time getting the words out, I'll explain why we both need brides." Levi picked up Hannah's hand and held it in his. He made a show of looking deeply into her eyes.

Daniel made a mental note to throttle his baby brother when they got back to the ranch. "I—"

Before he could say anything more, Levi interrupted.

"Back in December, our mother made a declaration that whichever son got married and had the first grandchild would inherit our family ranch." His solemn gaze met Daniel's, the teasing light no longer there.

Hannah gasped and pulled her hand from Levi's grasp. Her eyes grew large and her breathing became rapid. Was she going to have a spell right there?

Daniel could only imagine what was going through her mind. Her green eyes screamed shock and disbelief. He'd planned on telling her once they were married and settled comfortably in his new house. Why did his mother's words have to sound so cold when spoken out loud?

His bride-to-be cleared her throat before taking a delicate sip of her tea. She lowered the cup. "I see."

Did she really? Daniel didn't think so. The Westland Ranch should rightfully be his. He was the oldest, worked the hardest and he'd poured his blood, sweat and tears into the land. Daniel doubted any woman could understand.

Hannah turned her gaze to Levi. "In your letters to Miss Summer, did you tell her why you wanted to get married?"

He nodded his head, his gaze focused on his coffee cup. Daniel could almost hear his brother thinking that he shouldn't have written that part of his letter. If he hadn't, Millicent Summers might have arrived, too.

Hannah cleared her throat again, drawing his attention from his brother. "So why didn't you tell me?" Her soft voice held a sharp edge.

Daniel captured her gaze with his and sighed. "Would you have come?" He didn't think so, and in this instance supposed he hadn't been truthful with Hannah. He sent a silent prayer heavenward asking forgiveness.

His not being honest and her stubbornness would probably cause him to lose his ranch. *Lord, please help Miss Young and me work through this. I don't want to lose my ranch.*

Had she mistaken God's gentle nudge to answer Daniel Westland's ad? Hannah studied his handsome features. Strong jaw line, firm chin and the prettiest green eyes she'd ever seen. All that aside, Hannah had to ask herself, would she have still come had she known his real reason for taking a wife?

Truth be told, she probably wouldn't have. Getting married was one thing, but expecting a child immediately afterward was another, unless they were in love. And they were not. It was bad enough when her fiancé had left her at the altar. What would have happened had they gotten married, she came up with child and then he'd decided he didn't love her and left?

Hannah had thought she was doing God's will when she'd answered Daniel's ad. Now she had to wonder about that, as well. If she had known why he was looking for a bride, and it had still been God's will for her to come, Hannah knew she would have obeyed the voice of her Lord.

Heat filled her face as she realized that a number of minutes had passed since his question. She raised her chin and answered, "I would like to think that if God had deemed it so, I would have."

Bertha chose that moment to make her way to their table. She balanced three plates of food, a small basket of bread, silverware and a pot of tea on the large tray she carried.

She set the tray on the empty table next to theirs and then skillfully positioned everything before them. The rich aroma of the stew floated to Hannah as Bertha worked. When she had everything where it should be, she grinned. "Will there be anything else?" she asked.

"I think that about does it. This smells wonderful, Bertha. Thank you," Levi answered for them all.

Daniel nodded his thanks as well, but kept his eyes trained on Hannah. "Just holler if you need anything," Bertha replied, leaving to greet a couple who'd entered the restaurant.

After saying a quick prayer of grace over their meal, Daniel continued their conversation. "Now you can see why we have to get married today." He picked up his spoon as if to say the matter was closed.

"No, I don't." He started to protest and Hannah raised her hand to stop him. She struggled to keep her voice strong and even. "I will not get married without being courted or without love. Your mother said you have to get married and have a child. I never agreed to her terms, even if you did." She picked up a piece of bread and tore it in two.

Hannah focused on the bread. What if he said, "Fine, I'll order a new bride who will do what I tell her to"? Would Levi be willing to court her, as he'd declared earlier? Hannah instantly rejected that thought. She refused to come between brothers, especially since, from what she could gather so far, their mother had already placed one invisible barrier between them. Hannah wouldn't do the same.

The desire to get up and walk out pulled at her. She

fought the need to run. But where would she go? If only she could return to Cottonwood Springs…. But even as the thought teased her, Hannah knew she couldn't.

The people of Cottonwood Springs thought she'd tried to have a romantic relationship with one of their local teens, so they'd stripped her of her job, and most of the local gossips had lost all respect for her. Everyone seemed to have turned against her except her two best friends, Rebecca Billings and Eliza Kelly.

No, she couldn't return there. Self-doubt began to plague her. Was it foolish to hold out for love? Should she up and marry Daniel Westland just to have a roof over her head?

She thought about her limp and all the years she'd been teased, ignored or pitied because of it. Hannah wanted to prove to Daniel that she'd make a good wife. That she could work on the ranch and not be a hindrance to her husband. She wanted him to love her, not just feel sorry for her.

Hannah wanted love, she wanted security and she wanted respect from her husband, not pity. To have those things, she felt that she had to insist on courtship and the words "I love you" said before they said their vows. With that thought in mind, she squared her shoulders and lifted her head.

Her gaze clashed with that of Daniel, who seemed to have been studying her. Hannah lifted her chin even as despair ripped through her heart, taking her breath away. Did Daniel realize how much power he held over her at this moment? She prayed with all her might that he did not.

Chapter Three

Hannah still couldn't believe that Daniel had simply nodded and begun to eat his meal after she'd told him that she hadn't agreed to his mother's contest. Shock must have shown on her face, for Levi had grinned and winked at her. Then he, too, had turned his attention to the food in front of him.

When they'd left town in Daniel's buckboard wagon, Levi had followed on a white stallion. Every so often Hannah would hear the animal snort and Levi reassure him with gentle words. She wondered what had happened to Millicent Summer. Had the other woman gotten cold feet? Or would she show up in a couple days? If she did arrive, would that give Levi an advantage over Daniel's chances of winning the ranch?

"Oh, it's beautiful out here," Hannah said, bouncing along on the seat of the supply wagon. Red, blue, yellow and purple wildflowers dotted the deep green, grassy pastures. Cedars, elms and other short, bushy trees and shrubs peppered the landscape.

"Are we on Westland land now?" She gripped the bench she was sitting on tighter.

Daniel nodded. He'd been quiet the whole trip. Hannah wasn't sure if that was his normal nature or if he was punishing her for not marrying him immediately.

Levi brought his horse alongside the wagon. "We like it. Pa worked hard to settle this land and build the house and barn."

She noticed that he looked over her head at Daniel. What was Levi thinking? Since she'd come along, did that mean he'd lost the contest their mother had set into motion? Heat filled her face as Hannah remembered the rules of the game. The first one to get married *and* have a grandchild would inherit the ranch.

If it all relied on her having a child, then Levi was still in the contest. She'd not marry without love and would never consider having a child without marriage first. To redirect her thoughts, Hannah asked, "How long ago was that?"

Levi's horse tossed his head. He patted the beast's neck and then answered, "About twenty years ago now. I was only ten when we settled here. Daniel was thirteen, so he can tell you more about how life was when we first moved to Texas." His gaze shifted from her to Daniel, to a house that stood to their right in the distance and then back to her. "I think I'll ride on ahead. See you in a little while." With those words, Levi nudged his horse onto a dirt road and into a trot.

They continued on in silence. Once more, Hannah wondered if Daniel was a quiet man by nature. If so, he and Levi seemed to be complete opposites.

For a brief moment their eyes met. Tension crackled in the air between them. She jerked hers from his and looked at what she now knew was the Westland Ranch. *Lord, please help us,* Hannah silently prayed.

"I hope you will like it here, Miss Young." His low voice was like an answer to her prayer.

Hannah slowly returned her gaze to him. Daniel's lips twitched as if he'd thought about smiling but at the last minute changed his mind. He faced forward once more.

This was more difficult than she'd thought it would be. "I'm sure I will like it just fine." Hannah straightened her skirt and focused on the pretty scenery.

Sturdy oak and cedar trees towered above her on both sides of the driveway that led to the house. The wind filtered through the tall grass, giving her the illusion she was riding in a sea of green. Beauty abounded all about her. If only things were different between her and Daniel, she'd enjoy her surroundings more.

Hannah took a deep breath and then blurted, "Would you stop the wagon for just a moment?" Her hands began to tremble.

Daniel pulled back on the reins and turned to face her. His green eyes searched hers.

To halt the shaking of her hands, Hannah clasped them together on her lap. "When I answered your letters, I thought we had an understanding of what we both wanted. You wanted a wife and I wanted to be a wife, but I wanted us to be in love before we wed."

He nodded. "Go on."

"But since you didn't get the letter explaining about the courtship, and didn't understand the terms of the agreement, I feel as if we are total strangers. Is it possible to start over?" Hannah held her breath. She hated confrontations like this. She released the pent-up air in a gush of words. "Or should I simply ask you to turn the wagon around and take me back to town?"

There, the question was out. Now Daniel Westland could decide if he wanted to court her, and he could do it on his own terms. Although giving him an escape put her in a bad situation. She had no idea what she was going to do once they returned to town.

He surprised her by asking, "Why would you want to go back to town? I thought we had an agreement." His gaze continued to study her face.

Hannah wondered if he really didn't understand. "I know you aren't happy that I want to wait to get married. And since you didn't get the letter, I don't want you brooding and blaming me because things haven't worked out the way you planned. So I was thinking, maybe it would be better if I returned to Granite." She swallowed hard to ease the lump in her throat.

She couldn't hold his gaze one moment longer, so she shifted and looked straight ahead, to the two-story white house with a wraparound porch. Movement to the right caught her attention and she watched as Levi dismounted from his horse beside a red barn. Hannah could see a vegetable garden on the left side of the house; small green shoots were poking through the rich soil.

So this was the Westland Ranch. She'd waited weeks for this glimpse of a Texas ranch. Her heart gave a little lurch at the thought that at any moment, Daniel was going to turn the wagon around and take her away from the place she'd planned on making her future home.

A heavy sigh drew her gaze back to him. "I'm sorry, Hannah. I haven't made you feel welcome. To be honest, I really don't know how to act now. When we were going to be wed, I figured we'd work through the details of married life, but now…" He rubbed the knuckles of his right hand with his left palm and sighed again. "I just don't know what to do or how to do it. I'm sorry. I haven't been very friendly."

Hannah felt hope swell in her chest. "Is there a chance we can start over?" She captured her bottom lip between her teeth and waited.

His green eyes searched hers. "That's just it—I don't feel as if we've started anything." He looked toward the house. "I'm a man who thought he had a plan, but now that's changed."

"I see." The words caught in her throat. Hannah licked her lips and looked toward the ranch house in turn.

A harsh laugh tore from him. "No, you don't. If Levi marries before me, he'll get the ranch." Daniel took one of her hands in his and tugged on it to get her attention. When she looked at him, he continued, "I've worked hard all my life on this spread. My blood, sweat and tears are in the soil. Hannah, I can't let Levi have it."

She raised her chin and wet her lips with the tip of her tongue. He was asking her to give up her dream of being respected and loved because he wanted a piece of dirt. "And I can't marry you right now, Daniel."

He dropped her hand. "Because you want love?"

"Yes. I want to fall in love. I want to be the center of my husband's world. I won't settle for less." Having love jerked from her before had hurt her too deeply to take the chance it would happen again. Tears filled her eyes. She couldn't bring herself to finish that thought with, *and I want you to forget I have a handicap. I want to be treated like a normal human being.*

Hannah sighed. Where was she going to go? It was

obvious she wouldn't be staying here. Daniel wanted only the land—he didn't really want a wife.

"We have time, Miss Young. Levi's mail-order bride didn't arrive today. Until she does, I am willing to court you. I can't promise you love, but maybe we can become friends." He rubbed his chin. His five o'clock shadow scratched against the calluses on his hand. "I've heard that friends have been known to fall in love and marry. Who's to say it won't happen with us?"

Hannah mulled his words over. She needed time. If Daniel was willing to court her, she'd use the borrowed time to pray and decide what to do about her future.

Daniel watched her face closely. Did she realize her thoughts flittered across her delicate features like a butterfly flutters from flower to flower? Even before she nodded her consent, he knew she'd agree.

He also knew it was a stretch, but maybe he could make her fall in love with him and he'd still win his ranch. He offered her a grin. "Good. Are you ready to go meet the rest of my family?"

She ran a trembling hand over her hair and readjusted her hat. Hannah turned to look at the house. "I believe so."

Reaching across to her clasped hands, Daniel gave them a gentle squeeze. "You will do fine. My mother is going to love you."

As for him falling in love with her, he had no intentions of doing that with anyone. With Hannah having a limp, like his sister, he couldn't allow her to enter his heart. He'd made the decision to take care of Hannah, and keep her off the ranch and out of harm's way.

But as for loving her…

Daniel didn't think he could lose another person he loved to ranch life. His sister, Gracie Joy, had been ten when she'd been killed. He tried not to relive that night, but the memories started flooding his mind and he couldn't stop them.

Gracie Joy had loved the ranch and wanted a horse of her own. Because she'd had one leg shorter than the other since birth, their mother had insisted they get her a Shetland pony instead of a full-size mare. He'd tried to explain that Shetland ponies were often mean-spirited and had no sense of personal space, but his mother hadn't listened.

The morning they'd gone to get the little Shetland, Gracie Joy had been thrilled, and rode with Daniel over to the Carlsons' ranch to get him. She'd listened carefully how to care for the little horse, and had named him Lightning because of a white blaze that ran down his nose in a zigzag pattern. Mr. Carlson had laughed, and then explained that Lightning was afraid of storms.

After a week, Daniel began to doubt his own judgment of the pony. Lightning and Gracie Joy took to each other like kittens take to fresh milk.

And then it happened.

A storm blew in from the west. In his rush to get the newborn calves in out of the wet weather, Daniel and Levi had hurried to the pastures to gather them. Gracie Joy remembered that Mr. Carlson said Lightening was afraid of storms, and she'd sneaked out to the barn.

When Daniel and Levi returned, they'd found their little sister's broken body inside Lightning's stall. The doctor said it looked as if the little horse had kicked her in the head and then run over her chest in his hurry to get out of the barn. He said Gracie Joy probably never even felt the impact.

Daniel sighed. If he had been there, then Gracie Joy wouldn't have gone to the stables. If he'd refused to get the Shetland as he'd first planned, she would still be alive.

A soft voice pulled him from the nightmare of memories. "Daniel, are you all right?"

He looked into Hannah Young's heart-shaped face. Soft blue eyes studied him with concern. Daniel cleared his throat. "I'm fine."

He released her hands and focused on guiding the horse to the house. If he lost his heart to Hannah, and she died, too, Daniel was sure he'd not survive. In desperation, he turned to the Lord. *Father, I don't know why You have allowed this woman to enter my life, but I will do my best to make her happy and keep her safe. But please don't ask me to love her.*

Chapter Four

Gravel crunched under the wagon's wheels as Daniel pulled it up to the front porch. The sweet fragrance of roses drifted from the rosebushes beside the house. It teased Hannah's nose as he set the break and hopped down.

She watched as a woman opened the front door and stepped out onto the porch. She wore a peach-colored blouse and a tan riding skirt, and brown boots peeked out from under the hem. Her blond hair was pulled back in a braid that hung over her left shoulder. Hannah wondered if this was one of Daniel's sisters. She had the same green eyes, the same nose.

Daniel jumped from the wagon and then turned to offer Hannah his hand. She studied his stormy eyes. No longer did they look pain filled and haunted.

She laid her hand in his. He helped her down and then turned her toward the woman. "Hannah Young, this is my mother, Bonnie Westland. Ma, Hannah is my mail-order bride."

His mother?

The same shock that Hannah felt at discovering this

was his mother filled Bonnie Westland's voice. "Your mail-order bride?"

"Yes, ma'am. You said to get a wife. Here she is." Daniel pulled Hannah's bags from the wagon.

Hannah stepped forward and extended her hand. "It's nice to meet you, Mrs. Westland."

Bonnie took her hand and gave it a hard shake, then released it. "Same here."

Hannah felt like a cow at auction as Daniel's mother walked around her, studying her as if she were sizing her up before making an offer.

"What was wrong with JoAnna Crawford?" Bonnie asked Daniel, placing both hands on her hips and standing in a manner that indicated she expected an answer from her son, and fast.

Daniel stomped past them up onto the porch, his neck and cheeks bright red. "Ma, that girl doesn't have the sense that God gave a goose." With that he used his booted foot to push the door open, and then slipped inside.

Mrs. Westland took off after him. "I was talking to you, Daniel Westland. You get yourself back here." She slammed the door behind her.

Hannah crossed her arms. She didn't know whether to be insulted, annoyed or happy that they seemed to have forgotten all about her. Obviously, Bonnie Westland didn't like the way her son had chosen a bride. Had Daniel realized his mother would be displeased?

"I see you've met Ma."

She turned to find Levi approaching. His steps were long and even, as if he was never in a hurry to get anywhere. "I did."

Levi laughed. "Ma doesn't make a good first impression, but she's as good as gold."

A smile touched Hannah's lips. "I'm sure she is. But she doesn't seem too happy that Daniel sent for me when JoAnna Crawford is available."

"I reckon she isn't. Ma's wanted him to take up with JoAnna ever since we were kids." Levi walked to the horse and gave its harness a little tug. "Why don't you come with me to the barn? We'll let them hash that out before we go inside."

That sounded fine by Hannah. She nodded and fell into step beside him. "Why didn't Daniel want to marry JoAnna? It seems to me that would be easier than sending off for a mail-order bride."

Levi looked over at her. "Probably for the same reason I won't marry Lucille Lawson." He kicked a stone and watched it skip across the ground.

When they got to the barn, Hannah knew he wasn't going to elaborate without a little prodding. "And that would be because…"

"The girls around here are simpleminded and most of them are too young for us, anyway." Levi's face flushed the same shade of red that Daniel's had a few minutes earlier. He hid his embarrassment by unhitching the wagon.

Hannah leaned against a stall door and inhaled the sweet fragrance of hay. A mama cat looked up from the corner of the barn, where three kittens nuzzled at her. Contentment could be found here on the Westland Ranch, if things were different.

The mama cat licked her babies' faces.

When Hannah was a child she'd been content. Until the horse stepped on her ankle and shattered that contentment, along with the bones. She'd been saddling her horse to go for an afternoon ride when a snake spooked it and sent it sidestepping. Unfortunately for her, the animal had stepped on her ankle, shattering the bone. Hannah remembered the doctor and her parents whispering in the next room when she'd come to and the doctor telling her father that he should probably put her away. She wasn't ranch life material anymore. Her world had changed that day. People's behavior toward her changed.

Her father had no longer wanted his favorite child working beside him on the family farm. He'd swiftly made the decision she was a cripple and not good for farming. Horses were to be kept far away from her, and as soon as she was old enough, Hannah had been sent off to school, where she was trained to be a teacher. Feelings of hurt and anxiety filled her as she recalled being put on a stagecoach and sent as far away from home as one could go. After all these years, resentment and pain still lingered in her heart. Then she'd met Thomas, and he'd promised to marry her and create a home she could be proud of. Only that, too, had shattered with no more than a moment's notice. She'd pretended like neither mattered, but as soon as she'd completed her education, Hannah had run to New Mexico, as far from Missouri as her money would take her. She'd found working for the school in Cottonwood Springs rewarding, but not having her own place had left her far from content.

Then Eliza had invited her to come live with her, and Hannah had been happy for a while. She felt sick to her stomach as she remembered the humiliation she'd felt when Mr. Miller entered the school and found his sixteen-year-old nephew, John Miller, trying to kiss her.

"Miss Young? Are you all right?" Levi stood in front of her with his hands on his hips, reminding her of his mother. His concerned green eyes studied her.

In a shaky voice Hannah answered, "I'm fine." She straightened. Earlier, Daniel had said he was fine, too, but Hannah wondered again what had put that haunted look in his eyes.

His brother reached forward and brushed a strand of hair from her eyes. "You sure?" Levi's gaze studied her.

"What's going on in here?"

Hannah jerked her eyes from Levi's. Daniel stood in the doorway, staring at them. Anger seemed to radiate from the man like hot sun off a flat rock. She sighed and looked back to Levi, who dropped his hand.

"Are you feeling any better?" he asked, just loudly enough for her to hear.

"Yes, thank you," she whispered back.

Levi winked at her and then muttered, "Then time to have fun with my brother." In a robust voice he said, "I'm sorry, big brother, I thought since you left Miss Young standing in front of the house, it was all right for me to get to know her a little better."

Daniel stalked into the barn. He passed Levi and came to a stop at Hannah's side. "Get to know her like a sister-in-law and not like a sweetheart and we'll be just fine."

Levi tilted his head. "And if I decide to give you a little competition and see if she'd rather marry me, what then?"

Hannah couldn't believe what Levi was saying. She'd not led him to believe she'd choose him over his brother, but that's what he was insinuating. The first time they were alone, she was going to set him straight. She refused to come between the brothers. Although from the looks of things, they didn't seem very close. Still, Hannah planned on setting them both straight.

"I suppose that is up to Miss Young. She'll have to decide the right thing to do." Daniel directed Hannah to the barn door, leaving his brother standing there staring after them. Had he just called Levi's bluff? Or ignited the flame of competition in him? He wasn't sure.

And what about Hannah Young? She'd stared up at him like a newborn calf at its mother. Had she expected Daniel to fight his own flesh and blood over her? He continued propelling her across the yard toward the house. "Mother is waiting for you."

Hannah pulled her elbow from his hand. Anger flashed in her pretty blue eyes. "And whose fault is that?"

"I didn't say it was anyone's fault." If he lived to be a hundred, Daniel would never understand women. First his mother was angry with him for bringing home a mail-order bride, and now Hannah was angry with him, too.

She huffed. "No, you implied it was mine."

Daniel straightened his shoulders. "Well, you did run off to the barn with Levi."

"Because you left me standing in the front yard as if I was a stray puppy and not your fiancée. By the way…" she paused, then squared her shoulders, too, and tilted her head back to look him in the face "…I did not run."

"You two stop that squabbling and get in here!

You're acting like children," his mother called from the front door.

He had the satisfaction of watching mortification wash over Hannah's face. His pleasure was brief as his mother continued, "Wipe that smirk off your face, young man." She turned and stomped back inside the house, leaving the door open.

Daniel assumed that if she'd left the door ajar, his mother was getting over being mad. He'd known she wouldn't be too happy about him marrying a girl from anywhere else but Granite, but he hadn't expected her to be this angry.

His gaze moved from the door to Hannah. She looked ready to bolt. Once more he took her arm and propelled her toward the house. "Ma will be fine and so will you. You know, if we were already married, she wouldn't be able to say much."

Hannah seemed to ignore his comment. "You told her we aren't married yet?"

He followed her up the porch steps. "Sure did."

She sighed. "Good."

Daniel followed her over the threshold and swung the door shut behind them. Hannah stopped suddenly, causing him to bump into her, almost knocking her to the floor. He reached out and pulled her back against his chest and stomach.

Bonnie Westland stood in front of them with Hannah's suitcases propped in front of her. Her arms were crossed and her mouth was set in a hard line. She hadn't looked at him like that since he was a little boy. And then it had been a baby skunk and not a girl he'd brought home. "Daniel, I suggest you take your future bride back to town. She'll not be staying under my roof."

Chapter Five

Hannah gasped at the venom in the older woman's words. She thought Daniel's mother would have been happy that her oldest son had brought home a prospective bride. Hadn't she been the one to set up this contest? Hannah squared her shoulders and asked, "May I ask what you have against me, Mrs. Westland?"

Bonnie's eyes narrowed. "No, you may not." She looked over Hannah's head at her son. "Get this woman out of my house now." With that, she spun on her booted heels and stomped up the stairs.

The way she'd said "woman" made Hannah feel dirty. She spun on her heels in turn and stepped around Daniel. As she did so, Hannah saw that his mouth was gaping open and his eyes were wide. Obviously this wasn't normal behavior from Bonnie Westland.

Still, it hurt.

Hannah fought tears.

She stopped at the porch railing and looked out over the Westland Ranch. Cows grazed in the pastures and horses stood in the corrals. A pond could be seen in the distance and dots that might be ducks floated on its watery surface. Chickens scratched in the dirt. Several fruit trees stood off to one side, with blooms of various colors promising a healthy harvest. To Hannah it was the most beautiful place on earth.

"I'm sorry for my mother's brisk behavior. Normally she is not this ill-mannered."

Hannah turned her head and looked at Daniel Westland. His dazed expression spoke volumes about his confused feelings. She sighed. This day hadn't gone well. "Maybe she's right."

"No, she isn't." Daniel's gaze moved to the orchard. "She wanted me to marry and I will. But I will chose who I wish to wed." His chin rose stubbornly. The glint in his eyes matched that of his mother's.

"But where will I stay?" Hannah didn't know what else to say. Right now she was homeless, and disliked by the only woman she'd seen on the place.

"The schoolhouse." He picked up her bags and headed down the steps.

"You have a schoolhouse?" Hannah hurried after him. "Won't the schoolteacher need it?"

"School's not running right now." Daniel continued across the yard. His feet carried him over a grassy pasture to the edge of the orchard.

Hannah picked up her skirts and hurried after him. The sounds of a gurgling stream played in her ears as she looked about. Green, lush trees surrounded them as they continued on. She wondered how much farther they'd have to go. Just as she opened her mouth to ask, they came out of the orchard and she saw the schoolhouse sitting on a hill.

It was whitewashed and rather large, with two big windows looking out over the yard. She wondered if more windows were on the other side. A tall tree stood in front and she saw where a rope had been hung over one limb. A loop at the bottom indicated it was a swing.

Daniel's legs were too long for Hannah to try to keep pace with, so she gave up and looked about. Her sides were aching and she felt out of breath. The stream she'd heard earlier wound behind the school, with tall cedar and pine trees lining its banks. Birdcalls filled the early evening air.

A sense of peace enveloped her. The schoolhouse felt like a beacon in a storm. Could she be happy here? At least for a little while? Hannah believed she could.

She slowly began to follow Daniel again, watching his wide shoulders sway as he climbed the hill. He'd seemed annoyed with his mother, but not truly angry. Had Hannah chosen a man with a slow temper for a future husband? She hoped so.

He put her bags on the porch and then turned to wait for her. She was aware of his eyes upon her as she climbed the short hill. He had yet to comment on her limp. Hannah tried to walk without favoring her injured ankle.

She pretended to ignore him, and took in her surroundings. Wildflowers grew about the building and she wondered when the school had been built. It looked and smelled new.

Once she'd climbed the steep, widely spaced steps and stood beside him, Daniel asked, "Ready to go inside?"

"Yes." She felt a little out of breath.

He must have heard it in her voice because he said, "Good. I hope you can manage that climb. When I built the stairs it didn't occur to me that…" He let the sentence hang between them as he opened the door.

Hannah took mercy on him and continued his sentence. "That a small child might have trouble making the climb? Maybe if you added another plank between each step that would help. They are a little steep."

He nodded. "I'll get on that first thing in the morning." Daniel retrieved her bags once more.

"Thank you," Hannah said, entering the room. The scent of fresh-cut wood filled her nostrils and she inhaled deeply.

The bags looked small in his large hands. Hannah knew they were heavier than they looked. She had packed at least ten of her favorite books, along with her dresses and two pairs of shoes. The muscles in his arms bulged. What would it feel like to someday have those same arms around her in a tender hug?

She shook the thought off and turned from him to focus on the large room. A bookshelf filled each of the four corners. He'd placed a blackboard on the far wall. She turned and looked back the way they'd come. There were several hooks beside the front door, low enough for children to hang their coats and jackets on, but there were no desks.

A fireplace rested on the west wall, between two large windows that matched the ones she'd seen while coming up the hill. It was made of red bricks, and he'd placed a metal screen in front of it—to keep the children out and the wood within, she assumed. She'd expected to see a stove there, but was happy the fireplace was so large.

To the right of the blackboard was another doorway.

"What is through there?" she asked, even as she walked toward it.

His boots clopped on the wooden floor behind her. "That would be the storage closet, but I think we can fit a bed in it, and maybe a side table for you to use, until we get married."

Hannah opened the door to find a nice-size room. About ten feet wide and twelve feet long, it was much larger than she'd expected. Built-in bookshelves lined the far wall, and a window on the west end let in the setting sun. A smile touched Hannah's lips. It was perfect.

"Yoo-hoo!" The call came from the front door.

Hannah looked to Daniel. He'd already turned and was heading in that direction.

"Well, hello, Opal, girls," he said as he walked toward an older woman and two little girls.

A warm sensation enveloped Hannah at the pleasant kindness in his voice. It curled around her heart, creating a space of its own. During the past few hours she hadn't heard that tone from Daniel, but decided it was one she'd love to hear all the time.

Opal wore an apron over her day dress and a flush tinged her cheeks. "Your mother sent me. There is a bed and bedding in the back of the wagon, and I brought a basket of food, just in case you two might be hungry." She handed Daniel the basket and stepped around him.

Hannah watched her approach. After the reception she'd received from his mother, she wasn't sure what to expect from this woman.

"I'm Opal Dean and these are my granddaughters, Daisy and Mary." She pulled the girls in front of her and offered a wide smile.

Daniel set the basket on the floor and headed toward the door. "Thank you, Opal. I'll go unload the bed."

Hannah smiled at the children. Daisy looked to be older, perhaps eight or nine. As Mary chewed her fingernail and stared up at her, Hannah decided she was probably five or six. "It's nice to meet you all. My name is Hannah Young."

"That's a pretty name," Daisy offered.

"Thank you. I think Daisy is a pretty name, also." Hannah raised her gaze to Opal.

"I'm sorry about Bonnie's behavior earlier. I don't know what has gotten into her lately. She's normally very kind and levelheaded." Opal shook her head as if trying to figure the other woman out.

Hannah wanted to ask how she knew Bonnie, but felt it wouldn't be appropriate at this stage of their relationship. "I'm sure she was having a bad day," she murmured politely.

"No, she's just gotten ornery over the past few months. I'm her housekeeper and best friend, so I should know. It's not like her to be so rude." Opal stroked Mary's red curls.

Hannah didn't know what to say. If this woman really was Bonnie's close friend, then it would be best not to say anything at all. She was saved from answering by the tugging on her skirt.

Mary stared up at her with big brown eyes, looking almost like a miniature image of her grandmother. She pulled her finger out of her mouth and asked, "Are you our new teacher?"

Daniel set part of the bed down and answered before Hannah could. He must have seen the look of dismay cross her features at the little girl's question. "She sure is. I told you I found a teacher to start teaching you those ABCs, didn't I?"

Daniel snuck a peek at Hannah. Confusion marred her lovely features. His gaze returned to the kids, who were laughing and jumping about. These two little girls were a big part of why he'd chosen Hannah's letter from the stacks of others he'd received in answer to his newspaper ad. She'd been the only schoolteacher to respond.

His announcement was rewarded with a smile from Mary and a frown from Hannah. To avoid a confrontation with Hannah, he turned his attention to the younger female.

Mary's front tooth had fallen out sometime between yesterday and this evening, he noted, as the redheaded urchin nodded.

Daisy clapped her hands. Her pigtails bounced against her shoulders as she jumped up and down. "Oh, I'm so glad! We've been waiting forever for you to get here. I can't wait to tell John Paul. He hates school."

He realized he couldn't ignore her forever, and walked to her side. "I thought you understood that part of the reason I chose you was because you are a schoolteacher." He tried to keep his voice from carrying to Opal, who was squawking at the girls to settle down.

"How would I have known that?" she whispered back.

He ran a hand through his hair and tried to remember if he'd mentioned the new schoolhouse, or his expectations that she'd agree to teach the children on the ranch. With a sinking feeling, he realized he hadn't.

"Did you and Mr. Daniel get married?" Mary asked

Hannah, and then poked the tip of her finger back inside her mouth.

Daniel coughed to cover up his embarrassment. Surely Opal had already heard from his mother that they weren't married yet.

A nervous laugh exited the older woman. "Girls, girls. Let Miss Young get settled before you start asking her personal questions."

"John Paul says Mr. Daniel isn't the marrying kind. John Paul's sister has been trying to get him to marry her for years, and he keeps saying no. You didn't marry him, either, did you, Miss Young?" Daisy asked, moving out of range of her grandmother.

Daniel felt his face burst into flames. Hannah answered by shaking her head. Her eyes searched his face and he could hear the unasked question. Why hadn't he married John Paul's sister?

"I need to go get the rest of the frame for your bed." He hurried away from her accusing eyes.

Opal's embarrassed voice filled their ears. "Daisy Dean! Go play on the swing and take your sister with you! Don't get dirty!" She shooed both girls out the door.

Just as they passed him on the stairs, Daniel heard Opal say to Hannah, "I'm sorry. This hasn't been a good day for you, has it, dear?"

It hadn't been a good day for him, either. He stomped down the stairs and yanked another piece of the iron bed from the wagon as he recalled his day.

The west fence had been cut and had to be mended, so he'd had to rush to get to the stagecoach on time to meet his bride. She'd refused to marry him, and his brother had tried to steal her from him. His mother refused to believe he was going to wed Hannah and had forced him to find a new home for her, and now had sent the heaviest bed in the house for him to haul inside and assemble for the woman who wouldn't marry him.

Daniel tugged the heavy section of bed frame into the schoolroom and dumped it next to the one he'd brought in earlier. Opal stood hugging Hannah around the shoulders and talking softly to her. He headed back outside.

The sun was steadily sinking and he still had a bed to assemble and chores to do before he could eat and turn in himself. He jerked at the next piece of metal framing. This was not the way he'd thought his wedding day would go.

A movement to his right caught his eye. Cole Winters, Daniel's right-hand man on the ranch, stepped out of the shadow of the building. The serious look on his rugged face caused Daniel to pause. Cole normally greeted everyone with a lazy smile. As he came closer, Daniel could see he was covered in mud and a fresh, bloody cut marked his face.

"Boss, we've got trouble."

Daniel wanted to groan. Trouble seemed to be in abundance today. *Lord, I should have stayed in bed.*

"What kind of trouble?"

Cole grabbed the other end of the bed and helped him pull it from the wagon. "Jack Tanner kind of trouble."

Jack had been a thorn in Daniel's side ever since the day he'd hired him. The man drank too much and always brought some sort of bad attitude with him wherever he landed.

Cole walked toward the steps with his end of the frame. "The kind that started with us both in the horse trough and ended with him sprawled out in the mud beside it."

That explained the scratch down Cole's face. "So you were fighting." Daniel heaved his end of the bed up and followed him inside.

"'Fraid so." Cole laid his end down beside the other pieces.

"What started it?" Daniel asked, standing. He didn't see Hannah or Opal in the schoolroom, then detected the soft sound of their voices coming from the supply room.

Cole removed his hat and swept his chestnut hair off his forehead. "He came back from town drunk and as mean as an ole polecat."

Daniel shook his head. "Well, help me get this bed set up for Miss Young and we'll escort him back to town."

"So you're gonna fire him this time?" Cole asked, stooping over to pick up the bed again.

"Yep, no choice. He was warned. It's a shame, too. He's a good hand when he's sober." Daniel and Cole carried the bed frame into the storage room. He really did wish there was another way to deal with Jack. Letting men go wasn't his favorite part of running a ranch.

"I'm going to fill this shelf with the books I brought from Cottonwood Springs," he heard Hannah say as she dusted off one of the many shelves.

"Miss Young, where do you want the bed set up?" Daniel asked.

She turned and gave him a gentle smile. "Really, Daniel, just call me Hannah. After all, we will be married, so we might as well start using each other's first names."

So she was planning on marrying him. Daniel felt

as if she'd lifted a hundred-pound bale of hay from his shoulders. He nodded in her direction. "Hannah, where would you like the bed?"

"Under the window would be nice."

Cole didn't move to where she'd indicated, but continued to stand there, staring at Hannah.

Daniel gave Cole a shove to wake the hired hand from his apparent awe of Hannah. "Cole, this frame isn't getting any lighter."

Hannah's cheeks became a pretty shade of pink before she turned her back on them. Her hands worked at dusting the shelves.

"Oh, sorry, boss. I, uh, had something in my eye." Cole ducked his head and began moving toward the window.

Opal grinned at Daniel. "You two bring in the rest of the pieces and we'll put it together."

Daniel didn't know what to make of his friend's behavior. "Thank you, Opal." They set the section down, then headed back to the wagon.

Cole didn't look at him, but walked ahead. "Sorry about that, boss."

Daniel nodded. "I'll get this piece while you grab the other two." He bent over and picked up the rail.

"I'll be right back." Cole hurried from the schoolhouse as if his boots were on fire.

Did Hannah really have that effect on men? Daniel answered his own silent question with another one. Hadn't he stopped to stare when he'd first seen her, too? He hoped she wouldn't have that effect on all the hands on the ranch or they might never get any work done.

Chapter Six

Hannah waved goodbye to Opal and the girls just as the sun slipped over the horizon. She shut the door and bolted the lock. The schoolhouse felt silent and peaceful. After the day she'd had, silent and peaceful seemed wonderful.

She walked back to the bedroom and dropped onto the soft mattress. Her gaze moved to her suitcases. This day had not turned out the way she'd thought it would. Daniel Westland wasn't the man she'd expected.

She'd assumed he would be open, talkative and thrilled that she wanted to get to know him and fall in love before they got married. Daniel was far from those things. He seemed angry all the time, except when he was with the little girls. The man hadn't said fifty words to her since they'd met, not that she'd been seriously counting, and he wanted a quick marriage and children so he could have the family ranch.

But he was handsome, and when he'd talked to Daisy and Mary she'd seen a soft side of Daniel that touched her heart and took away her anger at him for not telling her she was expected to teach the schoolchildren on the ranch. She'd also seen the sadness in his eyes that told her he was a wounded soul.

And what about Bonnie Westland? Hannah hadn't given his mother any thought when she was writing him letters and had agreed to come to Granite to be his mail-order bride. Now that she'd met the woman, Hannah wasn't sure what to think of her.

What kind of mother pitched her sons against each other? And of all things, over a plot of dirt? Why did she demand that they marry and have children if she wasn't going to be happy with the women they chose?

Hannah turned the wick up on the kerosene lamp that Opal had lit earlier, and then walked to her suitcases. She opened the first one and began unpacking her books. The Holy Bible was on top, and she caressed the cover before taking it to the small table beside her bed.

After that she arranged *The Adventures of Tom Sawyer, Through the Looking-Glass and What Alice Found There* and the remaining books on the shelf closest to the headboard. She ran her hand over the spines of her favorite stories.

Hannah took out her shoes and lined them up at the foot of the bed. Her gaze moved to the other suitcase and she wondered where she should put her clothes.

Weariness tugged at her. She slipped her shoes off and placed them with the others. Opening the second suitcase, she pulled out her nightgown and then proceeded to get ready for bed. Hannah decided she'd worry about the rest of her unpacking tomorrow. Carefully, she folded her dress and laid it on one of the many empty shelves.

Before climbing between the fresh clean sheets, she knelt beside her bed and prayed. She thanked the Lord for her safe travel from Cottonwood Springs, New Mexico, to Granite, Texas. She asked Him to help her and Daniel work through their new relationship, and she prayed that Bonnie Westland would learn to accept her as a potential daughter-in-law. Once her prayers were complete, she pulled back the covers and climbed into bed.

The sound of hammering woke Hannah the next morning. She quickly rose and pulled on a simple dress. The noise was coming from the back of the building, and with the room's one window facing west instead of south, she had no idea who was making the racket.

Running her fingers through the tangles in her hair, she rushed to see what was going on. Hannah took a deep breath before opening the back door. Daniel and the man who had been with him the day before were working on a small building. The rancher turned with a soft smile. "Good morning, Hannah."

"Uh, good morning." For the life of her, she couldn't figure out what they were building. It was too large for a wood box and too small for an extended room to the building.

"I see that we woke you. Sorry about that." Daniel was looking at the ground in front of her. A frown replaced the smile that had seemed so warm.

Hannah looked down, too, and realized her bare feet were showing. The scars on her right foot were pale but visible. She felt heat flood her face. "I'll be right back." As quick as her feet would carry her, she hurried inside.

The horror that he and his hired man had seen the scars filled her with a sense of illness. No one had seen them since she was a child. Hannah had always been careful to keep them covered. She even had special socks she wore at all time, except when she was sleeping.

Now that he'd seen the scars, what must Daniel think of her? She hurried to her suitcase and pulled out a pair of stockings, then proceeded to put on her shoes.

The sound of hammering resumed.

Taking a steadying breath, Hannah decided he'd have had to have seen them sooner or later. She would have preferred later, but the damage was done and she'd have to deal with whatever results it brought.

She sank down on the edge of the bed. The thought had come to her in the middle of the night that she would need supplies if she was going to live in the schoolhouse. And as soon as she could get up her courage, she'd go back outside and ask if Daniel would escort her to town. She wondered again what they were making as she combed her hair and pulled it into a braid.

The hammering stopped, and Hannah stood up. She inhaled deeply to soothe her nerves. *Be brave, Hannah Young,* she silently told herself as she walked to the door once more. *He's just a man and you need him to take you to town. You can do this.*

Even if he is as handsome as sin and has now seen your worst flaw.

Daniel turned toward the sound of the door opening. He saw that Hannah had donned shoes and fixed her hair. Color still rode high on her cheeks, but her blue eyes held his. "I thought you might need a storage shed."

Hannah smiled. Even white teeth flashed in the morning sun. "So that's what you are making. I wondered."

"Ma sent over a washtub and a small armoire. I

thought you might like to have a place to store the tub and any supplies." He took his hat off and wiped sweat from his forehead. Hannah looked as pretty as the flowers Levi had given her the day before.

"That was very considerate of both you and your mother." She played with a ribbon on her dress. "Speaking of supplies, do you think we could go back into town today so I can pick a few things up?"

Daniel thought of all the jobs he still had to do. They needed to finish the shed, a stall in the barn needed to be mended and he wanted to check his fence line in the north pasture. The thought came to him that he could send one of his men. He turned to Cole.

The man was grinning at Hannah as if she was a slice of his favorite pie. He tipped his hat to her and said in a husky voice, "Good morning, ma'am."

No, sending her with one of the ranch hands was out of the question.

"Sure. Let me talk to Cole here and then we'll be on our way." He enjoyed the sweetness of her smile, which brightened her eyes and face. Strands of black hair had escaped the braid and curled about her rosy cheeks. She almost looked like a porcelain doll he'd once seen in a city shop.

"Thank you. I'll go start a list." Her skirt swished as she turned and reentered the school.

Daniel glanced back at Cole, who had picked up another board and was about to resume working. "I need you to take care of a few things while I'm in town."

"Sure, boss, you name it," he said, hammering the board into place.

He was a great worker, but at some point Daniel knew he'd have to talk to him about Hannah. She was going to be Daniel's wife, so Cole was going to have to stop looking at her like a lovesick schoolboy.

"Go to the house and get Levi to finish this shed. Tell Tucker and Sam to check the fence on the north pasture. Miguel and Rowdy can do the feeding today. Once you get all the men working, come back here and help Levi." Daniel put his hat back on his head and tried to decide if there was anything else that needed doing.

Cole laid his hammer down. "Sure, boss. You'd mentioned earlier that you might set up a spot for Hannah to have a garden. Would you still like us to start her a plot?"

Daniel didn't like him using Hannah's name as if he had a right to do so. "That's Miss Young to you, Cole. And while we're on the subject, I suggest that any interest you have in her, you put to rest."

The ranch hand coughed. "Uh, sorry. I don't really have an interest in her, but she reminds me of someone. I'll try to control my reactions when I'm around Miss Young."

Daniel walked over and clapped him on the shoulder. "That's all I'm asking." Cole was a hard worker and probably his best friend; Daniel didn't want Hannah to come between them.

He looked about the backyard. "How about we put the garden over there?" He pointed at a spot off to the right of the door, between the stream and the schoolhouse.

"How close do you want the garden to the tree?" Cole asked, surveying the land.

Daniel grinned. He could see Hannah sitting in the shade of the tree on a swing, sipping tea and enjoying the breeze. When he realized where his thoughts were headed, he squashed them. Yes, he wanted her happy, but he didn't want to be thinking of her in a warm way. He didn't want any feelings of love to cloud his better judgment. Daniel reminded himself that when he loved, others got hurt. They depended on him too much, and he couldn't allow either to happen again. "I'll leave that up to you."

"Would it be all right with you if young Adam had a look? He's good at planting things. He'll know better than I do where it should go." Cole piled the wood, hammers and nails together.

"I'd forgotten Adam. Yes, give him that job. I'll leave what you do up to you. I know you'll take care of whatever else needs to be done." Daniel wanted Cole to know he bore no hard feelings over Hannah.

Cole acknowledged the praise with a nod. "I'll get started, then." He walked to his horse and mounted. As he came even with Daniel, he stopped, leaned on his saddle horn and advised, "Daniel, enjoy your day in town today. You work too hard and don't play enough." He didn't give him a chance to respond, simply turned his horse and sent her into a gallop toward the ranch house.

Maybe Cole was right. He should try to enjoy the day. It wasn't like they were getting married while in town. Besides, the sooner he convinced Hannah she was in love with him, the sooner they'd get married, have a baby and he'd inherit the ranch. Winning the ranch was the true goal, and he'd have to wed to get it. With that thought in mind, Daniel squared his shoulders in anticipation of making Hannah fall in love with him without losing his heart to her.

Chapter Seven

Hannah held tightly to her list. She didn't know what to think of Daniel's easy, laid-back behavior today. He'd helped her into the wagon and then began telling her about the ranch he loved so much.

She learned that it was over one hundred acres of the best cattle land in the state of Texas, with three large ponds, and a spring-fed river running through it. The Larsons were on the west, the Montoyas' spread lay to the south, the Crawfords' land lay to the east and the Johnsons were on the north.

Daniel seemed to love every inch of the property, from the grazing pastures to the small patches of wood that surrounded the bodies of water. He talked about the wildlife and warned of rattlesnakes.

The thought of snakes sent a shiver down her spine. To take her mind off the reptiles, Hannah focused on Daniel. She watched his lips as he spoke.

"I am looking forward to the day I can take you down to the canyons. They are on the west corner of the ranch and are beautiful during the summer. The sunsets are perfect there. Would you like to go with me to see them? We could have an evening picnic." His lips parted in a smile.

Hannah would love to accompany him, but wanted to make sure he understood it would have to be a proper outing. "I'd love to, after we are married."

A grin tilted his mouth. "I'm sure the preacher would have no trouble hitching us today, if you'd like." The teasing glint in his eyes told her he wasn't really proposing they marry today.

"It's a mighty tempting offer, Mr. Westland, but I think I'll wait until your heart aligns up with your words before I say I do." She smiled back.

He winked at her and then turned his attention back to driving the team. "Fair enough." Daniel slapped the reins over the mares' backs and sent them trotting into town.

Since it was Saturday, the main road was busy with families in buckboards and lone riders on horseback traveling from business to business. Dust kicked up from all the traffic. Hannah covered her mouth with her handkerchief and glanced about.

Yesterday she hadn't taken the time to really look at the place.

Granite seemed to be a working town, with no frills that she could see. Each store looked the same: raw wood fronts, no paint, no trees and no flowers. A few of the rustic buildings, such as the general store, had benches sitting on the boardwalk beside their windows. Water troughs were lined up on the dirt street in front of the mercantile, the hotel, the bank and what looked like a saloon toward the end of town.

Hannah jerked her gaze away from the saloon. It

wasn't a bad town; it just wasn't as pretty as Cottonwood Springs, at least not in her eyes.

Up the hillside sat the church, which also served as
the school. It was the only building in town that sported
paint. Unlike her school, this one had no trees to offer
shade to the children.

She missed the new trees that had recently been
planted and the freshly painted flower boxes that stood
in front of most Cottonwood Springs businesses. Hannah wondered if there was a ladies group she could
join. Perhaps they could work together to beautify the
town a little.

Daniel stopped in front of the general store. "It's
not much to look at, is it?" he asked, setting the break.
Hannah smiled at him.

"Not now, but it could be." She watched as he leaped
from the wagon and came to her side to help her down.

"Miss Young, I don't believe I like that glint in your
eyes," he teased, as her feet touched the hard ground.
"Makes me think you might be up to something."

She held on to his arms. "Who, me? I just arrived,
Mr. Westland. What could I possibly be up to?"

Daniel laughed down at her. His green eyes sparkled.
The richness of his laughter quickened the beat of her
heart and tickled her funny bone, causing her to giggle.

His hands felt warm against the fabric at her waist.
Hannah thought she could get used to being around
Daniel when he was in this mood. Maybe her first impression of him, that he wanted her around only for
business reasons, had been wrong. Dare she hope?

Daniel released Hannah and tucked her small hand
into his. He enjoyed the sound of her sweet laughter

and the feel of her soft palm. "Get whatever you need at the general store and have it put on my personal account."

A frown creased her forehead. "I don't know."

He stopped her by shaking his head. "You are going to be my wife, so you should go ahead and start getting things you think we will need. No one will question that." He opened the door and allowed her to enter first.

Hannah whispered, "But it might get too expensive. I'd prefer you look at my list and then decide what I should and shouldn't buy today." She held it out to him.

Daniel glanced toward the back of the store, where two gentlemen were playing checkers by the window. He nodded as he recognized the town doctor and Mr. Carlson. Daniel returned his attention to Hannah, not bothering to read her list. "Get everything."

She murmured for his ears only, "But you didn't even look at the list. It's going to be expensive." Her blue eyes echoed the concern in her voice.

Daniel grinned. She really didn't know that if she married him, she'd be wedding a wealthy man. He turned her toward him, leaned forward until their cheeks were almost touching and whispered, "I can afford whatever you want or need. I'm not a poor man, Hannah."

Her eyes widened as understanding dawned. "Oh, I see. I should have realized. Well, thank you."

Daniel enjoyed the way color filled her face, the soft smile she offered and the way her eyes turned into a river of deep blue. It was no wonder Cole couldn't seem to tear his gaze from her. Hannah Young was a beautiful woman.

"I, uh, need to go to the livery and see a man. I'll

be back in a little while." Daniel dropped her hand and spun on his heels, not liking the path his thoughts had taken.

Hannah watched as his long legs carried him from the store in a rush. The bell jingled as the door closed behind him. Why had he left so quickly? Was it something she'd said? Or had he embarrassed himself by confessing his wealth?

"Is there something I can help you find?" The soft voice came from behind her.

Hannah turned to discover a tall woman with blond hair and clear blue eyes studying her with interest. A dimple graced her cheek. She wore a simple dress with a large apron over her swollen stomach, and a pencil was stuck in the hair over her left ear.

Hannah returned her smile. "I hope so, as my list is rather long." Once more her gaze moved to the woman's swollen stomach and she felt bad that she had bags of sugar, flour, beans and rice to buy.

The woman took the list. "I'm Carolyn Moore. My husband and I own the store. I'll be happy to help you find everything you require." She chuckled as she looked over the paper. "At least I hope we have everything on here."

"Thank you, Mrs. Moore." Hannah wanted to introduce herself, but didn't really know how. If she followed Carolyn's example, she'd have to say something like, "I'm Hannah Young, Daniel Westland's mail-order bride." She really didn't want people referring to her that way.

"I see you have five slates on your list. Are you a teacher?" Mrs. Moore asked.

Hannah almost sighed. There was her answer. "Yes, I'm Hannah Young. I'll be starting classes out on the Westland Ranch for the children who live too far from town to attend here."

"That is wonderful. Those kids really do need an education. I was just telling Wilson—that's my husband—the other day that I wish there was someone who could teach those young'uns." She walked over to a shelf and pulled out the slates. "When will you be starting classes?"

Hannah followed her and said, "I'm thinking next week. We'll have classes during the middle of the day, when it's the hottest. That way the children can do their chores and still get an education. During harvest season we'll take a break and then start up winter sessions at the beginning of the year."

Hannah ran her hand over the books on display. Would her budget allow her to splurge and buy a couple? She missed the books she'd had to leave behind. Hopefully, Cottonwood Springs's new schoolteacher would find some use for them.

"That sounds like a great schedule to me. You've considered the children, the parents and the best way to get their education in." Carolyn Moore moved to the counter and laid down the requested slates.

Hannah continued to study the books. "Thank you." She didn't recognize several of the titles. Were they new, or just new to her?

The shopkeeper continued to gather items on the list and place them on the counter. "Mr. Richards, the schoolmaster here in town, has almost every book on that shelf. He's always ordering something new. I try to order two copies. That way I have an extra for our customers." She reached behind her for a tin of mint tea.

What was Mr. Richards like? Was he older? Younger? Hannah wondered if she should introduce herself to him.

"It's going to take me a little while to get everything on your list boxed up if you'd like to walk over to the school and meet him," Carolyn offered with a knowing look.

Hannah nodded. "I would like to introduce myself to him. He will probably know where the ranch children are in their studies." She glanced about the store. It would be nice to just browse, but that could wait for another day. "Would you let Mr. Westland know I've walked up to the schoolhouse?"

"I will. You might beat him back. The men at the livery love to talk."

A man at the back of the room made a huffing noise. "And you womenfolk don't."

Hannah peered at the gentleman who had spoken. A twinkle lit his grayish-blue eyes. He appeared to be in his late sixties or early seventies.

"Now, Pa…" A stern warning sounded in Carolyn's voice. "You best pay attention to your checker game or Doc Bryant is going to beat you again."

The man opposite her father laughed. He was younger, probably in his thirties, and as handsome as sin. His brown hair was a little wild and his brown eyes were as soft as a doe's. "Ole Phil here has already lost." He removed his opponent's last checker.

"Well, it's those womenfolks' fault. They were talkin' too loud," Phil answered as he frowned down at the board.

Dr. Bryant stood and clapped a hand on his shoulder. "Thanks for the game, Phil. I need to be heading out to the Larson place. Jack Larson has a nasty cut on his leg that needs tending."

"Thanks for letting Mr. Westland know where I'll be, Mrs. Moore," Hannah said, turning to leave.

The doctor beat her to the door and held it open. As they stepped out onto the boardwalk he asked, "Mind if I walk with you for a bit?"

"You are free to walk wherever you please, Mr. Bryant," Hannah answered kindly. She wondered why the doctor wanted to walk with her.

"The Larsons live just over the hill from the schoolhouse. We're going in the same direction," he said as he slowed his steps to match hers.

Had he read her unspoken question on her face? She looked down and noticed his empty hands. "Won't you need your bag?"

"Not for this visit. I'm basically going to check the wound and make sure it's clear of infection. Whatever I might need, Mrs. Larson will have on hand." He grinned across at her.

The doctor was handsome, but Hannah couldn't help but compare him to Daniel. Her future husband had a rugged quality about him that she discovered she appreciated more than the doctor's clean-cut look and soft brown eyes. Hannah looked to the schoolhouse that now stood a few feet away.

"Thank you for accompanying me to the schoolhouse, Doctor." Hannah hurried her footsteps. When she had climbed the steps, she turned back to him.

He grinned and bowed at the waist. "The pleasure

was all mine." Then the doctor put his hands in his pockets, whistled a merry tone and walked away.

She watched him go. Yes, if she'd had to choose between the two men, Daniel Westland would have been her first choice. The doctor reminded her too much of Thomas and the scar he'd left upon her heart.

Chapter Eight

Daniel sat across the table from the minister. They'd met by the livery and then walked over to The Eating House. Sitting at the table, he held his coffee and blew into it. "I thought I'd be a married man by today, but Hannah wants love before marriage." He sipped the bitter brew. "And Ma seems to have lost her mind. She insisted I get a bride, but when I brought one home she wouldn't even let her stay in the same house."

Reverend Robert Lincoln shook his head and laughed. "I imagine your mother thought that if Hannah didn't have a place to live, she'd marry you, and the two of you would move into that big house you had built. You did ask Hannah to marry you again, didn't you?"

Daniel lowered his cup. "You mean after Ma kicked her out?"

"That would have been a good time to do so, don't you think?" The minister's twinkling blue eyes revealed he'd already guessed Daniel hadn't thought of that.

Why hadn't he? Had he subconsciously avoided marrying Hannah? The impulse to smack himself on the forehead overwhelmed him, and he did just that. "No, I took her to the new schoolhouse."

The preacher chuckled. "Where is she now?"

Daniel groaned. "Over at the general store buying supplies." He picked up his cup again and cradled it in his hands. "I don't know the first thing about making a woman fall in love with me." He stared into the dark liquid.

A serious tone entered the preacher's voice. "Be yourself, Daniel. A woman wants to know the real man, not someone made up to please her."

He looked into the minister's eyes. "You don't understand. If Levi's mail-order bride shows up and he marries her and they have a baby first, then my brother inherits the ranch. Not just a corner of it—the whole thing." Daniel heard the desperation in his voice and avoided the other man's gaze by looking out the window.

Gentleness entered the preacher's voice. "I know the terms of your mother's demands, but I also know a woman's heart."

Whose heart did the reverend think he knew? His mother's? Or Hannah's? Had his mother been trying to push them into marriage? Daniel hadn't really spoken to her about what had happened the day before.

And then there was Hannah. She'd seemed to enjoy the ride into town and had even teased him. If Daniel continued to be open with her and tell her about his life, maybe she'd fall in love with him and be ready to marry before Levi's mail-order bride arrived.

"I do believe you are right." He gulped the rest of his lukewarm coffee and stood. "Thanks for letting me bend your ear, Reverend, but I think it's time I go pick up my future bride."

Daniel paid for the coffees and then headed back to the general store. The bell over the door jingled as he entered. Several boxes lined the counter, with his name printed on each wooden crate.

"That little gal sure can shop." Phil Carlson stepped out from behind the counter. "Carolyn had to run to the bank, but said to tell you she put everything on your account. Want me to help you carry these to your wagon?"

Daniel looked about the store. He and Mr. Carlson were the only ones there. "I got it, thank you." He reached for the nearest box. "Did Miss Young go with Mrs. Moore to the bank?"

Mr. Carlson walked in front of him to the door. He pulled it open before answering. "Nope. She and the doctor were headed to the schoolhouse last I saw her."

Daniel carried the box to the wagon and looked toward the school. Children played in the yard, but he couldn't see Hannah, the doctor or the schoolmaster.

"Doc seemed awful interested in Miss Young. He beat me at checkers and then hightailed it out of here with her," Mr. Carlson called from the doorway.

Daniel headed back inside for the next box. The doctor was a single man and about his age. Was he interested in Hannah? They'd just met; surely the doctor hadn't taken a liking to her that quickly. Daniel scooped up the crate and walked back outside.

As he passed, Mr. Carlson added, "Miss Young seemed in a hurry to meet the schoolteacher, too. When my Carolyn told her about all his books, she decided to go see him. I never did cotton to reading. Suppose some folks enjoy it, but I'd rather be playing board games."

Daniel set the crate in the bed of the wagon and headed back for the last one. It made sense that Hannah would be interested in the schoolmaster's books. She was a teacher herself. But why would the doctor go with her?

He crossed the store threshold again. Mr. Carlson asked, "Would you like to play a game while you wait for her to come back?"

Daniel wiped sweat off his brow and then replaced his hat. "No, thanks. I think I'll go get Miss Young and then head on back to the ranch. Tell Mrs. Moore thank you for me."

Her father grumbled something and then walked back inside.

Daniel climbed aboard the wagon and turned the horses toward the schoolhouse. Both the doctor and the schoolteacher were single and about his age. Were they competing for Hannah's attentions? And if so, where did that leave him?

As far as he knew, only the minister and Daniel's family were aware that Hannah was his mail-order bride. The ranch hands knew also, but none of them had come to town yet and leaked the news. He pulled the wagon to a stop a few feet away from the school.

Children laughed as they played chase and other games in the schoolyard. He took the steps two at a time. The door was open, so he walked inside.

Hannah and the teacher were looking down at the big desk positioned off to the right, at the front of the room. She glanced up at Daniel and offered a dazzling smile. Her eyes seemed to sparkle with excitement. "Mr. Westland, I am learning so much about the children on your ranch."

So they were back to addressing each other formally. He moved to the front pew and sat down. "I'm glad to hear that, Miss Young. Are you about finished here?" Daniel watched as the schoolmaster studied Hannah's profile. He didn't care for the way the man's gaze seemed to take in her every feature.

"I think so." She straightened and picked up several books.

Jonah stood also, his white teeth flashing in a smile. "I'm so glad you came by to see me today. If you have any other questions, please feel free to stop by. I'd love to visit with you again, when we have more time." He held a piece of paper out to Hannah.

She took it and smiled back. "Well, I will have to return these books, and I'm sure Mr. Westland wouldn't mind if you came out and looked over my small collection."

Jonah followed her around the desk. "I might just take you up on that offer."

Daniel stood. His eyes bored into the schoolteacher's. "We'll be glad to see you." At the moment he felt anything but pleased to invite the man out to his ranch. But the invitation had been made, and there was no reason to deny him a visit.

Other than the fact that he was handsome, not married and kept looking at Hannah as if she was a fresh flower ready to be picked. Daniel took her elbow and escorted her out to the wagon, very aware that Jonah followed.

"Thanks for everything," Hannah called as Daniel helped her onto the high seat.

The teacher nodded and gave the school bell cord a good tug. The sound of it ringing filled the little town.

Daniel climbed up beside Hannah and slapped the reins over the horse's back. There was something about Jonah that he didn't quite like. Could it be he didn't trust him because of his obvious interest in Hannah? Daniel mulled over the idea.

He looked back at the schoolteacher, who was talking to the children as they entered the building. He was a big man who wore jeans and boots. A white shirt covered his wide shoulders. Daniel turned his attention back to guiding the horse home. Jonah's appearance was more that of a rancher or lawman than a teacher.

Trying not to be obvious, Daniel glanced in Hannah's direction. She seemed absorbed in the book on her lap. Her hair shone in the midday sun. The back of her slender neck was exposed, revealing creamy white skin. He had to admit that Hannah Young was a fine-looking woman. Why hadn't she already married?

She chose that moment to look up. "Oh, we're heading out of town." Disappointment filled her voice.

Daniel pulled back on the reins. "Was there something else you needed to do while we're here? I can turn us around."

Hannah closed the book. "No, I just assumed we'd be having lunch in town. But since we are already on our way, I'll fix us a snack from the supplies."

"I'll turn the wagon around." He really didn't want to. The fence on the west side of the ranch needed to be looked at, and he had a herd of cows over there that he wanted to check on, also.

Hannah's soft laughter took him by surprise. "No, I can tell you have work to do. My pa used to get that same look on his face when he had chores that needed doing but didn't want to disappoint Ma. Trust me, I'll be fine eating from the supplies, and so will you." She turned on the seat and rummaged through the boxes.

Daniel grinned and clicked his tongue to get the horse started again. "I take it your pa was a rancher."

They hadn't talked about her family in their letters and Hannah dreaded the questions she knew were now coming. She turned back around and sat down on the seat. Their fingers brushed when she handed him a green apple. "More like a farmer. He doesn't hold as much land or livestock as you do."

The apple crunched as Daniel bit into it. The scent of green sweetness drifted to her. She took a much smaller bite of her own fruit and chewed.

Daniel swallowed and then asked, "Where is his spread?"

"Missouri." She took another bite to avoid adding to her answer.

Daniel nodded, as if he understood she didn't want to talk about her family. "I hear that is beautiful country."

"Pa says Missouri is the closest he can imagine that heaven will look like. The trees are tall, and in the summer the grass is deep green and the sky royal blue, with fluffy white clouds. But my favorite time of the year is autumn. The leaves turn colors and it's like God got out His paintbrush and began to work." Hannah turned and found Daniel studying her face. She felt heat enter her cheeks and looked away.

Birds sang and the sound of buzzing insects filled the silence between them. Did he think her silly for describing the Lord as a painter? She put the rest of her apple on the seat and picked up the book she'd laid aside earlier.

The wagon wheels crunched grass and weeds as Daniel pulled to the side of the road. Hannah looked up. They were cutting through tall vegetation. "Where are we going?" she asked.

"There is a nice spot over here by the river where Mabel can get a drink and we can talk. There is something we need to discuss." Seriousness laced his voice like cinnamon laced a peach pie.

Hannah nodded and focused on Mabel's ears. They twitched back and forth, as if she were listening to their every word. Hannah swallowed the lump of uneasiness that was beginning to form.

Had he decided he didn't want her for a wife, after all? Or that he wasn't willing to wait until she fell in love with him? And if so, what was she going to do?

She cut her eyes to look at him. His set jaw and the furrow on his brow made her even more uncomfortable. Hannah clasped her hands over the book and prayed silently.

Lord, please help me not to panic. I know that what I'm asking of Daniel is a lot, but, Lord, You know that I have to have the assurance that he loves me and will never send me away, like my family did when I was a child. If that is what he is planning now, please help me to not react in front of him. I know You will take care of all my needs. Thank You. In Jesus's name.

Chapter Nine

Daniel led Mabel to the water's edge and let her drink her fill. The little mare bumped him gently as if to say thank you. He rubbed her ears as he tried to think how to begin the conversation with Hannah.

She sat on a log not far from where he stood. Her hands were clasped in her lap once more and worry filled her eyes. It hadn't been his intention to worry her. He led the horse to a nice lush spot to graze and then walked back to Hannah.

He knelt down in front of her. "I've been thinking about us and what the town is going to think when they find out you are my mail-order bride." Daniel searched her eyes for a reaction.

"Why do they need to find out?" She twisted her hands in the material of her dress.

He offered what he hoped was a gentle smile. "Hannah, the town is small and people talk. As soon as the ranch hands get off on Friday afternoon, they will head straight to the saloon, and soon everyone will know our business." Daniel stood and took his hat off. He rubbed one hand over the back of his neck, trying to ease the ever-tightening muscles. He hadn't liked the look of confusion and alarm that had flitted through the pretty blue depths of her eyes.

She cleared her throat. He heard the concern when she said, "I see. What do you suggest we do about it?"

Daniel turned to face her. "I know you don't want to wed me right now, but I think we need to make it clear that we are planning on getting married in the future."

Hannah looked down at her hands. "I see."

Nothing in her tone told him what she was thinking. "Please stop saying 'I see' and talk to me." Daniel hadn't meant to growl at her, but he wanted to know how she was feeling.

Seeing Hannah with the schoolteacher and hearing that the doctor had seemed interested in her made him feel possessive.

He inhaled deeply, taking in the soothing smells of the earth and the calming sound of the running water behind him. Daniel realized he wanted other men to know that Hannah was spoken for, though he couldn't exactly come out and say that to her. He needed to explain his feelings, but how could he explain them to her when he really didn't understand them himself?

Hannah tilted her chin upward, a movement he was beginning to recognize as stubbornness. "I'm not sure what you want me to say, Mr. Westland."

Daniel knelt in front of her again and took her hands. "For starters, my name is Daniel. You don't need to be so formal. Second, you can tell me if you want to become engaged." He rubbed the back of her hands with his thumb, enjoying the softness of her skin.

She lowered her chin and spoke in a soft tone. "I don't know. Engagement is the promise to get married.

We aren't sure love is in our future, and without love we have no future." Her eyes searched his. "I'm really not trying to be difficult, Daniel. I just want to be certain that when we get married, we love one another, and no matter what may happen to either of us, we still will."

He nodded. "Do you believe that to fall in love we have to be totally honest with each other?"

Hannah pulled her hands from his. "I do."

"That sounds fair. Can you explain to me why you feel so strongly about this?" He missed the warmth of her touch.

She took a deep breath. "Well, I'm not sure I will ever feel totally loved, but I'm trying."

Daniel watched tears form in her eyes. Someone had hurt Hannah really badly. He could only assume it was someone she loved very much. Now he realized there was a ghost in her past standing between them, much like the one in his own past. Would they ever be able to overcome their fears and hurts?

It was hard for him to imagine getting over the death of his sister and his own role in it, of not being there when she needed him. He had sent off for Hannah only because of his mother's contest. "I think I can understand, but what I don't understand is why you answered my advertisement for a wife."

She pushed a stray hair from her face. "I want to be loved and have children someday, Daniel. A friend of mine, Rebecca, came to Cottonwood Springs as a mail-order bride. That didn't work out, but she did find love with the man who is now her husband, so I hoped I could find the same happiness as her. That's why I sent the letter, explaining that I wanted to be courted. Seth ended up courting Rebecca and they found true love. When I see them together, I know Seth will love Rebecca forever, no matter what might happen to her." Hannah ducked her head and studied the pattern on her dress. Her breathing was rapid, as if she'd run a mile.

Daniel stood. "How did Seth court Rebecca?" he asked.

A sweet smile graced Hannah's lips. "Well, he didn't really court her in the normal way. Seth is a U.S. Marshal and he needed a housekeeper, so he hired Rebecca to clean and cook for him. They spent time together and fell in love." Hannah's eyes gleamed with hope.

"And what did he do when other single men started coming around?" Had Daniel asked that question aloud? He felt his cheeks heat as he realized he'd just asked what he'd been thinking.

She giggled. "The other men were smart enough not to mess with Rebecca. Once Seth took her under his wing, they knew to leave her be."

Daniel pushed back the embarrassment and pressed his point home. "So, it was kind of like they got engaged. And that gave Seth the time he needed to fall in love?"

Hannah's forehead wrinkled in thought. "When you put it that way, I suppose." She grinned. "I can see where you are going with this, Daniel."

He grinned back at her. "Good. I was beginning to think I was never going to get through to you."

She stood and wiped the dusk off her skirt. "All right. We can announce that we are engaged, but I hope I've made it clear that I can't marry you until we are both sure it is love. Not just any ole love. I want the deep kind that will last forever."

Could he promise her that kind of love? Maybe someday, but how far in their future was that? If it ever happened. He needed to get married fast and have a grandchild before Levi.

Hannah watched his serious expression. He was a thoughtful man. Was it fair of her to ask him to wait until she was sure of his love? What if he never fell in love with her, or she with him? Then what? How long would he wait?

When she'd thought he'd received her letter and agreed to her terms, Hannah had felt it was a fair understanding. Now she wasn't so sure. A bird overhead sang sweetly, reminding her that God was in all things. *Lord, please let him be patient with me. And if this isn't Your will, please let us both know now.*

Daniel interrupted the silent prayer. "Hannah, these things take time, and our time depends on Levi and what he does. If he finds a wife before we fall in love, I'm afraid I'll have to break our engagement."

Hannah swallowed the lump in her throat. "I understand."

Daniel rubbed his neck again. "I would rather marry you now, and with time I'm sure we will grow into a comfortable relationship." His eyes pleaded with her to give up this fantasy of falling in love, and just get married and continue on with life.

But Hannah couldn't do it. "I'm sorry. I can't." She wanted to know that if she got sick, or couldn't walk someday, or talk, that he'd love her enough to stand by her and give her love and support. Was that really too much to ask?

Daniel replaced his hat and grinned at her. "Then I suppose you and I have work to do." He tucked her hand in his arm and then walked toward the horse. "So tell me, Hannah Young, what does a man have to do or say to make you fall head over heels in love with him?"

Hannah laughed. "I could ask you the same thing."

He helped her up on the wagon. "I'm not sure I can answer that. Most people don't go into a relationship thinking *I want to be deeply in love with this person.* It's all new to me."

She waited until he walked around the wagon, and when he was seated, said, "Then I guess we should just be ourselves and see where the Lord leads us."

Daniel flicked the reins over the little mare's back and guided her toward the road. "That sounds good to me."

The rest of the ride was completed in comfortable silence. Daniel drove around the back of the schoolhouse and unloaded her boxes.

Hannah took in the small shed with a woodpile beside it. She also noticed that someone had turned the earth to start a garden.

When Daniel helped her down from the wagon, his hands lingered on her waist for a moment longer than she had expected them to. She stepped back. "Thank you for the shed and garden spot."

He walked to the back of the wagon and pulled out a box. "It was my pleasure."

Hannah grabbed the smaller of the remaining two boxes and followed him inside her room. His blue eyes took in the changes she'd made the night before.

Hannah followed his gaze. Everything was in its place, but soon she'd be out of space. She smiled when he turned to face her.

He took his hat off and held it in his hands. "Tomorrow I'd like to come by and show you something. Would that be all right with you?"

"I would like that very much." She felt a blush warm her cheeks.

"Good." Silence filled the space between them. "I'll go get that last box."

Hannah grinned. "Thank you."

He returned within seconds carrying the last box, which he set beside the door with a frown. "Looks like you could use a table."

"I'll manage," Hannah answered, not wanting to be a bother.

"If you are all set here…" He paused, waiting for her nod. "Then I'll see you tomorrow." Daniel walked out the door and mounted the wagon.

Hannah sighed as he drove away. Would he ever love her the way she wanted him to? Would he ever love her at all?

She pushed the thoughts from her mind and began unloading the boxes. When she'd finished, she looked about the silent room. On a whim, she scooped up a book from the pile on the table and grabbed a blanket off the shelf.

A cool afternoon breeze greeted her as she headed down to the stream behind the school. Hannah spread the blanket out under a tree, and then sat down to enjoy her book. She'd just started it when the sound of a horse whinnying pulled her from the story.

Levi sat on his stallion a few feet from her. "I thought I'd drop by and see if you needed anything." He leaned against the saddle horn and grinned down at her.

Hannah stood hurriedly and moved away from the large animal. For a brief moment she allowed fear to grip her. Not fear of the horse, but of his hooves, which looked very large.

"I—I don't think so."

Her visitor's eyes narrowed. "Are you feeling all right?"

She smoothed her skirt before answering. "Yes, you just startled me."

"Beg your pardon. I guess I did sort of sneak up on you. But you really can't blame me—your nose was buried in that book." Levi swung his leg over the saddle and slid to the ground.

Hannah looked at the book lying on her blanket. "I suppose you are right."

He picked up the volume, glanced at the front and read aloud, "*The Vanished Diamond,* by Jules Verne." He handed it to her. "Is it any good?"

"I think so. I'd just started reading it when you rode up." She ran her hand over the cover. "Mr. Richards loaned it to me." Her gaze moved to Levi's, which seemed focused on the book. "Do you enjoy reading, Mr. Westland?"

He laughed. "Yes, I do, but if you are going to be my sister-in-law, I think we should put aside the formalities and you call me Levi." Once more his eyes strayed to the book in her hand.

Hannah could see the reasoning in his suggestion. If she was going to be a part of his family, they would use each other's first names. She smiled. "All right. Levi it is."

He nodded. "Well, if you don't need anything, I'll be going. Enjoy your reading."

"Levi, I was wondering if you'd like to borrow a book from me. I brought several with me. I'll be happy to loan one to you." She didn't know why she'd offered, other than he seemed interested in the book she held in her hands.

Hannah knew what it was like to want something new to read. After all, part of the reason she'd gone to visit the schoolteacher had been to see his collection of books. She hadn't been disappointed. Mr. Richards had a nice library of the latest fiction and nonfiction books and was generous in loaning them out.

"That's very kind of you, Hannah. I've been meaning to pick up a new book in town, I just haven't made the time to do so." Levi followed her back toward the school.

She laughed. "I'm not sure my collection will have something new, but you are welcome to browse through it."

He tied the horse's reins to the porch railing. "I haven't had much time for reading lately. The ranch has kept both Daniel and me pretty busy." Levi followed her inside.

"I am hoping to help Daniel with some of the ranch work once we are married, so that should take a bit of the burden off the two of you." She walked to the bookshelf and indicated the books he could choose from.

Levi snorted. "I doubt Daniel will let you do ranch work. He's a firm believer that women should stay in the house." Unaware of her frown, he continued. "He doesn't even like Ma helping out, and she owns the place."

Hannah leaned against the wall. She'd chosen to answer Daniel's letter because she'd thought she'd be able to work on a farm again and had decided ranch life wouldn't be that different, just a bigger operation. Now

Levi was telling her Daniel was against women working the land?

She studied his back as he pulled out each book and looked at the cover. "Your mother doesn't listen to him?"

Preoccupied, Levi answered in a low voice, "Naw, Ma does what Ma wants to. No questions asked."

If Daniel's mother could do ranch work, then Hannah decided she could, too. He would get used to the idea and that would be that. She straightened her spine.

Levi turned with a book in hand. "This one is by Jules Verne. Isn't that the author of the book you are reading?" he asked, never taking his gaze from the opened pages.

"Yes, he is one of my favorite authors. I have three of his books," Hannah answered. "Which title did you chose?"

Levi closed the volume and read the title aloud. *"'A Journey to the Center of the Earth.'"* He looked back up at her. "Are you sure you don't mind my borrowing it?"

"Of course not. I think you will enjoy it. Anytime you want to read one of my books, you are welcome to do so," she offered with a smile.

"That's very nice. Thank you." Levi tucked the book under his arm and looked about her room. "You could use a table and maybe a rocking chair."

Hannah laughed. Levi seemed to change subjects almost as fast as her friend Eliza Kelly. For a brief moment she wondered if Eliza had stayed to meet her future groom in Durango.

His footsteps moving toward the door drew her attention. "You have space for them here." He stopped and studied the area.

"Yes, I do, but circumstances being what they are, I'll make do with what I have." Hannah didn't want to be any more of a bother to Daniel or his family.

Levi didn't comment any further. He opened the door and moved to untie his horse. "Thanks for the book. I'll get it back to you in a few days." In one easy motion, he remounted the stallion.

Hannah admired the animal. Its coat shone in the sun and its big expressive eyes studied her in return. "He really is a beautiful animal." She sighed.

"Would you like a horse to ride? I'm sure we can find one for you in the stables."

"No, I haven't been on a horse in years." She didn't elaborate and say it had been close to twenty years.

He nodded. "Well, if you change your mind, let Daniel or me know. We've got some pretty gentle mares. You can have your pick."

"Thank you. I'll keep that in mind."

Hannah dreamed of riding a horse again as Levi rode away. She knew she'd have to overcome her fear of having one step on her if she was ever going to become a true helpmate to Daniel.

Chapter Ten

The next morning, Daniel sagged in the saddle. He'd given all the men jobs to do and was now headed to the schoolhouse to collect Hannah. Yesterday the thought of showing her his house—hers, too, if they got married—had seemed like a good idea. But now that the time had come, he wished he hadn't offered.

Both he and Levi had built houses on the ranch shortly after their mother had announced her desire to see them married and herself with grandchildren. Thankfully, the winter months had been mild and the men hadn't minded the extra work.

He stopped in front of the school. The front door was open and Hannah was sweeping. She shoved the dirt off the side of the porch and smiled at him.

"Good morning, Daniel." Her voice washed over him like heavy dew over a honeysuckle blossom.

Daniel nodded. "Morning. You look mighty busy this morning." He climbed down from his horse and walked toward her.

"Just doing a little housekeeping. I'm hoping to have the school running by Monday morning." She set the broom beside the door. "Would you like a cup of coffee?"

He didn't have time for coffee. Daniel wanted to tell her he had a ranch to run, but instead said, "No, thanks. I thought we could head on out."

Hannah cocked her head sideways and looked up at him. "Are we going to walk?"

"No, I thought we'd double up on Tornado." He indicated the horse.

Her face paled. "Um, I need to get my shawl." Hannah hurried back inside the school.

Daniel turned to the stallion and rubbed his nose. "You be a good boy. For the first time ever, you will have a lady riding on you. I expect only good behavior. You got that?" He looked deeply into the animal's eyes. Tornado might not understand the words, but Daniel knew he understood the tone.

The stallion's head bobbed in answer.

"Good boy." He rubbed the horse's neck. Daniel looked toward the schoolhouse door, but there was still no sign of Hannah. What could be keeping that woman?

Ten minutes later, just when he'd decided to go in after her, Hannah appeared on the porch. Her blue eyes searched his. "He's really tall. Do you think you could lead him over here and maybe I could just sit on his back?"

Daniel looked from the woman to the horse. Tornado was tall, but not that tall. "I don't know, Hannah."

"Please," she said. "You don't have to do anything but hold him steady. I can do it."

Hannah studied the boards under her feet. She wore a big straw hat that covered most of her face from his view. He didn't understand why she wanted to mount

Tornado from the porch, but if it would get her on the horse faster, he'd give it a try.

He pulled Tornado toward the porch and positioned him so that Hannah could lean over and climb aboard, which she did without too much trouble. Since his mother straddled a horse all the time, he wasn't surprised to see her get on like that. What did surprise him was the pretty blush that colored her cheeks.

"Daniel, would you look away, please?" Her gaze refused to meet his.

He averted his eyes and listened to the rustle of her skirt against the leather of the saddle. Tornado snorted and tried to pull his head around to the side, but Daniel held firm. "Is everything all right?"

"Fine. You can turn around now." She sounded breathless.

He turned to find her sitting sidesaddle, on the rump of Tornado, hanging on to the back of the saddle with both hands. A smile brightened her face and pride shone in her eyes. "I'm on," she announced, as if he couldn't see her.

Daniel laughed in spite of himself. "So you are. Wouldn't you be more comfortable in the saddle?"

She shook her head. "Oh, no, I'm perfectly fine where I am."

Careful not to kick her, Daniel mounted his horse. He reached behind him and pulled Hannah closer. "Wrap your arms around my waist so you don't fall off."

He didn't have to ask twice. Her arms came around him and she hung on tight, almost slamming into his back. Daniel laughed and scooted up farther.

"I've never ridden sidesaddle before," Hannah

confessed, clinging to him tighter with each step the horse took.

When it became apparent that soon he wouldn't be able to breathe any longer if he didn't do something, Daniel pulled Tornado to a stop. "Let go of me and grab the saddle again. I need to get down."

She released him and clung to the leather, looking about. "Is this where you wanted to take me?"

He looped the reins around the saddle horn and slid off. Hannah clung to the saddle as if her life depended on it and offered him a weak smile.

"No, but we need to change places."

Fear laced her face and her voice shook. "Why?"

"If I can breathe, I won't pass out and fall off the horse." He grinned up at her.

"Oh." She looked at the saddle and the stallion's flowing mane. "I'm not sure how to move up."

Daniel shook his head. "Well, you could get down and then climb back on."

Hannah's head swung from side to side. "No, I don't think I can do that." Her knuckles turned white on the leather.

What was she so afraid of? The horse? Falling off? The only way to find out was to ask. "Hannah, what are you afraid of?"

"Snakes, spiders, just about anything that bites." She sent him another wobbly smile.

He wished he could tell her that Tornado didn't bite, but that wasn't exactly true. Everyone knew you had to watch stallions or they would take a hunk out of you, and a horse's bite hurt. "I promise to hold Tornado's head so he won't get you."

"No, I'm good. I'll just sit like this."

Frustration laced his voice. "Hannah, we have to switch places. You were squeezing the air out of me."

Again she shook her head. "I'm sorry. I won't squeeze so hard."

Daniel felt his teeth grind and his jaw work. The lady was proving to be one stubborn, irritating, mule-headed woman. Could he pull her down and then set her in the saddle?

Hannah knew she was being unreasonable, but the thought that this huge animal could step on her sent reason right out of her mind. Was there a way she could pull herself into the saddle without getting down?

She wiggled her bottom and felt the material of her dress slip. Hannah twitched forward to keep from falling off. The action caused the horse to jerk sideways. Her palms had begun to sweat and slide off the leather. Tornado must have felt her descending, and bunched his hindquarters.

"Easy, boy," Daniel soothed.

But it was no good.

One moment she was clinging to the saddle, and the next Hannah felt herself go airborne. All she could do was pray nothing would break when she hit the ground, and that she'd land far enough away from the horse not to frighten it further. She saw Daniel move to catch her but knew he'd never make it in time to keep her from hitting the ground.

Air whooshed from her lungs when she hit the packed earth. Hannah sat up as fast as she could. Concern laced Daniel's face, so she tried to smile. "I'm all right."

He released the reins and Tornado lowered his head

to munch on the grass. "Are you sure?" Daniel extended a hand to help her up.

Hannah felt the warmth of his palm scratch against her soft skin as he pulled her to her feet. "I'm sure." She released his hand and dusted off her skirt.

"Well, if you're certain. We need to get going." He walked to Tornado and picked up the reins. "I'll hold him steady and you climb up."

She could see the schoolhouse in the near distance and realized they hadn't gotten very far. "Can't we just walk to wherever we're going?"

"No. It's not far by horse but walking would take too much time." His brow furrowed.

"I'm sorry, Daniel. I can't get on the horse again. I can't." She heard her own ragged words and saw the disappointment on his face.

"Then we'll have to go another day. I don't have time to go hitch up the buckboard." His own words came out sounding harsh and irritated.

"I really am sorry," she offered.

He studied her face and his own features softened. "If you are afraid you'll fall off again, I promise to hold Tornado steady, and once you're on, I'll hang on to you, too."

He obviously meant it, but Hannah knew there was no way she'd get close enough to the big black stallion to mount him. She shook her head. "No, you ride him and I'll walk along beside you."

"Well, it's too far to go without riding a horse, so we'll have to plan our outing for another day. Besides, I have work to do and I need to get some of it done before lunch. I'll walk you back." He headed toward the school.

Hannah ran to catch up with him. "That's not necessary. If you need to go back to work, go. I'll walk my-self home." She hurried past him so that he couldn't see the tears building behind her eyes.

She heard leather creaking behind her and knew Daniel had mounted the big stallion.

Disappointment filled her ears as he sighed and then said, "I'll see you at dinner."

It took all her willpower not to look back to see how close he and the horse were to her. She nodded to let him know she'd heard him. The resonance of thundering hooves let her know he'd spun around and ridden away.

With misty vision, she turned and watched him ride off. She'd made a mess of their outing. Hannah took her time walking back to the school. Tears streamed down her face as disappointment filled her heart. How was she going to help run a ranch when she couldn't even mount a horse?

A cool breeze picked up. Hannah sat down on the schoolhouse steps. She couldn't get the tears to stop. The past couple days were taking their toll on her. She didn't normally cry like this. Since no one was around, she buried her face in her hands and let the tears flow.

After several minutes someone cleared a throat, snagging her attention. She didn't want to look up. Had a parent came to welcome the new schoolteacher? Or worse, had Daniel returned?

What would her visitor think of her appearance? Hannah knew her eyes were red, swollen and bloodshot. Her face was probably a splotchy mess. Why had she given in to her impulse to just let it all out? She inhaled deeply, knowing she couldn't ignore her visitor forever.

Hannah felt some relief at seeing Levi sitting on a buckboard instead of Daniel on his stallion. She wiped at the moisture on her face. So deep was she in her emotions she hadn't heard him pull up.

Sorrow and regret laced her voice, and it cracked as she said, "Hello, Levi."

He was off the wagon and by her side in an instant. "Are you all right, Hannah? Are you hurt? Should I go get Ma? Or Daniel?" His big hand patted her shoulder.

It was nice to hear the concern in his tone. "I'm fine, Levi. I just needed a good cry."

She felt him ease down beside her. "Here. You might need this." A large white handkerchief was stuffed into her hands.

"Thank you." Hannah tried to be ladylike as she blew her nose. She didn't know what to say, so they sat in silence for several moments.

Her gaze moved to the wagon, where a little brown mare stood chopping grass. Hannah saw a table, two dining chairs and a rocking chair stuffed in the back, and she looked to Levi.

He squirmed. "I brought you a wedding gift."

"Oh, Levi, you didn't have to do that," she protested, even as warmth spread in her heart. Of all the Westlands, Levi had been the kindest by far.

He grinned. "It was no bother." He stood and walked to the wagon, pulled out the chairs and handed them to her. "Think you can take those inside?"

"I believe so." She balanced them against her hips and then climbed the stairs to the schoolroom.

Levi followed carrying the table. It wasn't very large, but Hannah knew it would fit perfectly in the spot he'd been studying the day before. He set it down and spun on his heel to retrieve the rocking chair.

Hannah placed a chair on each side of the table, leaving enough room to walk past it. Now she had a place to eat and entertain guests. She glanced about and realized the rocking chair wasn't going to fit in her space. She'd have to tell Levi thanks, but to take it back.

His boots clomped on the wooden floors. "I'm going to set the rocker beside the fireplace. I don't think it will fit in your room." Levi positioned the chair so that it sat facing the hearth.

Why hadn't she thought of that? Hannah ran her hands over the crafted wood. "This is beautiful, Levi. Won't your mother miss it from the house?"

"Nope. This is my rocker, and I know she won't miss it because it wasn't at her house." He indicated Hannah should sit down in it.

She eased into the chair and sighed. It fit her body perfectly. "This is great. I don't think I've ever been more comfortable in a rocking chair."

Levi's chest puffed out a little. "Thank you. I wasn't sure if it would be low enough for you or not. But I'm glad to see you like it."

His stance and the way he rocked happily on his heels reminded Hannah of the little boys in her classroom throughout the years. When they'd done their work right, they seemed to puff up just as Levi was right now. There was pride in his green eyes.

"Did you make this chair, Levi?" she finally asked.

He grinned. "Sure did. All I had to do to make it yours was readjust the height."

Hannah stood and ran her hand over the vine design that decorated the chair back. "It is beautiful."

"Thank you, again."

She looked at him. A strand of brown hair rested on his forehead. His deep green eyes seemed calm and full of joy. Levi was so much like Daniel, and yet so different. Of the two brothers, he was easier to talk to. Maybe because he felt more relaxed around her. Levi seemed to want to please and make her comfortable.

Did he think she'd fall in love with him instead of Daniel? Hannah realized that could be the motivation behind his gift giving. She sighed. Why did this all have to be so complicated? She knew she had to set Levi straight. She'd promised to marry Daniel, and marry him she would, if they fell in love. If not, Hannah knew she'd not come between the brothers. Now, how was she going to explain this to Levi without hurting his feelings?

Chapter Eleven

"Look, Levi. I know you are trying to be nice and everything, but I want you to know that if you are trying to court me—"

Levi raised both hands. "Hold up there, Hannah. That is the furthest thing from my mind. You are Daniel's girl. I don't mind teasing him a bit about you, but I've no intention of being anything more to you than a friend, or someday a brother-in-law."

For a brief moment, Hannah felt foolish. She'd assumed, and she shouldn't have. Warmth flooded her cheeks. "Good," she replied.

He rubbed his neck, probably unaware his actions were the same as his sibling's. She smiled. Levi was a good brother, and deep in her heart she knew that Daniel was, too.

"I guess I should go." Levi started backing out the door.

Hannah sighed. "I'm sorry I embarrassed you, Levi." She followed him down the steps.

He turned and studied her. "Well, since you did, I don't feel so bad about asking you a question, even if it does embarrass you a mite." A teasing glow filled his eyes.

Dread filled her. He was probably going to ask why she became a mail-order bride, and why she wanted to fall in love and be loved before she married. They were reasonable questions. Hannah took a deep breath and nodded.

"Why were you crying?" Concerned green eyes studied her face.

She released the air from her lungs. "Your brother came to get me today to show me a surprise. But we had to turn around because I wouldn't ride on his horse. That's what started it, but then I just decided to have a good cry."

Levi crossed his arms and stared down at her. "Let me get this straight. You were crying because my brother wouldn't take you for a surprise? Because you refused to ride Tornado?"

Hannah nodded. "Yes, but don't forget I was feeling sorry for myself, so it wasn't really Daniel's fault."

Levi shook his head as if to clear it. "Why wouldn't you get on Tornado?" When she didn't answer immediately, he pressed, "Are you afraid of horses?

It was going to come out sooner or later. Hannah sighed. "No. I'm afraid of getting stepped on again."

She knew the moment understanding dawned. His gaze moved to her injured ankle, then up to meet her eyes. "So that's what happened. A horse stepped on you."

Hannah nodded. "Yes, and for the first time in twenty years I have an opportunity to ride again. I love horses, but every time I get close to one, close enough for it to shift sideways and step on me, I panic." Tears filled her eyes once more. She forced herself to hold them in. He'd seen her cry once already and that was one too many times.

"Do you know how to get over that fear?" Levi asked.

Hannah knew to overcome the fear she'd have to face it, but how? "Yes, but I can't."

"Sure you can, and I'll help you." He grabbed her by the arm and began pulling her toward the wagon. "We'll go to the barn and I'll saddle up ole Clover. She's Ma's old horse. Children can play at her feet and she won't budge."

Even as he shoved her up on the wagon seat, Hannah protested. "I'm not so sure, Levi."

He ignored her and swung up in turn. "You want to help Daniel run this ranch someday?"

She nodded. Hannah wanted to work the ranch more than she could express. The desire to brand calves, mend fences and ride the range overwhelmed her. More than anything, Hannah Young wanted to prove to herself she could still work a ranch.

Daniel wiped the sweat from his brow. The sun shone directly overhead and his stomach growled. His gaze moved down the fence line to the wire that still needed to be mended. Whoever had cut it the night before had done a fine job.

It had taken him half the morning to round up the cows and calves that had gotten out. He'd taken ole Jeb with him. Jeb was his best tracker and had found the cattle in record time.

Daniel tried to figure out who had cut his fences. Had a new cattle-rustling gang decided Granite was the place to stop off? He'd need to meet with other local ranchers and see if any of them had had their stock taken or their fences cut. Or perhaps this was more personal. None of the calves or cows were missing, and the fence had been cut in such a way that whoever did it knew it would take a couple days to replace.

Ole Jeb had taken the whole situation in stride. He'd only shrugged when Daniel had asked him who he thought might have done the job. That was Jeb's way. He was quiet and did his work.

Daniel had left him with Miguel to corral the cows and calves. He knew without having to double-check that Jeb had gone back to working on the loose boards in the barn, and Miguel would be working his mother's massive vegetable garden.

Now he and Cole were mending the fence. Daniel couldn't help but wonder where his little brother had gone off to. "Where is Levi?" he asked.

Cole stood a little taller. "Said he would come around this afternoon, had something he needed to do this morning. I didn't ask what, boss."

It was just like Levi to be off doing who knew what when there was plenty of work for him right here on the ranch. "Let's break for lunch. I'll find my little brother and he and Sam can finish this job this afternoon."

"I hate to ask, but what are you and I going to be doing?" Cole gathered their tools and piled them beside the fence post.

"We need to round up the rest of the cows and calves and get the calves branded. Whoever did this probably has a few head of our cattle already. We can't afford to lose more." He pulled himself into Tornado's saddle.

Cole mounted his own horse. "I'll head to the bunkhouse for grub, then meet you at the barn."

Daniel nodded and turned toward the big ranch house. He'd wanted to show Hannah his home, and had hoped when she saw it she'd give up the notion of wanting love before marriage.

What had spooked her this morning? She'd seemed to be afraid of the horse. If that were the case, he'd handled her fear of Tornado wrong and hoped to make it up to her. But now, well, he'd have to explain that the branding had to be done before he could take her to see the "surprise."

Would he ever understand her? She'd said she wasn't afraid of the horse, but refused to ride him. Daniel knew he'd have to learn to talk to her and ask questions. He had asked what she was frightened of and she'd made a joke of it. How could he help her when he didn't know what the problem was? Daniel shook his head. One thing was sure, running the ranch and courting a woman at the same time was not going to be easy.

He approached the house from behind. Tornado snorted at the knowledge that he was close to the barn and fresh grain. Daniel's own stomach gurgled, reminding him breakfast had been hours earlier.

The sound of Hannah's laughter floated on the breeze. He climbed off Tornado and led the stallion around the house. What was she doing here? Not that she wasn't allowed to be at the house—he just hadn't expected to find her there.

Hannah was leaning against his mother's little brown mare, Clover. Her legs were far away from the horse and she rested her arms on the saddle, reminding him of a leaning ladder. What was the woman trying to do?

Levi's laugh joined hers. "You have to get your feet closer to her, Hannah. You've done this a time or two now." He was behind her, trying to push her legs toward the mare.

Daniel continued on toward the barnyard. When he was within normal speaking distance, he asked, "What are you two doing?"

Levi straightened. "Can't you tell a riding lesson when you see one, big brother?" he asked with a cocky grin.

"Is that what you are calling this?"

Hannah's hair had begun falling down. She turned her head and offered him a smile. Her cheeks were flushed and her eyes sparkled. "It's more a lesson on how not to get stepped on by a horse," she said, pushing away from the horse and windmilling her arms until she stood upright.

Daniel pointed at the mare. "That's Clover. She wouldn't step on a child."

"That's what Levi said, but I'm not a child and she might change her mind about adults." Hannah twisted her hands in her dress as she eyed the old mare.

He had a choice to make. Go eat lunch and leave his brother with his fiancée to bond over how to ride a horse, or ask her to lunch and offer to teach her how to get on the horse himself. Daniel felt someone watching him and looked at Levi.

His brother was smiling like a jack-o'-lantern at Halloween. "Maybe you should take over the lessons, big brother. I haven't done very well. The closest I've gotten her to Clover is what you just witnessed."

"Is this what you've been doing all morning?" Daniel asked.

"Not all morning. I went to the school with a small

load of furniture and then we came here." Levi tucked his hands in his back pockets and rocked on his boots.

Hannah walked over to stand beside Levi. "I'm sorry, Daniel. I should have realized Levi had chores to do."

Daniel didn't like the way she took the blame for his brother. Her soft blue eyes met his. "No harm done."

"Glad that's settled. I'm starving. What about you, Daniel? Is that why you returned to the house?" Levi asked. He started walking toward the ranch house, not bothering to stay and hear Daniel's answer.

"As a matter of fact, it was." Daniel offered Hannah what he hoped was an inviting smile. "Come have lunch with us, Hannah. Ma and Opal always fix way too much." He held out his hand, wondering if she'd take it.

She hesitated. "I'm not sure your mother will be happy to see me at her dinner table, Daniel."

"Ma has never turned anyone away from her table. Come on." He wiggled his fingers.

Hannah rewarded him with a slow grin. Her hand slid into his. "Are you sure?"

"I'm sure." He wasn't, but they'd find out soon enough what kind of mood Bonnie Westland was in today.

He led Hannah around back to where the wash supplies were sitting just outside the kitchen door. The smell of baked bread filled his nostrils.

Hannah washed first. He could see her hands trembling in the water basin. Bonnie Westland could be intimidating, he supposed, but she was his mother and sooner or later she'd have to come to an understanding about Hannah.

Opal opened the door. "About time you all came in.

Bonnie has decided to have lunch in the formal dining room."

Levi patted the housekeeper's cheek. "Thanks for waiting for us," he teased, and continued into the house.

"Hello, Opal," Hannah said warmly, and then followed Levi, unsure what to expect. Bonnie Westland had made it clear she was not to sleep there. Did that include eating, too?

Her gaze took in the spacious kitchen. A small table with four chairs sat under the only window in the room. The rest of the area reminded her of a horseshoe. The sink and counter rested against the back wall. A large stove filled the next wall, along with a wood bin. Then the door that led to the formal dining room loomed before her.

Levi walked through it, but Hannah stopped. Would Mrs. Westland send her packing, as she had the day she'd arrived? Hannah swallowed the lump in her throat, suddenly wishing she'd declined Daniel's invitation to lunch.

She felt his warm hand on her back. His breath fanned her ear as he whispered, "It will be all right." Then he gave her a gentle shove through the door.

Hannah glared over her shoulder at him. Didn't he understand how nervous she was? His mother hadn't been very welcoming, and surprising her by arriving for lunch was a bit unsettling.

Bonnie Westland's voice demanded, "Are you two going to stand there all day? Or have some lunch with the rest of us?"

Hannah took a deep breath and slowly turned to face Daniel's mother, who sat at the head of the table. Steaming plates of food filled the table and created a hearty aroma in the dining area. Bonnie nodded toward a chair and Hannah moved to sit down.

Daniel followed her and took the seat at the other end of the table, so he and his mother faced each other. Hannah couldn't help but wonder if this was their normal seating arrangement. Levi sat across from her and winked.

Bonnie cleared her throat. Hannah looked in her direction and saw that she had her arms resting on the table, her hands palm up. Levi laid one hand in hers and then extended his other hand for Daniel to take. Hannah immediately followed suit, realizing the Westlands held hands during prayer time.

"Daniel, you give the blessings," Bonnie ordered.

Hannah's mind wandered as Daniel blessed the food. She wondered if Bonnie had always been this firm with her boys. They seemed to jump whenever she barked. Her own mother had been a soft-spoken woman who seldom raised her voice. She ran her home with a sweet disposition, unlike Bonnie, who seemed to run hers with an iron fist.

When Hannah felt both Daniel and his mother release her hands, she picked up her napkin and laid it in her lap. Her gaze fell to the ham, cheeses, fresh vegetables and bowls of potatoes, green beans and other food choices. The Westlands ate like kings and queens, she thought. Her stomach growled, reminding her that she had skipped breakfast. "Everything looks lovely, Mrs. Westland," she stated.

"It's not there to look at. Dig in." Bonnie picked up the platter of ham and dished herself two thick slices, then handed the plate to Levi.

Dishes were passed around the table and plates were filled. Hannah listened as Daniel told his mother and brother that the west fence line had been cut and that several head of cattle had to be gathered up.

"Levi, you and Sam will be mending the rest of the fence while Cole and I corral the new spring calves. Tomorrow we'll start branding." Daniel stuffed a slice of ham into his mouth and looked at Hannah.

A frown marred Levi's face. "Seems I get the fence-mending job again. How many times does that make this month, Daniel?" he asked.

His brother swallowed. "They have to be fixed, Levi. It's a part of ranching. You know that."

"Yes, but it's also your favorite job to give to me," Levi retorted.

"Would you rather muck out stalls? I'm sure Adam would trade you jobs this afternoon," Daniel answered around a piece of buttered bread.

Bonnie spoke up. "Boys, we don't argue at the table and we don't argue in front of our guest." She used her eyes to indicate she meant Hannah.

"Hannah's not a guest, Ma. She's my fiancée," Daniel retorted.

Bonnie placed her fork and knife on her plate. She looked Daniel squarely in the eye and said, "Until the ring is on her finger or I dos are said, Daniel Westland, she's a guest."

Hannah wanted to melt into the floor. She hated being the center of attention, and right now all eyes had turned to her. What did one say at a time like this? She searched her mind for any etiquette she might have read or been taught in school that would apply to a situation such as this. None came to her rescue.

What she wouldn't give to be in her room at the schoolhouse, munching on an apple, a hunk of cheese and a slice of bread right now.

Desperation filled her as she silently prayed. *Lord, please help me to get through this meal.*

Chapter Twelve

Hannah was thrilled when Daniel pushed his chair back and thanked his mother for a hearty meal. She laid her napkin down and started to rise.

"Not so fast, Miss Young. Around here, everyone helps with chores, and since you ate at our table, you can help with the cleanup."

Her heart sank.

Daniel growled, "Ma."

"Don't you sass me, young man," Bonnie warned. "You're the one who pointed out she isn't a guest here."

Hannah turned to face him. "It's all right, Daniel. Your mother is right."

She could tell by the look on his face that he was still ready to argue with his mother. Hannah tried to reassure him. "Really, I will be perfectly fine cleaning the kitchen. It's the least I can do after such a fine meal."

Daniel took her by the hand and pulled her through the kitchen and to the back porch, away from the rest of them. "You do not have to clean the kitchen, Hannah."

"Look, if it will help your mother come to terms with us eventually getting married, I'll wash every dish in this house." Hannah offered him what she hoped was a silly grin and prayed that he couldn't read on her face the panic she was feeling.

He swept his hand over her cheek and tucked a wayward strand of hair behind her ear. "You really want this to work, don't you?"

The feel of his rough palm on her face and the deepness of his voice had her heart fluttering. "Of course. All I'm asking for is unconditional love."

Her words hung between them. Was it really too much to ask? Was she being unreasonable? He nodded, turned and walked away.

Hannah steadied her heart and thoughts. She had a mother to face, and wasn't sure how she'd fare during the encounter. But true to her word, she would try to help Bonnie Westland come to terms with the idea that her eldest son would someday marry her.

An inner voice taunted, *Then why not marry him now?* It was obvious that they would eventually marry. Hannah pulled her head up. No. She would wait until she felt sure Daniel loved her above all else, even the ranch.

She entered the kitchen to find Opal already at the sink.

"Would you mind getting the other plates for me, Hannah?" she asked, swishing the tea glasses in the soapy water.

Hannah smiled even though she dreaded entering the dining area, where she felt sure Bonnie Westland waited. "Not at all. I'm happy to help." She walked through the door with her head held high.

The room was empty. It looked as if Bonnie Westland

had decided not to help out in the kitchen. Hannah released a sigh of relief and began collecting dirty dishes.

She reentered the kitchen and said, "Here you go, Opal."

The housekeeper was sitting the cups on the counter to air dry. "Just put them down here." She indicated the counter to her left.

Hannah did so and then turned to go collect the remainder of the food. "I'll be right back to start drying," she said.

"Thank you, Hannah." Opal dumped the plates into the water. "This job seems to get bigger and bigger."

Hannah laughed "Well, you do have an extra cup, plate and silverware today."

The woman joined her in laughter "I do, don't I?" She waited until Hannah returned, juggling food bowls and platters. "I'm glad you stayed for lunch. I'm sure Bonnie wasn't expecting that."

Did Opal enjoy seeing her employer upset over an extra lunch guest?

"You have spunk. Bonnie likes folks with spunk. She'll warm up to you real fast once she gets the notion out of her head that Daniel isn't going to marry that Crawford girl."

Hannah set the food on the sideboard, not sure what to do with it. She picked up a dish towel and began drying glasses and plates. "I hope you are right."

"I know I'm right," Opal declared. "Can't say I blame Daniel for looking outside town for a bride. The girls around here are too immature for grown men. They giggle and try to catch those boys' eyes every time they go to town. Not that I'm accusing anyone, but I'd say those young ladies are looking for rich husbands. Yep, can't blame Daniel for placing that ad." She tsked and handed Hannah another wet plate.

Hannah looked about the spacious kitchen while she dried. It had every modern appliance money could buy. The Westlands probably had more money than the whole town of Granite. Was that why all the local girls wanted to marry the Westland men? And if so, was Opal right about the reason Daniel and Levi had gone outside of their town looking for wives?

She pulled her thoughts from the two men. "Where is Mrs. Westland?" Hannah asked the question that had been silently plaguing her since she'd realized Bonnie wouldn't be helping with the dishes.

Opal grinned. "She's headed to her quilting bee this afternoon."

For a brief moment, Hannah wished she'd been invited to the bee. It would have been fun to meet with other women and sew.

But then again, it was probably for the best that Bonnie hadn't asked her. The women would have been curious not only about her being a mail-order bride but about her limp. At times like this, Hannah missed her friends. Eliza and Rebecca never asked a lot of questions about her limp, and had accepted her for who she was, not what she looked like or how she walked.

"There. Done!" Opal tossed the dishwater out the back door.

Hannah put the last plate away and then scooped up the broom. "I'll sweep and then head on back to the school. I really should be working on lesson plans."

Opal rested a hip on the counter. "When are you starting classes?"

"Monday morning." She moved about the room, swinging her broom.

Opal's words took her by surprise. "Then I suppose Bonnie will want to call the monthly ranch meeting before supper."

That old familiar feeling of dread crept up into Hannah's stomach. She stopped sweeping and asked, "What is a monthly ranch meeting?"

Opal looked at her as if she'd grown two horns. "A meeting where we all get together and discuss important things that impact everyone living on the ranch." She said it as if she were explaining to a child why he or she shouldn't touch a hot stove.

"Oh." Hannah swept the dirt out the back door and replaced the broom.

"I take it Daniel hasn't told you about this Sunday?" Opal asked, pulling out a chair at the small table.

"No." Even as she said it, Hannah knew whatever the housekeeper had to reveal about Sunday wasn't going to be pleasant for her.

Opal indicated she should sit down. Once Hannah had done so, the older woman settled in also, then began. "Sunday morning we all load up and go to town for worship service. Usually it's me, my daughter's family, Bonnie, Daniel and Levi. Now you will be riding with us." She paused, waiting for a reaction from Hannah.

"That's lovely. I'm looking forward to attending church on Sunday." Hannah listened carefully as Opal continued.

"This is the first Sunday of the month, the day we always have the ranch meeting. Bonnie and I will pack a light picnic and we'll eat it on the way home. Once here, the work begins. We usually have a big barbecue dinner, where we supply the meat. At the end of the meal Bonnie gives out any information that might be important for the families to know."

"That's very nice," Hannah murmured, when Opal paused again.

"Yes, and this Sunday she plans to announce your and Daniel's engagement, and that you're the new ranch schoolteacher. She'll want to know what time the children should arrive and when the parents can expect them to be home."

Hannah felt her face lose all its color. "She's going to announce our engagement?"

"I thought that part might bother you a mite." Opal moved to the stove and pulled a teakettle from the back.

Dizziness enveloped Hannah. She'd agreed to the engagement but hadn't expected it to be announced officially. What if she changed her mind? What if Daniel did? Would he have to officially break it to the ranch hands on a Sunday evening, as well?

Opal thrust a mug at her. "Here, drink this."

Hannah's hands shook. She took a sip of the hot beverage, a delicious mixture of honey, lemon and tea. The warmth from the hot drink helped soothe her shattered nerves. "Thank you."

"It's really not that bad. You were planning on marrying the boy, weren't you?" Opal sipped from her own mug.

How did she answer that? It was one thing to make an arrangement with Daniel that they'd only marry if they fell in love, but explaining it to Opal made her feel childish. "I…"

"You know, I overheard Daniel explaining to his

mother how he sent off for you as a mail-order bride. He said there'd been a misunderstanding and that the wedding wasn't going to happen immediately. Why do you suppose that is?" Her brown eyes bored into Hannah's.

Hannah straightened in her chair. "I think you already know."

Opal lowered the cup. "Nope, he wouldn't tell his mother. But he did say to get JoAnna Crawford out of her mind as future daughter-in-law material."

Hannah studied the design on her mug. So Daniel had spoken to his mother about her, but not given a reason as to why they weren't married yet.

She sighed. "This may sound foolish to you, Opal, but the reason I didn't marry him the moment I stepped off the stage is because I want a man who will love me unconditionally."

"That is wise." The older woman stared out the window.

"Do you really think so?"

"Yes, but you should have told the boy before you arrived."

Hannah heard the disapproval in Opal's voice. "I did. Only Daniel says he didn't get my letter, so when I got here he was a little taken by surprise."

The housekeeper laughed. "I'm sure he was. Like his mother, Daniel likes things done the way he's planned, and he hates when the plans have been changed. Always has." She sipped from her cup and then smiled at Hannah. "I think you are just what that boy needs."

She didn't want to tell Opal she wasn't so sure. Daniel sometimes acted warm and caring, but then seemed to pull away. As he'd done outside on the porch. One moment he'd seemed concerned for her, but then when she'd mentioned falling in love, he'd pulled back.

Why couldn't Daniel love her? Was it because of her limp? Or had he been expecting a stronger woman? One who could get on a horse without using a porch?

Chapter Thirteen

Daniel paced the barn like a caged lion. Why did his mother have to be so stubborn and demanding? Why couldn't she just for once accept things the way they were?

"If you keep that up, I'll have to spread more hay in here just to cover the poor floor." Jeb sat a few feet away, chewing on the end of a hay straw.

"Jeb, you've known Ma a number of years. Why is she acting so rude to Hannah? Doesn't she realize that the meaner she is to her the harder it will be for me to get Hannah to marry me?"

The old man chuckled. "Have you ever thought that might be her plan?" He pushed himself off the bale of hay and put his floppy hat on his gray head.

Daniel stopped pacing. "Why? What does she have against Hannah? They've just met."

Jeb shook his head. "Think about it, son. If you don't marry Hannah and you marry JoAnna Crawford, what do you have to gain?" He picked up a pitchfork and began tossing hay into the stall.

Daniel frowned. "More land?"

"Adding the Crawford spread to yours would be very profitable to both your mother and Mr. Crawford." Jeb paused to lean on the fork handle.

"So that's it." Daniel took his hat off and slapped it hard against his thigh. "That woman is not going to meddle in my life."

Jeb's throaty laugh filled the barn. "She's been meddling in your life since the day you were born. What's going to stop her now?" He returned to his work.

Daniel stared at the old man. Normally Jeb didn't say more than ten words a day. So why was he being so chatty today? "I will."

The old hand just shrugged and continued working. Daniel tightened the cinch on Tornado and led him out to the barnyard.

Adam was helping Daniel's mother up onto the buckboard. She glanced his way and frowned. Determined to ignore her, he mounted the stallion. He always felt better at this height.

Cole rode up beside him. "I hope you don't mind, but I'm sending young Adam to town with your ma."

He turned the black toward the west pasture. "Why? She's fully capable of driving the buckboard."

"Yes, but I got to thinking about it. What if whoever cut the fences was still hanging about? I'd hate to send our womenfolk off alone." Cole slumped in the saddle, his hat pulled low, the picture of ease.

Daniel nodded in agreement, noticing the extra rifle attached to the other man's saddle. He had been so focused on Hannah that he hadn't considered the bandit who'd cut his fence might mean harm to his family, too. Drat! That woman was already consuming too much of Daniel's thoughts.

He pulled Tornado to a halt. "Hannah's at the house, and as soon as she's finished, I'm sure she'll be heading to the school. Maybe one of us should stay behind and escort her home, as well."

A slow grin spread Cole's lips. "Yeah, I thought of that, also. Levi has agreed to take her back."

"I'll take her back," Daniel growled. He turned the black horse toward the house.

Levi rode out to meet him, a toothy smile on his face. He stood up in the stirrups and called over Daniel's shoulder to Cole, "Told ya he wouldn't cotton to me being the one to take her home."

Daniel shook his head as Cole and Levi rode away, laughing. He turned Tornado toward the barn. Hannah probably wouldn't ride him, and since his mother had just taken the buckboard, Daniel saw no other way of getting her back to the school other than walking.

"Back already, boss?" Jeb stepped out of a stall toward the back of the barn.

He slipped from the stallion's back. "Yep. You still in the mood to talk?"

"Depends."

"On what?" Daniel began to take off the stallion's saddle.

"You, I reckon."

He leaned against the horse and looked at the old man. "Have you ever been in love, Jeb?"

"Once."

"Did she love you?"

"Said she did." Jeb sat down on a bale of hay and picked up a feed sack and a needle with thread.

Daniel turned his attention to caring for his horse.

"How did you make her fall in love with you?" He didn't want Jeb to see his face, so he stayed behind Tornado.

A snort sounded from Jeb's direction. "What kind of fool question is that?" he asked.

"The kind I need an answer to. Hannah wants me to fall in love with her, and her with me, but for the life of me I can't figure out how to make all that happen." He prayed Jeb would keep their conversation to himself. The last thing he needed was for the men to know that he was asking advice on romance from Jeb.

"Aw, so that's the reason you didn't come home married. Me and the boys were wonderin' about that." He poked the needle through the fabric.

"I'd just appreciate it if you didn't share this conversation with the boys." Daniel placed a feed bag over Tornado's nose.

"Don't see no call to tell them your business, boss." Jeb continued sewing.

"So?"

Jeb looked up from his stitching. "So what?"

"So how do I make her fall in love with me?"

"Aw, well, son, you don't." He went back to the sack.

Daniel sighed. "Then what do I do? She won't marry me until she falls in love with me, and I have to be in love with her."

"Back in my day, if a man wanted to marry a gal, he asked her pa. Nine times out of ten, they'd be married by supper." Jeb chuckled.

If only it were that simple. "Well, it doesn't work like that anymore," Daniel said, sighing.

Jeb laid his work aside and came to stand beside him. "Son, treat her like a real lady. Give her flowers, buy her small gifts and listen to her when she talks. But if you want her to fall in love with you…" he paused and laid a hand on Daniel's shoulder "…then be yourself. Don't try to act like someone you aren't."

The old man started to walk out of the barn. "Jeb? One more question."

He turned around. "All right."

"What does it feel like to be in love?" Daniel had to know what it was he was looking for in himself before he could confess his love for Hannah.

"Some men say they can't eat, but I never went off my feed. And some say they kind of feel sick, but I never felt that way, neither." He stared at the hay at his feet and swirled his boot in it. A faraway expression crossed his face.

Daniel heard himself whisper, "What about you? What happened to you?"

Jeb's old gray eyes came up to meet his. They were filled with tears and memories of long ago. "I gave up everything to be with my Lilly. On the day I realized I could lose her, my heart ripped. She became my heart, and my life, and I never looked back. I believe that's true love." He walked out the barn door.

Daniel realized he didn't really know the old man.

Jeb had been the first hand his pa hired when they'd moved here. Even then he hardly ever spoke, but had always been ready to listen. When Daniel's father died, Jeb had been there to guide him on how to run the ranch. The more Daniel learned about ranching, the more the old man had pulled back. Now Jeb was the handyman. He stepped in when needed. It dawned on Daniel that he'd never told the old man what to do. He didn't need to; Jeb always stayed busy.

Daniel tried to wrap his mind around Jeb's advice.

If he understood correctly, then there were only three things he had to do to make Hannah fall in love with him: take her flowers, buy her small gifts and listen when she talked. He smiled, figuring even he couldn't mess that up. And with him doing those things, she'd believe he loved her deeply. So both of them would be happy.

After putting Tornado away, Daniel stood at the barn door and waited for Hannah to come outside. He inhaled the various ranch scents of hay, dirt and livestock.

Here was where he wanted to remain. His eyes scanned the house, the yard, the corrals, the chicken coop and the vast pastures that stretched in every direction. He'd worked hard to keep his father's dream alive.

Everyone called him boss, but Daniel knew who the real boss was. His mother. If he could get Hannah to marry him and they had a baby within the next year, Daniel felt sure the ranch would be his, and then he really would be the boss and owner of the Westland Ranch.

Hannah stepped out of the kitchen door, seemingly unaware that he watched her. Her cheeks were flushed and she appeared to be deep in thought. She'd almost walked passed him when he said the first thing that came to mind. "A penny for your thoughts."

Her head came up and her eyes shone. "I'm not sure they are worth a penny, Daniel."

He moved to her side and smiled. "Tell me what they are and I'll decide the value." He took her elbow and began strolling in the direction of the schoolhouse.

She pulled her arm from his grasp but continued walking with him. "I was thinking of all the things I need to do to start school on Monday, and I was wondering what the ranch hands are going to say when your mother announces our engagement on Sunday. The thought entered my mind that falling in love may not be a simple thing for either of us, and I was wondering if I should just go to town and find a job and forget this whole business of being a mail-order bride."

So she was having doubts about their future. Daniel didn't want her to go back to town. It wasn't because he loved her, but he did care for her. And what would she do there in town? "I'd say your thoughts are worth more than a penny," he volunteered, as they continued to walk.

"You think so?" Doubt filled her voice.

He nodded. "Let's take them one at a time. Your first thought was about the job ahead of you, preparing for school. Haven't you taught before?" He knew from her letters that she had, but wanted her to see that she would have no trouble preparing for the job ahead.

"You know I have." Her forehead furrowed in thought.

Daniel stopped under a large oak tree. "Then you will have no trouble getting started on Monday. As for the announcement on Sunday, everyone is going to love you and be pleased that we are planning to marry." He reached out and ran the back of his hand over her soft cheek. "Opal, Cole and Levi already like you. You have shown them that you are a kind person, Hannah. The others will feel the same."

Her eyes turned to pools of blue. He cupped her chin in his hand and looked deeply into their depths. In a softer voice he said, "As for it being hard to fall in love, we won't know until we give it a try. I'm still willing to work on it. Are you?"

She nodded. "I just don't want you to feel I'm being unreasonable."

"I won't lie to you—I am disappointed that we didn't get married when you arrived. But I also realize that your needs and feelings are important to you. I don't want you to feel forced into a marriage that you will be unhappy in. So let's agree to get to know one another and try to make it a happy union."

Hannah took a step back from him. He missed the feel of her face in his hand and the sense that she was focused totally on him.

"All right. But to be fair, let's agree that if we don't have some feelings for each other by the end of six weeks, then I will return to Granite and you can begin a new search for a bride more suitable to your needs." She looked up at him, sorrow filling her eyes.

Daniel took a deep breath and then exhaled. "I can't agree to that, Hannah. Six weeks isn't enough time."

She started to protest and he stopped her. "No, I'll only agree to your terms if you make it six months."

"But Daniel, Levi could marry, and then where will you be? I've been giving this a lot of thought. I know you love this ranch and don't want to lose it."

She'd thought about him and his love for the ranch? It both surprised and pleased him that she'd considered his feelings. He stepped forward and took both of her hands in his. "You're right, he might, but I don't think that he will."

"But what if he does?" Her hands felt cold in his.

What would he do? Daniel stared into her pretty blue eyes. He'd have to make Hannah Young fall in love with him as fast as possible, and to do so, he'd start by kissing her.

Chapter Fourteen

Hannah felt Daniel's warm breath upon her lips before his mouth descended. The smells of leather, outdoors and sweet coffee blended and filled her senses. His hands released hers and he pulled her closer, deepening the kiss. Her heartbeat quickened and her mind went blank.

When he pulled back, Daniel looked as confused as she felt. He cleared his throat. "We should get you back to the school. We'll worry about Levi and his potential bride when the time comes."

Hannah nodded, afraid to speak. Her voice might crack, and then what would he think of her?

How had one little kiss affected her so? Weakness had entered her knees and the rest of her limbs. How could that be so? Was she coming down with a sickness? Surely it couldn't have been the kiss. She'd been kissed before and hadn't felt this way afterward.

She felt his hand grasp hers, and walked beside him, curious as to why he was holding her hand. Was he trying to court her the right way? A smile played across her face at the thought. The next six months might not be so bad after all.

When the schoolhouse came into view, Daniel said, "Tomorrow, I'll need to be gone. We have to brand the calves and I have to be there to oversee the work. I'm afraid we'll have to postpone our outing a few more days." He pushed his hat back off his forehead.

Disappointment filled her. She'd been looking forward to spending more time with him. "I understand. I'll be busy myself, getting the schoolroom ready and creating lessons for the children."

He stopped at the stairs and released her hand. "Hannah, with the fences being cut, I'd appreciate it if you'd stick close to the schoolhouse until we catch whoever is doing it."

"Daniel, I'm perfectly capable of taking care of myself."

She didn't like the idea of having to stay at the schoolhouse all the time.

A handsome smile spread his lips. "I'm sure you can."

She nodded.

"Well, do you need anything to make your stay here any more comfortable?" His green eyes held hers.

"No. Thanks to Levi's thoughtfulness I think I have everything I need now. He brought me a table and two chairs for meals and lesson planning at night, and he also gave me a beautiful rocker. He said they were his wedding present to us. Would you like to come in and see them?" Hannah turned to lead the way inside. She could tell Daniel wasn't happy that Levi had brought the furniture. Maybe showing him would make him feel better.

His words stopped her. "No, thanks. I have to get back to work." He turned on his boot heels and headed back toward the barn, where Tornado waited. His voice gentled. "Maybe I can look at them later."

Hannah nodded. She expelled the air in her lungs as she watched him ride away. Hannah didn't know what to think of Daniel's mood swings. One moment he was Mr. Romantic and the next Mr. Grumpy.

That evening and the next day she prepared the classroom for students. On Saturday morning Hannah woke up and decided it was time to start doing work around the ranch. She pulled on her boots and headed to the barn.

As a little girl she'd mucked stalls, collected eggs and fed the chickens. She could do that now, too, if no one else had already done so. The dew on the grass soon had her boots damp. She smiled up into the heavens and thanked the Lord for such a beautiful morning.

She crossed the barnyard, where Jeb came out to meet her. "Good morning, Mr. Jeb."

"Howdy. What can I do for you this morning, Miss Hannah?" he asked around a piece of hay.

Hannah grinned. She'd met Jeb the day of her riding lesson and found she liked his quiet ways. "I was hoping I could do something for you."

Jeb frowned. "What did ya have in mind?"

"I thought maybe I could help clean out the stalls, feed the chickens or maybe collect their eggs. I'll do just about anything to help out."

He shifted the straw from one side of his mouth to the other. "Does the boss know you're down here?"

Hannah wasn't sure if he meant Daniel or his mother. She didn't relish the idea of having to ask either of them if she could to do a few chores. "No, I didn't think I needed to ask permission to work. On our farm back home, people just did what needed to be done."

Jeb chuckled. "I like your way of thinkin'. Come with me." He led her into the barn.

The smell of hay and dust filled her nose and she sneezed. Clover nickered in her stall. Hannah walked up to the little mare and rubbed her muzzle. "What's wrong, ole gal? Did they leave you behind today?"

The mare bobbed her head as if to say yes.

"Can ya paint?" Jeb asked from behind her.

Hannah turned to see him holding a bucket of white-wash and a brush. "Sure can."

"Follow me."

He led her down the fence line to a large chicken coop. "When you get the henhouse done, work your way down the fence thataway." Jeb set the bucket down, handed her the brush and walked off, whistling a happy tune.

Hannah picked up the paint and carried it inside the chicken yard. She pulled the gate closed behind her. Chickens scattered and squawked at her. She ignored them and dipped the brush into the whitewash.

"Well, at least I'm not cooped up in the schoolhouse today." She giggled at her own joke.

As she painted, Hannah noticed that the chicken coop had seen better days. It needed more than just paint; it needed new boards in some places, and she could tell the inside needed a good cleaning. She finished painting, and then moved into the henhouse.

It was big, with two rows of nests. They were dirty and the hay had seen better days. Spiderwebs hung up high where the chickens couldn't get to them. She decided to clean it all up. As she worked, Hannah hummed. The hens that were trying to nest eyed her suspiciously.

Once the place was a little more livable for its occupants, Hannah headed to the barn for fresh hay. The coolness there surprised her. She hadn't realized how hot she was until that moment.

An old brown hat hung on a nail and she plucked it down and plopped it on her overheated head. Then she grabbed as much hay as she could carry and headed back to the chicken coop.

The sweet smell of hay filled the air. Hannah worked quickly, filling boxes and fighting off pecking hens. She collected the eggs and set them outside the gate. Her hair felt plastered to her head and her cheeks were hot, so she stood in the shade of an oak tree, attempting to cool off.

The water trough could use a good cleaning, too, she thought, enjoying a soft breeze. Hannah wondered whose job it was to take care of the chickens. Whoever it was, they were sorely neglectful, in her opinion.

Her gaze moved across the yard to the green pastures that stretched out for miles. Where was Daniel today? Were they still branding calves? Hannah wished she could go and see him. She took the big hat off and wiped her forehead. Well, since she couldn't, she decided to continue working.

How were she and Daniel going to fall in love if they didn't see each other for days? She dumped the water from the trough and proceeded to scrub off the algae with handfuls of sand.

A plan began to form as she worked. If he couldn't stop farming to spend time with her, maybe she could spend time with him. She finished the trough and then refilled it with fresh water from the well.

"You've done a really good job out here."

Hannah spun around on her heels. Opal stood beside the gate. "Thank you. I only planned to paint the hen-house but then saw where it needed a bit more work."

Opal held an egg basket in her hands. "Thanks for collecting these. I've had a slow start this morning. Why don't you come on up to the house for a spot of tea?"

"I'd love to." Hannah looked down at her dirty dress and boots. "But I'm a mess."

"Nonsense, you've been working. You're expected to be a tad dirty. Dust yourself off and come along." The housekeeper walked away, leaving her to follow.

Hannah hurried to catch up with her. "Thank you. Tea sounds lovely." She immediately wished she had one of her friend Eliza's sticky buns. Her stomach growled at the thought.

Opal laughed. "Sounds like you could use lunch, also."

She felt her face flush. "Oh, no, I don't want to be any trouble."

"No trouble at all. Wash up and come on inside," the woman instructed, and then went into the kitchen.

Hannah hurried to do as she was asked. She hung the brown hat on a nail by the door and then dipped her hands into the basin. The water felt wonderful on her palms, so she splashed it on her neck and face, also. She dried off and hurried inside to find Opal sitting at the table with a pot of tea, two cups and a plate of food.

The housekeeper looked up. "I hope you are in the mood for a chicken salad sandwich. I've added a couple of pickles and sliced tomatoes."

"Thank you." Hannah slipped into her chair and said a quick blessing over her lunch. When she finished, she looked up to find Opal studying her.

Dark circles rested below the woman's eyes. "Thank you for taking care of the chicken house. I've been meaning to get out there, but my daughter is having a rough time carrying this newest baby and, well, between helping her and my inside chores, I just haven't had time to get to the henhouse."

Hannah liked the older woman and wanted to help. "It was my pleasure. I wouldn't mind lending a hand around here, if you'll let me." She began eating as she waited for her to answer.

"You wouldn't mind?" Opal asked.

Hannah took a sip of tea. "I would enjoy it. I'll be honest with you—I'm bored at the schoolhouse." She reached for the sugar bowl and added a teaspoon into her cup.

Opal's face brightened. "It would be nice to have some help. Would you mind tending the chickens and collecting the eggs in the mornings?"

Those were chores Hannah had done on her father's farm. She smiled. "I'll be glad to."

Opal frowned briefly. "Will it interfere with teaching the children?" She took a sip of tea.

"Not at all. I'm going to start classes midmorning and carry on through the heat of the day. Midafternoon the children will be released to go home and help with chores." She pushed her empty plate back. "I will be happy to help you with your morning tasks."

"Thank you. And I'll make sure that you have a proper breakfast and lunch." Opal grinned from ear to ear.

"I'm not sure that's a good idea. Mrs. Westland might object." Hannah folded her hands in her lap. She needed to find a way to befriend Daniel's mother, and eating her food probably wasn't the way to do that.

"Oh, pish posh! Bonnie isn't going to care if you eat a few vittles in exchange for helping me get the chores done around here." She picked up her teacup and carried it to the sink. "Besides, I'm looking forward to having another female around to talk to." Opal returned for Hannah's plate and cup.

Hannah liked her spunk. "If you're sure, then it's a deal." She held out her hand for Opal to shake.

The older woman surprised her by ignoring her hand and grabbing her in a swift hug. "I'm so glad our Daniel found you."

The sound of the front door slamming and Daniel's voice bellowing, "Opal! Ma! Have either of you seen Hannah!" pulled the two women apart.

Was that fear she heard in Daniel's voice? If so, what did he think had happened to her? Did the emotion in his voice mean he cared about her? So many questions raced through Hannah's mind as she hurried to assure him she was there.

Chapter Fifteen

Daniel's breath came hard and heavy. He couldn't believe Hannah was gone. He stood in the middle of his mother's living room, waiting for her or Opal to appear. He'd told Hannah not to leave the schoolhouse. How long had she been gone?

Guilt ate at him as he realized he should have gone to see her yesterday or sent someone else to check on her. Daniel jerked his hat off and slapped it against his leg. His other hand moved to rub the back of his neck. Had she gone back to town? Given up on him loving her? He inhaled another deep breath, and just as he planned to yell for his mother again, he heard Hannah's voice.

"I'm here, Daniel. What are you yelling about?"

His gaze swung to the dining area. Hannah stood in the doorway with Opal behind her. Her hair was sticking out in all directions and straw and dust clung to it. The dress she wore was covered in mud and muck. He gasped. What had the poor woman gone through to put her in such a state?

"What's all the yelling about?" Bonnie Westland

came down the stairs at a run. She saw the direction Daniel was staring, and turned to look, too.

Daniel ignored his mother and hurried to Hannah. A smudge of dirt marred one creamy cheek. Her nose and cheeks had been sunburned. "Are you all right?" he asked, reaching up to wipe away the dirt.

"I'm fine. I was having lunch with Opal." Her blue eyes stared up at him in confusion.

He said the first thing that came to mind. "Are you sure? You don't look so good."

Hannah gasped.

Bonnie laughed.

And Opal scolded, "You wouldn't look so great yourself if you'd cleaned and painted the chicken house this morning. Where are your manners, Daniel?"

He looked from one woman to the other. "I'm sorry, Hannah, I didn't mean to insult you. Mother, stop laughing." His jaw tightened and he reached out and grabbed Hannah's hand. "If you will excuse us, I need to talk to Hannah in private." Relief and anger fought for control of his emotions. Anger won. Why hadn't she stayed at the school as he'd told her to?

Her hand felt small and warm in his as he pulled her across the room and out the front door. Just as he shut the door behind him, he heard his mother call, "Play nice, Daniel." Her laughter followed them down the steps.

He slapped his hat back on, grabbed Tornado's reins as they passed the stallion and continued on across the yard.

"Daniel, slow down." Hannah pulled against his hand.

"I'll slow down once I get you back to the school," he answered, continuing at his fast pace.

She dug her feet into the earth.

Daniel growled deep in his throat. Turned around, scooped her up and then seated her up onto Tornado's saddle. Confused blue eyes searched his face before he mounted behind her and wrapped his arms around her waist.

Hannah clung to the saddle horn. Her hair had come down from his rough treatment and curled about her shoulders.

Tornado took off like a shot across the yard, through the strand of trees and then on past the school. Her hair brushed against his face. The soft material of her dress brushed his arm.

She called over her shoulder, "I thought you were taking me to the schoolhouse."

He ignored her. Right now all he wanted to do was ride with the wind in his face. He wasn't sure who he was angry with, her for disobeying his orders or himself for caring so much about what could have happened to her. What if she'd been kidnapped? Hurt?

She relaxed against him, releasing the saddle horn. Why? Did Hannah trust him not to let her fall? He'd never understand women. She had no reason to trust him, and yet here she sat with her back resting against him, her eyes closed and her head on his shoulder.

Daniel pulled Tornado to a walk.

Hannah opened her eyes and looked at him. "Why are you so angry?"

He leaned forward and answered in a low, throaty voice, "Because I told you to stay at the school."

She moved forward in the saddle. "And I told you I can take care of myself."

"Hannah, there is danger on a ranch this size. Anything could happen to you. Just this morning we found two of our cows and their calves butchered in the west pasture. Someone is on Westland lands who shouldn't be." He guided Tornado up a steep hill. Hannah slid back against his chest once more.

She reached up and cupped his jaw. "Does this mean you were concerned for me?"

"Of course I was concerned for you." Her fingers felt soft against his cheek. The urge to lean into her touch was tempting.

She dropped her hand as Tornado lurched to the top of the rise. The big stallion snorted and shook his head. Daniel pulled him to a halt.

Below was his house, the home he'd hoped to be sharing with Hannah already. He loved this spot. The structure stood in a grove of oak trees, with a stream running alongside, far enough away not to flood the place but close enough that he could listen to its music. A meadow lay in front of it and in the evenings deer would come and drink from the stream.

"Oh, Daniel, what a beautiful place," Hannah said, her gaze taking it all in.

He didn't respond with words, not sure what to say. Daniel eased Tornado down the incline toward the house, where he stopped the stallion and slipped off his back. Reaching up for her, he answered. "This is our home, Hannah."

Once on the ground she stepped out of his arms and walked to the front porch. "Our home?"

Daniel came up behind her and placed his hands on her shoulders. "Yes."

"I thought your mother started this contest at Christmas. That was only six months ago, Daniel. You built this place that fast?"

He looked at the large house, which was shaped like a capital L. It had taken longer than six months to get it finished—more like eight. "No, I started working on this house last fall. I completed it a couple of months ago." At the time he'd started building it, it had been for him alone. Now he knew he'd be sharing it with Hannah. The thought both annoyed and pleased him. *Get it together, Daniel. You are marrying for the ranch, not for love.*

"Oh, I see," Hannah said. She'd hoped he'd built the house with her in mind, but now knew that wasn't possible. To hide her disappointment she asked, "Can we go inside?"

Daniel gave her shoulders a gentle squeeze. "Sure can. I want to show you what I added after I started writing to you." He grabbed her left hand and pulled her forward.

So there was something in the house that he'd created with her in mind. Hannah smiled. They climbed the three low steps and he opened the door.

He held it for her. Hannah passed him and the scent of leather and the outdoors enveloped her. She smiled up at him, and then turned to see the room she'd just entered.

It was a nice-size living room, with a big fireplace against the back wall. A large brown chair sat beside the hearth, but there was no other furniture. She could see that the room opened into the kitchen and a dining area. The fresh scent of wood filled her with a sense of happiness, something she couldn't really explain.

Hannah walked to the kitchen. It was a spacious room, but again wasn't furnished, and she frowned. It was almost as if Daniel had never really planned on living in the house. She turned to him and asked, "Where is the furniture?"

A light pink color moved up his neck and into his face. "I was waiting for you to get here and planned on letting you pick out the furnishings."

She walked over and hugged him. "Daniel, I think that's one of the nicest things you've said to me."

His arms wrapped around her and he hugged her back. "I haven't been very nice, have I?" He chuckled.

Hannah pulled out of his embrace and slapped his arm. "That's not what I meant and you know it."

Her attention went back to the house. She stepped out of the kitchen and into the dining area. A bay window took her breath away with its beauty. It allowed a lot of light into the room. She gasped. "Oh, Daniel, it's beautiful. I love the window."

A smile creased his face. He stood with his hands in his back pockets and rocked on his heels. "I hoped you would. At first it was just a small window, one I thought you could put a flower box on. But the more we wrote, the more I realized you'd be the type of woman who enjoyed lots of sunshine."

She walked to him until they were standing inches apart. Hannah stared up at him. "You added it because of my letters to you?"

His hands came out of his pockets and he stopped rocking. "I wanted you to be happy. You said in one of your letters that you were looking forward to living on a ranch again because you missed the open spaces and the sunshine."

This time Hannah impulsively rose on tiptoe, cupped his handsome face in her hands and kissed him. His arms snaked around her and he returned the kiss, until she pulled away and said, "Thank you."

He released her reluctantly. "Want to see the rest of the house? I'm interested to see if any of the other rooms will garner more kisses."

She saw the teasing glint in his eyes. "I do, but don't expect kisses in every room."

Daniel took her hand again and escorted her through the rest of the house. There was a small staircase that led upstairs, where three bedrooms had been built. She noticed there was no furniture in any of those rooms, either.

When they came back downstairs, she realized they hadn't explored the rest of the first floor. Daniel dropped her hand and let her precede him into what proved to be a large bedroom. There was a huge bed in the center and a chest of drawers against one wall, with a basin and water pitcher sitting on top.

Hannah realized this was the master bedroom. She saw an armoire sitting against the other wall with a dressing table beside it, and knew it was meant for her. He'd done the room in soft blues and greens. The wedding-ring quilt covering the bed reminded her that he'd prepared this room for them.

He cleared his throat. "There is another room through that door."

She turned to see that he'd leaned against the door-jamb. His arms and ankles were crossed, and his deep green eyes studied her. Hannah felt her face flush, and turned away.

The next room was smaller, but it, too, had furniture. A small dresser and bassinet lined one wall. He'd covered the window with light blue curtains.

She walked over to the bassinet and looked down to find a small pillow and blanket covering the little mattress. Had Daniel dreamed of the day when a baby would sleep there? Or had this been part of winning his mother's contest?

Hannah turned to face him but saw that he hadn't followed her. She retreated from the room and discovered him missing from the bedroom, as well. Daniel wasn't in the living room, either. The house held no sound, so she assumed he'd stepped outside.

She walked back to the dining room. Her feet carried her to the window that he'd taken such pains to put in for her. Hannah loved the house. She loved the thought of living there happily forever. Daniel had admitted earlier that he was concerned for her. Could he fall in love with her? And if so, would it be an unconditional love?

Hannah took one more look about the dining room and then turned to leave. Would they share more kisses in this house or was she doomed to be disappointed? *Lord, if it be Your will, please let him love me, and let me be wise enough to know what real love is and what it isn't.*

With that silent prayer, Hannah closed the door of the house and went in search of Daniel.

Chapter Sixteen

Daniel stood by the stream's edge, letting Tornado drink his fill. What had Hannah thought of the nursery? He'd hoped it would be a room she'd enjoy. He thought they could have the babies close when they were little, and then eventually move them to the bedrooms upstairs. Once the last child was up there in his or her own room, Hannah could convert the nursery into a sewing room or sitting room.

Ducks floated on the stream, creating a sense of peace within him. He couldn't help but wonder, what would it be like to have children with Hannah?

He'd enjoyed the two kisses they'd shared and felt as if they would be compatible once they were married. She was smart, beautiful and had a quick sense of humor. To his way of thinking, any children that might come from their union would be much like her. He'd built the house with four spare bedrooms and had thought they could have three children and an extra room for a guest.

Daniel picked up a piece of driftwood and drew circles in the sand at the water's edge. In his mind's eye he envisioned little ones playing along this bank. Their children would have black hair and blue eyes or brown hair and green eyes. If he was lucky, he'd have a little girl who looked just like Hannah. He smiled at the thought.

When he was building the house, he'd thought about children a lot. They'd seemed unreal and no threat to his plan to not fall in love. But now, with Hannah in the house, looking down on the bassinet, he'd grasped just how real a family would be.

How would he guard his heart from loving them too deeply? Daniel honestly didn't think he could, and that scared him. If he couldn't guard his heart, then there was always the chance it could be broken. With small children on a ranch there was always the danger of one of them getting hurt, or worse, dying.

Was that part of the reason he hadn't left Hannah in town and sent off for a new bride? As long as she refused to marry him, his heart was safe from both her and any future children they might have.

He felt as if a thunderstorm was building in his brain. If he didn't marry before Levi and have the first grandchild, then his brother would get the ranch. Daniel knew he wanted it himself. But to have the ranch, would he take a chance on love, and on losing another loved one to the hazards of ranch life?

Thankfully, it seemed as if Levi had given up on sending off for a mail-order bride. Daniel had bought six months with Hannah, but after that, what was he going to do?

He closed his eyes, and immediately the night of his sister's death came racing back. He and Levi had returned during a thunderstorm and found her small, trampled body in the barn. Remembering took his breath away.

Gracie Joy had only wanted to comfort her pony, of that he was certain, but instead the little Shetland had pushed her down and run over her in his fear. The doctor said she'd died instantly, but he wasn't so sure.

"Daniel?" He opened his eyes to find Hannah staring at him. "The house is very nice."

He tried to smile, but the action felt stiff upon his face. "I'm glad you like it." And he was glad. But now that she was here, and it all seemed so real, Daniel was beginning to think he should have bought a house in town. At least there the children would be safe from ranching dangers.

"Do you think we can go back now?" she asked, eyeing Tornado doubtfully. It was clear she didn't want to get on the horse again.

Daniel picked up the reins and walked toward her. She backed away. He stopped and asked, "Want to talk about it?"

"You'll think I'm… Well, I don't know what you'll think, but I feel foolish." She tucked a wayward strand of hair behind her ear.

He reached out and grasped one of her hands, which felt cold in his. Daniel gently pulled her to him. "I know Tornado scares you, but you didn't seem to mind riding on him this afternoon."

She didn't drop his hand, but moved to the right, placing Daniel between herself and the big stallion. "I don't mind riding Tornado."

Daniel began walking. "Then what are you afraid of?"

"Promise not to laugh?" she asked, twisting her free hand in her skirt.

…ough before they could make it their home. "Yes, please." The words came out soft and tearful, something Hannah decided she couldn't control at this moment.

He turned her toward the big stallion. "Will you trust me?"

She knew they'd come a long way on the animal and would need to return on him, as well. Hannah swallowed the lump of fear in her throat. She'd just poured her heart out to Daniel, told him what she'd never told another. Did she trust him? She raised her head and looked him in the eyes. "Yes, I trust you."

Daniel smiled in approval. He scooped her up into his arms and walked the rest of the way to the stal-

"I'll do my best."

Hannah pulled her shoulders back, raised her chin and said, "I'm afraid he might step on my foot."

She'd never told him how she'd acquired the limp, but Daniel thought he knew now. "You've been stepped on before?" he asked.

"Yes, when I was a kid. A stallion tromped on me." Hannah continued to stare straight ahead.

"I'd like to know what happened. Can you talk about it?" Daniel asked. Again his thoughts went to the possibility that someday his child could be hurt by a horse or bull, or bitten by a snake. The dangers of ranch life were endless.

Hannah nodded. "I was ten years old and my father and I were gathering the cattle out of the back pasture. I'd climbed off my horse and was trying to pull a calf out of the mud when Pa rode up. I'd gotten the calf out and had just turned to get back on my own horse when something spooked Blaze. He stepped sideways and my ankle ended up under his hoof."

She looked off into the distance, but not before Daniel saw the tears welling in her eyes.

"Pa said I screamed and passed out. When I woke up, the doctor was there, and I heard him tell my father and stepmother I'd probably never walk on that foot again." She took a deep breath. "But he was wrong." Determination laced her words. "I wasn't about to let a little limp keep me from working beside my pa on our ranch." A tear escaped and ran down her cheek.

Daniel stopped walking and turned her to face him. He wiped the tear away with his thumb. He looked deeply into her eyes and could see the hurt little girl

Wasn't that what he might have ⌐⌐⌐ could see the pain it was causing Hannah, Daniel kne he could never send a child away. Which still left h wondering what he was going to do about the ranch a about marrying Hannah.

After several minutes in Daniel's arms, Har calmed down. Her tears slowly dried and she wa feeling foolish once more. She'd never cried abo father's rejection. Why did she have to choose n do so?

She eased away slowly. "I'm sorry, Daniel." H turned from him and wiped at her damp face w dirty sleeve of her dress. She really was a mes there. "What happened next?" Something told him the worst was yet to come.

Her voice cracked as she said, "Pa didn't want me anymore. As soon as I could walk, he sent me away to school." Tears streamed down her face and her bottom lip began to tremble. The broken words tumbled from her lips. "He didn't love me anymore, Daniel. He wanted to get rid of me. I'd always thought he loved me, but he didn't." She sobbed, "He'd only used me as a ranch hand."

Daniel gathered her into his arms, then rubbed her back and held her tight. No wonder Hannah was asking for unconditional love. If she truly believed her own father didn't love her, how could she trust someone else to?

As she sobbed, he decided to see if he could find her parents and reunite Hannah with her family. Daniel couldn't help but think that maybe her father had sent her away out of fear of her getting hurt even more.

"There is nothing to be sorry for, Hannah. Your parents hurt you."

She wanted to tell him it wasn't her parents, just her father. Her mother had died six years earlier and her father had remarried. When she'd left home, Hannah had had a four-year-old brother and a two-year-old sister. Caught up in remembering them, she almost forgot about Daniel until he tugged on her hand.

He waited for her to face him, and then continued, "We all have things in our past that have hurt us. Thank you for sharing yours. I promise if we ever have children, I will not send them away."

Hannah didn't trust herself to speak. His kindness was bringing up the flood of tears again and she refused to let it burst a second time in front of him. She ducked her head and nodded.

"Are you ready to go home now?"

Home. She looked at the house behind them and wished it was home. Wished she and Daniel didn't still lion. He placed her in the saddle and then swung up behind her.

"That wasn't so bad, was it?"

When his arms snaked around her, Hannah relaxed. "No. Thanks."

As the horse set off, rocking them with a smooth canter, her thoughts returned to Daniel's kind words. He'd said, *We all have things in our past that have hurt us.* This troubled Hannah. What or who had hurt Daniel? He'd shown her that he was a kind, caring man. She didn't like the idea of him being hurt.

She tilted her head and looked up at him. His jawline was sprinkled with day-old stubble. He seemed more relaxed than she'd ever seen him as his eyes scanned the land about them. What was he thinking? Did he regret having sent for her, now that he'd seen her broken and crying?

"It's peaceful out here, isn't it?" he asked.

She wondered if he'd sensed her looking at him. Hannah allowed her gaze to follow his. Cows bawled softly in a pasture in the distance. Crows called to each other overhead, and the sweet scent of honeysuckle filled the warm afternoon breeze. "It is."

"Hannah, I wish I could keep it this peaceful, but I know that trouble is always near. If you are going to stay here, you should learn to be more aware of your surroundings." He tightened his grip on the reins.

She wanted to get angry with him for telling her that she'd been neglectful, but she knew he was right. Until he'd mentioned the peacefulness of their surroundings, she'd been unaware. "I will."

His arms closed around her in a brief hug. "Good.

I told you earlier someone is on Westland land that shouldn't be. I'd like to tell you the whole story."

"All right," Hannah answered. She saw a rabbit jump out of a bush and rush to another.

"They started with simply cutting fences, then moved on to running our stock off our land and now they have taken to slaughtering stock and completely destroying fences, so that it takes a couple of days to get them back up." Daniel shifted his weight.

Hannah wondered who would have done such a thing. "Do you have any idea who it might be?"

"Not at this point," he answered. His breath ruffled the top of her hair.

A shiver crawled up Hannah's spine. She tried to ignore the sensation. "Could it be a disgruntled neighbor?"

"I don't believe so. Most of the men will be at Sunday service. I plan on asking if any of them are having the same problems." He brought his left hand down and rested it on his leg.

Hannah nodded. "That's a good plan."

His voice hardened as he said, "Hannah, please stay at the schoolhouse. I don't want you wandering the ranch by yourself."

So now he felt he could boss her around. She straightened her spine. "I've promised I'll help Opal in the mornings, so I won't be staying at the schoolhouse, Daniel. I'll be walking over to the ranch house every morning." Hannah cut her eyes upward and looked at his jaw. Yep, as she'd suspected, it had tightened and no longer looked relaxed.

"Someone who doesn't belong here has been killing

cattle is on this land. I can't look after you all the time, Hannah." He stressed her name.

She shifted away from him. "I didn't ask you to, Daniel." She'd put emphasis on his name just as he had hers. "I told you I can take care of myself."

He ignored her declaration of independence. "What time will you be going over to the ranch house?"

"Before breakfast." Hannah realized as soon as the words were out of her mouth that she didn't know what time Opal served the first meal of the day.

Daniel laid his chin on top of her head. "You do realize breakfast is at five, don't you?"

Hannah prayed her voice sounded confident when she answered, "I grew up on a farm, Daniel." She said it as if that should be obvious, but the truth was she'd been young and hadn't really thought about time when she lived there.

"Good. Then I'll see you around four. I believe this is where you get off." He slipped from Tornado's back and turned to lift her down.

Hannah looked at the schoolhouse, and then slid into Daniel's waiting arms. She felt like a little girl again as he swung her away from the horse.

When her feet touched the ground she said, "Daniel, you don't have to come for me in the morning. I can make my way to the house alone."

He remounted Tornado and gathered the reins. "I'm sure you can, but I don't want you stumbling around in the dark. See you tomorrow." With that, he sent the horse into a gallop and rode away.

Hannah grinned. Maybe, just maybe, Daniel Westland was starting to care about her. She wouldn't label it love just yet.

The grin slipped from her face. Hannah knew she liked him, too, but she didn't want to fall for Daniel until she was sure that he loved her. Weariness weighed on her shoulders at the thought.

Chapter Seventeen

Daniel arrived at the schoolhouse a little after four-thirty the next morning, with Clover in tow for Hannah to ride. He knew she wasn't going to be happy to see the little mare, but if Hannah was going to travel about the ranch, she needed to overcome her fear of horses' hooves.

She answered the door with a big smile, until she saw the mare. It slipped from her face like hot wax dripping down a candle. "I see you brought Clover for a visit."

His gaze ran over her. Daniel was glad to see she didn't seem as distressed as the day before. It appeared she'd had a bath and washed her hair. The gown she wore was faded, but he assumed that was so that she wouldn't ruin one of her best dresses. "Yes, I thought it time you started riding again," he answered, moving aside so she could join him. "Think of it as a way to prove to your father that you can do anything anyone else can do."

"I don't have to prove anything to him." Her face had gone ashen, but she followed Daniel down the stairs. "Besides, I don't mind walking the short distance."

"True, but I do mind walking, and if you are going to start going places on the ranch, you really need to learn to ride again." Daniel turned and put both hands on her shoulders. "Hannah, you can do this. You taught yourself to walk with an ankle that a doctor said you'd never use again. You went to school and became a teacher. You can do this!" he declared.

"All right." Hannah nodded, but he could feel her shoulders trembling.

Daniel took one of her hands in his and walked to where he'd tied Clover's reins to a low branch. "Hannah, you know where your feet are at all times, right?"

Again she nodded.

"Then you can make sure they stay away from Clover's hooves." He went to the horse's head and petted her nose.

Hannah moved closer to the little mare. He watched as she checked the cinch, then took a deep breath and accepted the reins from him. Had Levi reminded her to check the cinch when they'd attempted to get her on the horse before? Or were her instincts kicking in? Daniel prayed it was the latter.

Hannah exhaled. She put the reins in her left hand and also grasped Clover's mane with it, then put her left foot in the stirrup and grabbed the saddle with her right hand. Hannah's memories must have taken over, because seconds later she was in the saddle.

He averted his gaze while she straightened her skirt. Daniel released the mare. He walked to Tornado, gathered the reins and swung up into the saddle.

"I did it." She beamed over at him.

He laughed. "Yes, you did. I knew you could."

Her smile warmed his heart. "Thank you, Daniel.

I can't believe how easy that was. All these years I've been afraid to climb on by myself." She looked like a kid who'd just won the pie-eating contest at the fair.

What he'd taken for granted was something she'd just experienced again for the first time in years. "You're welcome, but I didn't do anything but bring you a horse."

"You encouraged me." She patted Clover's neck.

Daniel prompted the stallion to walk beside Hannah and the old mare. "What are you helping Opal with this morning?"

"I'm going to feed the chickens and gather the eggs. Then I'll do whatever else she asks me to." Hannah allowed Clover to fall into step with Tornado.

Daniel made sure to keep the horses far enough apart that the stallion wouldn't act up. "Why?"

"Yesterday I was looking for something to do, and Jeb let me whitewash the chicken coop. Well, I noticed it needed a few repairs, and the eggs collected, so I took it upon myself to do those things."

Daniel felt guilty once more. If he had checked on her sooner, Hannah wouldn't have gotten bored. "That still doesn't answer my question. Why are you going to help today?"

Her soft giggle filled the crisp morning air. "Oh, I'm sorry. When Opal came to collect the eggs yesterday, we got to talking and she told me her daughter is having difficulties with the new baby. With all she normally does, and helping her daughter, she'd gotten behind on some of her chores. I offered to help, and here we are."

Hannah seemed to be talking more this morning. She sounded nervous and excited at the same time. Was it because of him? Or did she realize that since she'd gotten on Clover by herself, she'd have to learn to get down, too?

"That's very nice of you to offer to help her, but you don't have to do that. I'll talk to her and see if she wants me to hire another girl to help her out." He enjoyed the sounds of a rooster crowing. Mornings were his favorite time of day, with everything seeming fresh and new. His gaze moved to Hannah, who looked fresh and new this morning, also.

She flicked her ponytail over her shoulder and looked at him. "You'll do no such thing. I want to help. If this is going to be my home, too, I want to do all I can to make it successful."

Daniel grinned. He liked the idea that she was thinking of the ranch as her home. Holding his hands up in surrender, he laughed and said, "All right, but don't forget that after we're married, you'll have your own household chores to do. Speaking of which, we're here, and I have work to do, too, before breakfast." He spun Tornado around and headed across the yard to the east pasture.

As he rode away, he remembered Hannah might need help dismounting from Clover. Daniel didn't want her to think he was checking up on her, so he entered the edge of the woods, making sure she could no longer see him, and then turned to see how she fared.

She hesitated, twisting in the saddle and looking down. After she'd judged the distance, she swung her leg over the saddle and sort of leaped from the horse.

Daniel held his breath until she stood up, then he released it slowly. He chuckled and said to himself, "Well, I guess there is more than one way to get off a horse."

* * *

Hannah sat at the kitchen table with Opal, eating breakfast. She'd fed and watered the chickens, gathered the eggs, milked two of the five milk cows and washed most of the dishes while Opal served the Westland family breakfast.

"I can't believe how much we've gotten done this morning. Thank you for your help," the housekeeper said as she buttered a biscuit.

Hannah stifled a yawn and smiled. "You're welcome." She hated to admit that 4:00 a.m. came earlier than she remembered.

Breakfast consisted of eggs, bacon, ham, biscuits, gravy and grits. She'd watched as Opal carried platters in to the family and later returned with them empty. To keep herself busy, Hannah had washed the pots and pans Opal had used to cook the meal in.

"I didn't expect you to do the dishes, too, but it sure made my job easier this morning." Opal chewed the bread with relish.

Hannah dipped a fork into her scrambled eggs. "I'm glad I could help." She enjoyed the creaminess of the eggs and the saltiness of the bacon. After she swallowed, she added, "Thank you for inviting me to breakfast. I have to admit I haven't done any real cooking in the fireplace at the school, and this tastes wonderful."

Opal laughed. "You deserve every bite. Jeb stopped by yesterday afternoon and said that henhouse hasn't looked so good in years."

Hannah stopped eating. "He did?"

Bonnie Westland came through the kitchen door. "Yes, he did. It seems you've made quite an impression on Jeb." She walked to the stove and filled her coffee cup. "How come you didn't join us for breakfast, Hannah?" Those green eyes bored into Hannah as Daniel's mother waited for an answer.

"I didn't want to intrude." Hannah laid her fork down, no longer interested in the food on her plate.

Bonnie pulled a chair out and sat down. "I see. If you are going to become a part of this family, you need to start sharing meals with us." She set her cup on the table and played with the string on her cotton blouse.

Confusion filled Hannah's mind. Why was Bonnie showing a sudden interest in her now? "If you don't mind my saying so, Mrs. Westland, you haven't exactly made me feel welcome."

Daniel's mother sighed. "I know, and the Lord has been dealing with me about my attitude toward you. So today, after my prayer time, I realized I had to come and apologize to you. I haven't behaved well at all and I'm sorry."

"Why do you dislike me?" Hannah asked, giving no quarter. She needed to get on solid ground with Bonnie if she was going to be her daughter-in-law.

Bonnie looked to Opal, who nodded. "I don't dislike you, Hannah. When I tossed this contest into the wind, I thought my boys would marry local girls, but I was wrong."

Hannah said, "You're talking about JoAnna and Lucille." She picked up her tea and took a sip.

Bonnie nodded. "Yes. I'm sure the boys have told you all about them."

Instead of confirming what she'd said, Hannah asked. "Why did you pitch the boys against each other with this contest?" It was the question she'd been longing to ask ever since the day she'd heard they were competing for the ranch, and it was their mother's doing.

The woman released a deep sigh. "I didn't mean to set them against each other. The night I made my demands I was lonely for my husband. I looked at my boys and saw that they weren't getting any younger, and I wanted them to be as happy as I was with their father. I wanted grandchildren. I still do."

Hannah stared deeply into Bonnie's eyes and saw the truth of her words. She also saw the sorrow the woman felt for creating a wedge between the brothers. "You can call off the contest," she suggested.

Bonnie had started shaking her head before the words were completely out of Hannah's mouth. "No, I still stand by the contest. Those boys need wives and I need grandchildren. As for the ranch, well, I started something and now I have to stick to my word." She gulped down the last of her coffee and stood. "And Hannah, I like your straightforwardness. You are welcome to move into the house if you want to."

Hannah carried her plate to the scrap bucket and scraped it before answering. It was a kind offer, but she liked her small room and the privacy it provided. "Thank you, but I think I'll stay where I am for the time being, Mrs. Westland."

"Please, call me Bonnie. I'd like for us to become friends, even if you don't marry my son." She handed her cup to Opal. "Opal, I'll lay out a couple of my riding skirts for Hannah and a pair of trousers. If she's going to continue doing chores around here, she needs to be dressed appropriately." Bonnie spun around and headed to the door.

The idea of having more comfortable clothes sounded

good, but Hannah didn't want her to think she needed her help. "That isn't necessary, Bonnie."

Daniel's mother had one hand on the door and was about to leave. She turned around and smiled at Hannah. "Yes, it is. If you plan to get my son to marry you, you need to go where he goes, because he won't be an easy man to persuade. Besides, I want you to have them."

Hannah nodded absently. Her mind raced. She'd thought that if she told Daniel that she was ready to get married, he would marry her on the spot. But if Bonnie was correct in her insinuations, he didn't really want to get married. Hannah's head began to ache with confusion. What man sent off for a mail-order bride and didn't really want to get married?

Chapter Eighteen

Daniel looked across the dinner table at Hannah. Her hair was pulled up and small ringlets framed her face. She wore a blue riding skirt with a white blouse. A butterfly necklace rested against her chest, bringing out the deeper blues in her eyes.

He'd listened as she and his mother talked about the engagement announcement, the hours that the school would be open and what pies Hannah was going to fix for the Sunday get-together with the rest of the ranch.

Levi sat quietly, finishing up the coffee cake Hannah had made. Daniel noticed his younger brother seemed unusually silent tonight and wondered what was on his mind. Did it bother him that their mother and Hannah were getting along so well? Or did it have something to do with the ranch?

Daniel couldn't take it any longer and asked, "Is something bothering you, little brother?"

Levi looked as if someone had shot him. "Yes and no."

Frustrated, Daniel laid his fork down. "Well, which is it?"

Levi's face flushed as everyone turned their attention

to him. "Well, if you must know, I've been pondering which mail-order bride's letter to answer."

"Brides? As in more than one?" Hannah asked.

He nodded.

Bonnie's voice came out low. "You sent off for a mail-order bride, too?"

"Well, I placed the ad and one lady did answer—Millicent. But she didn't come. I have three more letters that came this week, and I'm trying to decide which one to answer." He pulled the letters from his vest pocket.

Daniel watched as his brother spread out the papers on the kitchen table. He frowned, not liking the fact that Levi could have a new mail-order bride there in just a few weeks. Daniel glanced at Hannah, who was staring at him.

"Here, let me get some of this stuff out of your way," Opal said, picking up empty dishes and bowls.

Levi's green eyes, so like Daniel's, came up to meet Hannah's. "I was wondering if you could help me write a letter to one of these ladies."

What? He wanted Hannah to help him find a bride? "Wait a minute. That's not a good idea." Daniel protested, looking from his brother to Hannah.

"Why not?" his mother demanded. "Your brother needs a wife, too. And since you're both dead set on mail-order brides, I don't see what harm it will do for Hannah to help him. She is a schoolteacher, after all."

Didn't his mother realize that Hannah would be helping Levi get married, and that Levi and his bride might have a baby before he and Hannah did? He looked at her and saw a small smile play across her lips. Yes, she knew. His mother was trying to speed up the process of getting grandchildren. He sighed.

Levi's face reddened and he rubbed the back of his neck. "I wouldn't ask, but I'm not sure how to respond, since Millicent didn't come. I think I did something wrong the first time." Levi kept his eyes trained on the letters.

"Do you mind if I read them?" Hannah asked, reaching for the closest piece of paper. He looked up and grinned.

"Feel free."

When Hannah picked the letter up, a strong smell of roses permeated the air. The scent became even stronger as she unfolded it.

"Woo-wee, someone likes flowers," Daniel exclaimed, covering his nose at the strong odor.

Hannah ignored him and focused on the words as she read them aloud.

"My dearest Mr. Westland,
After reading your advertisement, I decided to respond with a letter, telling you a little about myself. I am twenty-five years old. Have all my teeth and am a widow. My husband died a few weeks back from the fever, so I am in need of a husband who can take care of me in the fashion I am acquainted with. If you feel you can take care of me and provide me with all the comforts of home, I will be happy to come out and be your bride. I look forward to meeting you.
Sincerely,
Mrs. Elizabeth Marsh."

Hannah looked across at Levi. "What do you think about her?"

Daniel snorted and crossed his arms. Elizabeth Marsh seemed to presume a lot. Sounded to him that the woman was a money digger, but he kept that to himself when he saw the look his mother was shooting his way.

Levi grinned sheepishly. "She must smell pretty." He handed Hannah the next letter.

Bonnie and Hannah chuckled. "Well, her letter is heavily scented, that's for sure," Hannah said. She laid Elizabeth's letter to the side and began to read the next one.

"Dear Mr. Westland,
I am a teacher and would like to remain one. I know that is a lot to ask and your town may not allow it. Regardless, I promise to make you a good wife and take care of our children. Please consider sending for me, Mr. Westland.
Sincerely,
Anna Mae Leland."

Hannah looked at Levi again. "She seems nice."

He nodded. "I thought about sending for her. She can always have your job once you and Daniel marry. And since she already wants children, I wouldn't have to mention the contest."

Daniel didn't like the sound of that. He wanted Hannah to continue working at the school even after they got married. The children and school would keep her busy, and she'd also have to keep up with the house and chores, so he'd really only have to be around her at night. No way would he fall in love with a woman he hardly ever saw.

Sorrow filled Hannah's voice, catching his attention.

"No, you should tell her about the contest. Things might have been different if Daniel had told me."

"You didn't tell her about the contest before she got here?" Bonnie demanded. "No wonder she's not in any hurry to marry you."

Daniel didn't like where this was going. He reached across the table and scooped up the last sheet of paper. "Here's the third letter." He passed it across for Hannah to read, praying it would take the focus off him.

She tried to hide a grin by clearing her throat. Then she began reading.

"Dear Mr. Westland,
At my parents' request, I am answering your advertisement. My name is Emily Jane Rogers. I am twenty-three years old and am the oldest of twelve children. I've lived in the country all my life and would like to live in town. Your advertisement doesn't say what part of Texas you live in, but I'm praying that wherever you do live, it's in a town. My father says I am a good cook and will make you a good wife. I look forward to hearing from you soon.
Yours, Emily Jane Rogers."

Hannah laid the paper down.

Daniel could tell by the look on her face that the letter had bothered her. It bothered him, as well. The poor girl's letter sounded as if her parents were trying to rid themselves of the extra mouth they'd been feeding.

"What do you think?" Levi asked, looking from Hannah to his mother, and lastly to Daniel.

Hannah answered first. "I'm not the one who will

be married to the woman you choose. This is your decision. Which one do you like best?"

"I agree with Hannah, son."

Daniel shook his head, siding with the women. This was something Levi needed to do on his own. He'd been sent several letters, too, and had based his decision on the fact that Hannah was a schoolteacher. It never dawned on him that she might have a limp or that she would demand love before marriage when she arrived.

Levi sighed heavily. "I've read those letters so many times I have them memorized, and I still can't decide. Anna would be a good choice, if you decide not to teach after you and Daniel marry, Hannah. Elizabeth's letter smells good but she seems a little pushy. And I feel sorry for Emily. It sounds as if her family is trying to get rid of her." Levi rubbed the back of his neck again. "I just don't know."

Bonnie pulled Elizabeth's letter from the pile. "Well, if it were me, I wouldn't choose a bride based on how her letter smells. So I think you can eliminate Elizabeth. The other two are a little harder."

Levi nodded in agreement. "That leaves the other two."

Hannah laid the letters face up on the table. "Anna wants to teach and Emily wants to live in town. Anna is welcome to teach here. As for Emily, do you want to live in town?"

Daniel studied his brother. Did he want to live in town? Levi didn't seem to enjoy working on the ranch, at least not as much as Daniel did. He knew that Levi helped Jeb out quite a bit, most of the time without ole Jeb knowing about it. His brother had a heart of gold.

Daniel also knew that his brother enjoyed working with wood, so maybe he would prefer town. Dare he wish?

Levi avoided her question. He picked up the letters. "What a mess," he said, tucking them back in his pocket.

Hannah's gaze met Daniel's as she answered, "It's really not that big of a mess. Eventually, Daniel will marry—if not me, then someone else." She broke eye contact with him and looked to Levi. "So with that in mind, which woman would you choose?"

"Probably Emily. She sounds like she needs a fair husband. I can't help but worry about her. If my letter isn't the only one she's sent out, Emily might end up with someone worse than me."

Bonnie laid her hand on his. "If she marries you, she'll get a fair husband."

Levi looked up at his mother. "Thank you, Ma." He smiled at Hannah. "I believe things are going to work out for you and Daniel, also."

Daniel hoped so. Now that Levi was sending out a new letter, he needed Hannah to fall in love with him fast.

"Now that I've decided to reply to Emily, will you write the return letter for me?" Levi asked Hannah with a grin.

She laughed. "No. She will cherish that letter someday and it needs to be in your own words and your own writing."

Did Hannah cherish his letters to her? Daniel studied her face. She had the dreamy look of a girl who either was already in love or truly wanted to be.

Hannah pushed back her chair. "It's getting late and I need to get to the schoolhouse."

"I'll go with you. I want to make sure you get there safely," Daniel said as he, too, stood.

She smiled at him. "Let me go see if Opal needs any more assistance. I'll be back in a few minutes."

Levi called after her, "Thanks for your help, Hannah."

"You're welcome. Just make sure you are honest with her." Hannah pushed through the door and entered the kitchen. Opal sat at the table, sipping tea.

The kitchen was clean and the floors looked as if they'd been freshly mopped. "Seems like you have everything done in here." Hannah smiled at her friend.

"Yep, it goes faster when a body's not so tired they think they are gonna drop. Thanks for all your help today, Hannah." Opal grinned over her cup. "Now get back to that man. Looks like our Levi is about to give him a run for his money."

Hannah nodded. "It does look that way. 'Night, Opal." She went back into the dining room. "I'm ready."

Daniel walked with her to the front door. He opened it for her. "'Night, Ma. Levi."

"'Night," they echoed back.

Hannah descended the steps of the porch. How did Daniel feel about her helping Levi with the letters? Thanks to his mother's interrupting, he hadn't said much during the process of choosing which bride Levi should send for. Hannah walked to the barn and stopped.

The moon and stars shone in the cloudless sky, providing plenty of light. "Daniel, I'd like to walk back, if it's all the same to you." She turned to find him directly behind her.

He surprised her by reaching out and touching the

hair that framed her face. His knuckles brushed her cheek. "All right."

His husky voice mesmerized Hannah, holding her in place. Daniel ran the back of his hand along her jaw line and brushed her chin. "You are a very beautiful woman, Hannah Young."

She moistened her lips before answering, "Thank you."

Daniel's eyes focused on her mouth.

Was he going to kiss her again? Did she want him to? Her heart picked up speed. What was he waiting for? His hand still remained on her chin, holding it in place.

Daniel lowered his head and captured her lips. The kiss was sweet and gentle. He didn't move, simply sampled her lips.

Hannah returned his kiss. She wanted to fall in love with this man, but more than anything she wanted him to fall in love with her. With her lips, she tried to convey that message to Daniel. Hannah didn't examine her feelings too closely. She didn't want to admit that he was capturing her heart with each look and kiss they shared.

Chapter Nineteen

Hannah was glad to see Monday morning arrive, even though Daniel wasn't able to escort her to the ranch house. She missed him, but understood why. He'd told her the night before that he and a couple of the other ranch hands were going to be guarding fence lines all night. It seemed the rustlers were attacking on Sunday nights, and he wanted to be there to catch them.

As she walked, her thoughts were on Sunday and the flurry of activities that had taken place. They'd gone to church, ate lunch as a family and then rushed home to prepare for the evening meal with the ranch hands and their neighbors. Bonnie had played hostess and made sure everyone was happy.

The stressful part came when, just before the blessing was said over dinner, she'd pulled Daniel and Hannah to the front porch and announced their engagement. Hats had flown into the air and the women smiled. Well, most of them. JoAnna Crawford and Lucille Lawson had glared at her for the rest of the evening.

She'd tried to ignore them, and made a point of speaking to all the mothers who were present. Hannah had wanted to get to know them and their children before school started today.

Excitement rippled through her as she hurried through her morning chores. The first day of school was always exciting for her, and she tried to make it fun for the children, as well. Hannah finished gathering the eggs and carried them in to Opal.

"Good morning, Hannah. Today's the big day. My granddaughters are so keyed up that school was all they could talk about last night." She whipped a bowl of batter. "It took me an hour to get them settled enough to sleep." Opal yawned.

"I'm sorry they kept you up, but I am glad they are excited about school." Hannah washed her hands and then began cracking eggs into a skillet. While she scrambled them, Opal made pancakes. The two women worked as a team, preparing breakfast.

Opal glanced over at her. "Last night went well, don't you think?"

"I suppose. It was nice to meet everyone."

"Everyone?" she repeated doubtfully.

Hannah dished the eggs into a large bowl. "Everyone I met was very nice."

Opal grunted. "Uh-huh. Did you meet the Crawford and Larson girls?"

"Yes, when they first arrived."

"Before the big announcement." The housekeeper flipped a pancake in the skillet and set the sausages at the back of the stove to keep warm. "How were they after the announcement?" she asked.

"You were there." Hannah refused to say anything against the women.

Opal laughed. "Yes, and if looks could kill, you'd

be buried over in the north pasture this morning." She dished up the pancakes and looked about. "I think that's everything."

"I'll take the eggs and sausages in." Hannah picked up both platters and headed to the dining room.

Bonnie sat at the table. Dark circles lined her eyes. "Are you all right?" Hannah asked, placing the dishes on the table.

The older woman yawned. "Yes, just tired. Riding a fence line all night will do that to a body."

"I'll go get you a cup of coffee," Hannah offered. She hadn't realized Bonnie was riding fence lines, too.

"Would you be a dear and bring the pot back with you?" Bonnie asked.

Hannah nodded. "I'll be right back." She opened the door and Opal came through it, carrying the pancakes, butter and syrup. Together the two women set the table.

Levi came down the stairs, looking worn-out from a night in the saddle. Had all the Westlands ridden fence lines all night? Before Hannah could ask, Daniel came through the front door. His brown eyes sought her out and he smiled.

"Good morning, Hannah." He slipped into his chair at the end of the table.

She smiled back. "Good morning."

He looked from her to his mother and brother. "I take it you two had a quiet night, too?"

"Afraid so." His mother answered for herself.

Levi nodded. "Same here."

Daniel frowned.

"Go ahead and say the blessing, Daniel." Bonnie bowed her head, and the others followed suit.

As soon as the prayer was over, Levi asked, "How about Cole?"

"It was quiet on his side, also." Daniel scooped eggs into his plate. "I really thought they'd hit last night." He passed the eggs to Hannah and reached for the sausage.

Conversation began to fly about the table regarding the rustlers and their activities. Hannah learned that they'd stolen twenty head of cattle the night before last. They were randomly cutting the fences and they'd butchered two more calves just for the fun of it. Hannah felt left out as the Westlands discussed what to do next. It seemed as if they had forgotten she was in the room as she quietly ate her breakfast.

Bonnie listened to her sons and made suggestions on how to spread the men out about the ranch. The decision was made that at least one hand would guard each side of the ranch. They agreed that one wasn't really enough, but they couldn't put them all out there at night; no work would get done during the day if they did.

"I could help," Hannah offered.

The conversation went dead. All three Westlands stared at her as if she were a three-horned cow.

Daniel shook his head. "Thank you, Hannah, but no."

She stared back at him. "Why not? I can ride and shoot."

He stuffed food in his mouth and ignored her. Hannah turned to Bonnie. "Tell him. I can do this."

His mother looked down at her plate. "I don't think it's a good idea, either."

Hannah laid her fork down. Dread and sorrow filled her. Did they think she couldn't do it because of her limp? Did they see her as an invalid? "Why not?" she finally asked.

"Riding the range at night is dangerous," Daniel answered.

"Your mother did it last night."

Bonnie's head came up. She stared down the table at her son. It seemed to Hannah as if they were communicating silently.

She looked to Levi. He jerked his gaze from her and focused on his plate.

Daniel pulled her attention from Levi. "I know what my mother did last night, Hannah. But you aren't going to be riding the range now, or ever. So just forget it."

Hannah stood. She dropped her napkin on the table. "If you will excuse me, I have a class to teach today." With that, she held her head high and marched from the room.

Opal looked up from where she sat at the kitchen table, eating her breakfast. "What's wrong?" she asked as Hannah passed.

"Nothing. I'll see you tomorrow. Maybe." Hannah pushed through the back door and forced herself to walk across the yard. She wanted to run to the school, throw herself across the bed and cry.

The Westland family didn't think she was strong enough to work the ranch like them. It had to be because of her leg. There was no other reason that came to mind.

Lord, maybe this isn't where I'm supposed to be. I've lived my life trying to prove to others that I am just as fit as they are. And now, just when I think I've found a home and a man I could love, given time, I find out he and his family think I'm too weak. Father, I need Your guidance. Because right now, all I want to do is run away.

* * *

Daniel pushed his chair back to follow Hannah.

"Let her be," Bonnie ordered from her end of the table.

He looked at his mother. "But she's upset."

"Yes, she is." Bonnie sighed. "But if you follow her now, it will only upset her more."

Daniel eased back into his chair. He was tired and frustrated. Rustlers were stealing him blind, Hannah wanted more from him than what he felt he could give and he was still letting his mother boss him around.

Levi spoke. "Why can't she help out?"

"In case you haven't noticed, little brother, Hannah has a limp. I'm sure she gets tired when she's on that ankle too long." Frustration filled his voice.

"I've noticed, but I also noticed that since she's been here she has learned how to ride again, she's cooked and cleaned, not to mention handled all the chores she's been doing outside in the mornings. And believe it or not, Daniel, she did it all with a limp." Levi pushed his plate back. "I don't think you give her enough credit."

Bonnie looked at her youngest son. "Levi, there are times when we have to listen to Daniel and follow his lead."

Levi stood. "I do, Ma, but this time he's wrong. Hannah isn't Gracie Joy. She's a grown woman, not a ten-year-old little girl."

With that, he walked out the front door.

Daniel looked to his mother. Tears were in her eyes; Levi's words had cut deep. His ma was exhausted from being in the saddle all night, and her age showed. There was a time when Bonnie Westland could have ridden the range all night, done her household chores and rode all the next night before exhaustion claimed her.

She pushed back from the table. "I'm heading to bed." Bonnie turned away, but he'd seen the lone tear ease down her cheek.

Like him, his ma still mourned the death of Gracie Joy, and like him, she felt responsible. Life on a ranch was hard.

Bitterness ate at him as he thought that maybe he should allow Hannah to help out. She would learn what it was really like to work a ranch, and then she'd be happy to stay home and play school.

Daniel got up from the table in turn and headed to his own house. He didn't want to worry about rustlers, his mother or Hannah at the moment. Cole, Levi, his mother and himself had been replaced by Tucker, Sam, Miguel and Rowdy along the fence lines. Adam and Jeb could take care of anything else that might crop up. Right now, all Daniel cared about was getting some sleep.

When he got to his house, he rode Tornado to the corral, took off his saddle and released him. The stallion went straight to the water while Daniel filled his trough with grain and oats. He leaned against the fence as the horse pranced around the enclosure.

He couldn't help but think about Hannah. Daniel had seen the hurt in her eyes when she'd realized why he didn't want her out riding the fence lines at night. Her limp was only a part of his reasoning; the other part was that he didn't want her to get hurt. In the dark a horse could step into a gopher hole and break its leg while throwing its rider to the ground. Men had been crushed under their mounts because of a wrong step, or had their necks broken in the fall.

Hannah had pointed out that Bonnie rode the range, and she was right. His mother had been ranching since the day they moved out here, and he'd never worried about her falling from her horse. Was it because she'd always ridden the range?

Still, it scared him to think of Hannah lying hurt and alone. He shook his head and walked back to the house. He needed sleep. When he entered the house, Daniel found himself heading into the dining room. His gaze moved to the big window that Hannah had seemed so happy over.

She'd kissed him in this room. He closed his eyes and wished she was there to do so again. A smile touched his lips. When Hannah kissed him, Daniel felt warmth and happiness. It was as if she was a part of him. She belonged in his arms.

He jerked his eyes wide-open at the thought, then turned and went to his room. As he got ready for bed, he prayed.

Lord, I can't be falling in love with her. I'm just overly tired. Please, let her fall in love with me so that I can have the ranch, but Father, I ask that You harden my heart so that I won't be hurt. I know I sound selfish, and I don't mean to, but I'm scared. Loving someone is too painful when they are gone.

He slipped between the cool covers and sighed. Would God harden his heart against Hannah? He had hardened Pharaoh's heart in Exodus.

Daniel's final thought was, *Yeah, and look where that got Pharaoh.*

Chapter Twenty

Hannah couldn't hide the fact that her feelings had been hurt, and she didn't try. The next morning, Daniel sent Adam to escort her to the barn, with the explanation that he was busy watching for rustlers. She wasn't surprised when the young man continued to come each morning. Hannah told herself she didn't mind. Adam was quiet and she found herself becoming quiet, also.

So much for making a new life and becoming a more outgoing person. Her limp defined who people thought she was. Hannah couldn't change that.

For the next week, she helped Opal in the mornings, grabbed a biscuit with bacon or sausage and then headed home. Opal had taken to packing her a light lunch, and she continued teaching classes.

The old thrill of watching youngsters learn filled her each day. She enjoyed spending time with each child and learning about them and their families. She'd also learned that everyone loved Daniel and his family.

Hannah decided that she'd give Daniel his six months, but if he didn't court her and fall in love, well, she'd be leaving during Christmas break. By then,

Levi's Emily would be there and she could continue teaching the children.

The thought that she should pray about the situation filled her every waking hour, but Hannah stubbornly pushed the thought away. God knew the circumstances, and if He wanted to act on them, well, so be it. But for now Hannah was making plans of her own.

It was a nice afternoon; she picked up the seed packets and headed to the little garden spot that had been plowed beside her house. Daniel had been thoughtful in making sure the plot was there. She missed him, but refused to go in search of him.

The warm soil felt good in her hands as she worked, planting the seeds. Today she'd needed a quick refresher course on how to start a garden, and had turned it into a lesson for the older children. She'd been happy with their answers and the fact that they didn't realize they were teaching her.

"It's nice to see you smile again."

Hannah sat back on her heels and looked up at Daniel. He was seated atop Tornado, looking comfortable and lazy as he leaned on the saddle horn. His hat was pushed back and his green eyes seemed to be drinking in her appearance. She tried to ignore the way her pulse picked up a beat. "Good afternoon, Daniel." Hannah went back to planting seeds.

Leather creaked as he got off the stallion. He came and knelt beside her in the dirt. "I've missed you."

She titled her head sideways. "Really?"

Daniel tried to capture one of her hands.

She pulled it away and continued working. Her heart might be happy to see him, but her head said to be careful. Hearts could be broken and Hannah feared she was losing hers to him.

"Yes, really. I'm sorry I haven't been around to see you. I've been busy." He took his hat off and rested it on one knee.

Hannah scooted farther from him and continued to poke holes in the dirt, drop a seed inside and cover it. "So I've heard," she answered.

"You're still angry about the other morning, aren't you?" The tone of his voice said he couldn't believe she'd still be upset that he thought her weak and unsuitable for ranch work.

Hannah sat back on her heels once more. "I am. You basically said I'm not rancher's wife material. And you did it in front of your mother and brother." She couldn't keep the hurt from sounding in her voice.

"That's not what I meant, Hannah." He stood, towering over her.

She pushed up from the ground and dusted off her hands. He was still a head taller than her, but at least by standing she felt as if they were on even ground. "No? Then what did you mean?" Hannah crossed her arms and waited.

"I was tired, and what I said didn't come out right. I simply meant I don't want you to get hurt. There are too many things that can happen to a woman on a ranch. Especially at night. Horses step in gopher holes and spook when they hear odd noises. I want to know you are home, safe." His eyes pleaded with her to understand.

"I appreciate what you are saying, Daniel, but if we get married, I want to be a helpmate to you in every way. That includes working on the ranch."

He took the same stance she had, crossing his arms,

as well. "If we get married, Hannah, I will expect you to do as I ask." His green eyes studied her.

Hannah shook her head. Anger began to boil in her stomach. She used a technique she had perfected working with children and changed her tone slightly. "Marriage isn't about you telling me what to do and me doing it, or me telling you what to do and you doing it. It's about two people coming together and becoming one. That means we work together."

"I'm not a child, Hannah, so don't use that tone with me," Daniel replied.

"If you don't want me to use this tone, then stop acting like a child."

He raked his hand through his hair and then ran it across his neck. "Look, this isn't getting us anywhere."

"I agree." She turned to kneel in the garden and go back to work. Daniel was just being stubborn.

He caught her by the arm and swung her around. His lips captured hers and he held her tight. Hannah wanted to push away, but at the same time she wanted to stay where she was. Her arms snaked around his neck and she kissed him back.

If anyone had seen them, they might have thought her crazy. All she knew was that she'd missed Daniel and dreamed of his kisses.

His lips gentled and he relaxed his grip. After several long seconds, Hannah pulled away, but stayed within his arms. "That was nice, though I'm not sure it settled anything," she told him.

Daniel sighed and released her. "Me, either."

She missed his arms around her. "Daniel, I wish I knew why you are so cautious with me. Is it because of my limp?" Hurt filled her voice.

He looked deep into her eyes. "Hannah, I had a sister, Gracie Joy. She was born with a limp, similar to yours. Because of my bad judgment, she died. I don't want that to happen to you." The sincerity in his voice told her he meant every word.

Hannah wanted to reach out and hug him. She saw the sorrow in his eyes and heard the pain in his voice. "I'm sorry, Daniel."

He shook his head. "You didn't know."

She didn't want to cause him more pain, but had a question that needed answering. "Daniel, how old was your sister?"

"Ten." He picked up Tornado's reins.

"She was a child." Hannah thought about Bonnie and the pain she, too, must feel from losing a child. "How long has she been gone?"

Daniel mounted. "Five years."

Hannah walked over to him and placed her hand on his thigh. "I really am sorry and I do understand better what you are feeling. But Daniel, I'm not a child. Let me make my choices, and know that I will never hold you accountable for them."

He placed his hand over hers. "I wish it were that easy."

Daniel removed her hand from his leg and slowly backed Tornado away from her.

Hannah stepped back. She watched as Daniel and Tornado raced around the schoolhouse and out of sight. Had she just made things worse?

Hannah didn't know. Daniel was hurting, and for the life of her, she had no idea how to help him.

Daniel let Tornado have his head. The stallion flew across the pasture and through the woods. He leaped logs, ran through a stream and kicked his heels, happy to have his freedom. After a while, the big black slowed down to a walk.

Daniel patted the horse's neck. "Feel better?"

Tornado snorted and bobbed his head. Daniel wished he could run like the wind and feel better. He turned the stallion toward home.

He hadn't handled his visit with Hannah well at all. First he'd kissed her, to prove he wasn't a child but a man. Then, when she'd asked the hard questions, he should have been able to tell her the whole story, but couldn't. It was one thing to relive it in your head and another to verbalize what had happened.

Hannah said she understood, but he suspected she didn't. How could she? As far as he knew, she'd never lost a sibling to death. And even if she had, Daniel felt sure it wasn't because of the decisions she'd made. No, Hannah didn't understand and probably never would.

The words *I'm not a child* echoed in his thoughts. She was right about that. Hannah wasn't a child; she was a grown woman. He'd enjoyed kissing her and could even see her being his wife and coming home to this house.

He knew that each time he kissed Hannah and spent time with her she was working her way into his heart. Daniel worried he'd do as she desired and fall in love with her. He couldn't let that happen. He couldn't care that much for another person. He had to guard his heart.

Chapter Twenty-One

Normally after breakfast, Hannah returned to the schoolhouse and spent the next two hours preparing for the children to arrive. Not today. Today she was going to ride Clover around the ranch. She wanted to check the fence lines and see for herself what the excitement was about.

Not that there would be any excitement, she thought as she mounted Clover. The little mare blew air through her nostrils and seemed to grunt. Hannah wondered if the small animal was getting too old for this type of activity.

Since no one else was about, Hannah decided to see what other horses might be available. She dismounted and walked Clover back inside the barn, returning her to her own stall.

Hannah's eyes adjusted to the dimness and she began to walk toward the back. A brown head hung over the back stall and she frowned. She'd never noticed the horse before and made her way to that stall.

The pretty brown mare had no markings on her face, but her big brown eyes stared at Hannah. She patted her nose before leaning over the stall and looking at the rest of the horse, which nickered and swung her head, bumping Hannah on the shoulder. She laughed and nuzzled her face against the brown mare's nose. "How would you like to go for a little ride this morning?"

Another soft nicker was her only answer. Hannah smiled and returned to Clover. She took off the bridle and saddle and headed back to the brown mare. Would Daniel be upset with her for taking this horse instead? She didn't think so. At least she hoped not.

As she worked, getting the saddle on, Hannah told the mare what a beautiful horse she was. She ran her hands over her legs and belly, mindful of where her own feet were at all times.

The horse quivered and her ears twitched as she listened to Hannah's soft voice. Once saddled and ready to go, she led the mare out of the barn.

Hannah rubbed her nose once again. "Since I don't know your name, I think I'll call you Brownie." She eased to the side of the horse and got on as quickly as possible.

Brownie sidestepped a couple times and shook her head. Hannah patted her neck and murmured words of comfort. She walked her about the yard for several minutes, letting the horse get used to her weight and voice. Then Hannah did something she'd wanted to do for a long time.

She started the mare off with a gallop and then let Brownie have her head. With the wind whipping through her hair, they raced across the pasture and into the woods.

Hannah's youthful days of riding came back to her. She felt free again and happy. Memories of racing her horse through the woods and jumping logs and streams came flooding back to her.

With her knees, she directed the mare, riding low in the saddle. The thrill and feelings of freedom rushed up in her stomach and placed a big smile on her face. This was the life she loved; this was the life Hannah wanted.

They shot out of the wooded area and into another pasture. Birds flew for cover and Hannah laughed. She reached forward and patted Brownie's neck again. They made a good team.

The yell came from her left. "Woo! Woo!"

Hannah turned her head and saw the black stallion bearing down on them. She gently began pulling back on Brownie's reins. As the horse slowed, she sat up straighter in the saddle.

"What do you think you are doing?" Daniel demanded, coming alongside her.

"Riding." Hannah beamed at him.

"On this horse?" he exclaimed.

Hannah patted Brownie's shoulder. "What's wrong with this horse?" she asked.

Daniel frowned. "Well, up until today no one could ride her." His voice took on a note of awe. "What did you do to her?"

"I talked to her, stroked her and asked nicely if she'd like to go for a ride." Hannah laughed at the expression on his face. "Seriously, I didn't do anything unusual, but I do like her. What's her name?"

He pushed his hat back and stared at the horse. "She doesn't have one. I was planning on selling her."

Hannah's heart sank. She liked this horse. They seemed to have connected. "Oh. I didn't know." Brownie stomped and pawed at the ground.

Daniel shook his head. "You like her, don't you?"

She nodded. "Do you already have a buyer for her?" Hannah picked up the brown strands of mane and ran them through her fingers.

He turned Tornado around. "Yes, but I don't think I'll sell her, after all. It seems she has found someone who can ride her."

Daniel looked over his shoulder at her. His smile melted a small place in Hannah's heart.

"You mean I can keep her?" she asked, turning Brownie around to ride beside Daniel.

He nodded. "I think I'll ask Levi to build a lean-to behind the schoolhouse. If you want her, she will be your responsibility from now on."

Hannah laughed again. "Thank you, Daniel. I love her." She patted the horse and was rewarded with a soft neigh. The horse tugged at the reins. Hannah gave her her head and a small kick. "I'll race you back to the barn!" she called over her shoulder, and they took off running.

Daniel followed. He held Tornado back, knowing the black stallion could easily overtake them. Seeing Hannah and the little mare racing across the pasture earlier had just about given him heart failure. He'd thought the animal was out of control, but then saw Hannah handle her with grace and style.

The woman never ceased to amaze him. He'd forgotten to ask what she was doing out on the range this morning, but guessed at this point it didn't matter.

Her black hair whipped out behind her and she turned in the saddle to see where he was. She laughed again, merrily, and the little mare seemed to pick up speed. Today Hannah wore a beige blouse with a tan riding skirt. Her blue eyes had flashed joyfully when he'd said she could have the mare.

How was it that the horse had taken to Hannah? Ben Wilder, the ranch's horse trainer, had been trying to break her for months. It seemed Hannah had successfully mounted and ridden the horse within minutes of meeting her.

Once more Daniel couldn't help but admire his mail-order bride. It amazed him that Ben had brought the mare in from the training barn a couple nights before and suggested Daniel sell her to Mr. Johnson, because she couldn't be broken for riding but Mr. Johnson needed a broodmare. When Daniel had agreed, Ben made the arrangements. Now Hannah was riding the horse as if they'd been together for years.

He shook his head. Thankfully, Mr. Johnson was a neighbor. Daniel decided he'd ride over to the Johnson place and tell him personally that he'd changed his mind. He'd sold a couple of horses to the man before, with Ben's assistance, and knew his neighbor would understand.

Hannah and her horse were farther away now; Daniel grinned and gave Tornado his head. He felt the stallion's muscles bunch up under him and braced for the jolt of speed. Horse and rider passed Hannah and the little mare just seconds before entering the barnyard.

The dirt flew about them as the horses came to a stop. Hannah jumped from her mare, laughing. "You had me worried there for a moment. I thought you were going to try to be gentlemanly and let me win."

"Me, gentlemanly? Never!" He laughed, too, as he dismounted. "You are a very good rider, Hannah."

She led the mare into the barn. "You sound surprised."

"I am, a little." Daniel helped her take the saddle off. "Would you like to go out to the canyons with me after the kids get out of school?"

Hannah smiled. "I'd love to."

Daniel found himself watching the clock for the rest of the day. He'd enjoyed riding with Hannah that morning and wanted to spend more time with her. He told himself it was because Levi had mailed off his letter to his future bride, so his own time was running out. Daniel had to make Hannah Young fall in love with him.

When he arrived at the school, she was waving goodbye to her last student. Hannah smiled in his direction and waved again, this time at him.

Daniel nudged Tornado on toward the schoolhouse. He held a lead rope and tugged it to get the little mare to follow. Hannah's horse snorted but did as he bade.

A few minutes later, Hannah returned and shut the door behind her. She came down the steps with a smile on her pretty face. "Hi, Daniel. I didn't think school would ever get out. I've been looking forward to seeing the canyons all afternoon."

He noticed she'd changed from her dress to the beige top and tan riding skirt she'd been wearing that morning. "Well, I hope you didn't get your hopes up too high. They are just canyons." Daniel handed her the reins.

"Hey, Brownie, did you miss me?" Hannah nuzzled the horse's nose with her face. "They are part of the Westland Ranch. So I'm sure they are beautiful." She pulled herself into the saddle.

He liked that she thought his ranch was beautiful

and admitted to himself that the canyons were a favorite spot of his. As a kid he had camped there and pretended the small valley was his own.

Daniel and Tornado took the lead. After they crossed the stream behind the schoolhouse, Hannah pulled up beside him. "It is beautiful on this side."

The soft fragrance of honeysuckle once again greeted Daniel's nose. He'd begun to associate the scent with Hannah. Did she have a perfume that smelled of honeysuckle? Or was that her innate scent?

His gaze drank in her natural beauty. Hannah's skin was flawless. Her hair shone in the sunlight and her eyes sparkled with excitement. "Yes, it is," he stated, not thinking of the scenery around them but of her.

"What was it like growing up here?" she asked.

Daniel grinned. "You mean when we weren't working?"

She gave a peal of laughter. "Well, yes. I'm sure as a kid you didn't think the work was much fun at all. But I'm sure it wasn't always just work." She pushed a strand of black hair off her forehead and grinned.

"You're right. We did have free time. When we first moved here, Levi and I explored every inch of this land. I fell in love with it. On this ranch I feel free and close to God. I'm my own man here, everything is mine and I don't have to answer to anyone but God. Levi enjoyed it, but I think even then his heart was elsewhere." Daniel bent to avoid a low-hanging limb.

"What do you mean?"

"Levi likes building things, always has. He started with small traps. He's caught rabbits, squirrels, quail and a few times he caught skunks that were hanging around the chicken house. Later, he began to build bigger things. Pa was happy to let Levi oversee the construction of the barns and other outbuildings. The only thing I've ever seen him balk at is building fences." Daniel chuckled and added, "He hates that."

Hannah laughed with him. "I bet I can guess what his punishments were when he misbehaved."

Daniel nodded. What was it about Hannah's laugh that caused his heart to skip a beat? He decided not to ponder the question for too long. There were some things that were best left alone. "That and a trip to the woodshed."

They cleared the tree line and he could see the canyon in the distance. With his boot heels, Daniel urged Tornado to go a little faster. "It's not too far now."

He led the way across a small meadow and up a series of slopes. The canyon cut between some small hills. Green treetops and bushes concealed it from view.

Daniel smiled when he heard the expected gasp that sprang from Hannah's lips when they topped the ridge above the lush valley. His eyes drank in her beauty as excitement and wonder danced across her delicate features.

"Oh, Daniel. It's beautiful."

He had to agree with her. The small waterfall that fell from the side of the wall into a pool below fed a stream that ran through the gorge. Green grass, trees and flowers added to the beauty and wonderment of the canyon floor. It was one of his favorite places, and he'd known Hannah would love it, too.

Tornado picked his way down the small trail that led into the chasm. Brownie followed close behind. There were several animal trails like this one that entered the valley, and Daniel knew every one. As a teenager, he had spent the night here many times.

He knew that each morning the stream drew deer, foxes, quail and other wildlife to it. In the evening, the same animals would return. Often in the middle of the night he heard raccoons washing their food in the water.

At the moment, birds and butterflies flittered about. Wildflowers swayed in the breeze and bees buzzed close by. He'd always imagined this was what heaven would look like.

Hannah slipped off Brownie's back. Her rich blue eyes drank in her surroundings. "This place is beautiful. I'm surprised you didn't build your house here." She walked to the stream and knelt down. A fish jumped a few feet away, causing her to laugh.

Daniel enjoyed the sound and walked over to join her. "I thought about it, but in the winter it's not as beautiful and it's harder to get out." He knew this to be a fact, but didn't want to tell her he'd gotten snowed in one night while camping. It had been the coldest three days of his life.

As if she understood, Hannah nodded. "I can imagine. I'd hate to get snowed in down here." She looked around her. "But if you did, it looks like there are some small caves in the walls to shelter in."

Her observation surprised him. "Not many people noticed those caves."

She smiled. "I love caves. When I was a little girl I would go exploring around our farm. There was one spot that had a few caves and I'd play that I lived in one." Her eyes took on a faraway look and sorrow briefly touched her. She shook her head and stood. "Anyway, we should bring a picnic here someday."

He grinned. "Yes, we should." Would she be open to camping here after they married? Daniel thought about asking her, but then wisdom kicked in and he knew if he did, they'd be talking about falling in love and all that stuff. He shook his head. Nope, he was not going to open that can of worms.

His gaze moved down the rest of the canyon. He knew it went back about a mile and opened into a large horseshoe-shaped area at the end. It wasn't as pretty as here and he didn't see the point in taking Hannah to see it. "Are you ready to head home?"

She nodded and walked back to Brownie. The saddle creaked as she climbed aboard. "Thank you for bringing me here, Daniel."

Daniel saw a purple flower with big petals growing a few feet away. Impulsively, he walked over and picked it. He carried it to Hannah and held it up to her. "Here's a souvenir of our first visit to the canyon. I hope we have many more."

Her eyes and voice softened. "Me, too."

He walked back to Tornado as fast as his boots would take him. The impulse to pull her off Brownie and kiss her senseless had almost overtaken him. *I have got to stop kissing and thinking about kissing her,* he silently told himself.

But when he glanced over and saw her smelling the flower, looking all soft and sweet, Daniel knew he'd kiss her again and soon.

Chapter Twenty-Two

On Saturday morning, Hannah gently pressed the flower Daniel had given her between the pages of one of her favorite books, the dictionary. She would always treasure the blossom and the wonderful afternoon it represented with Daniel.

She picked up her brush and pulled her hair into a ponytail. Then she slipped into her new robin's-egg-blue blouse and dark navy riding skirt. Next, Hannah pulled on her freshly cleaned boots. A little thrill of excitement went through her as she thought about the trip to town she was about to embark on. She gathered up the books she'd borrowed from Jonah Richards, the schoolteacher in town, and put them in a burlap sack.

Brownie greeted her with a soft nicker. "Ready to go to town?" she asked the little mare as she laid a saddle blanket over her back. "We're going to go see Mr. Richards. I'm looking forward to telling him how the children are doing and—this is the best part of all—borrowing new books from him." Hannah tossed the saddle over the mare's back.

Soon the horse was ready. Hannah wrapped the book

bag around the saddle horn and turned Brownie toward the big ranch house. It didn't take long to get there, and she slid off Brownie and tied her up at the back porch.

Opal stood at the stove. A large pot of stew simmered on the back burner, filling the house with a wonderful smell. Hannah breathed in appreciatively. "I'm heading to town, Opal. Is there anything you need?"

The older woman looked at her. "I could use some more cinnamon. Who is going with you?" she asked, putting a lid on the pot.

"I'm going alone."

The older woman turned and looked at her with a frown. "Alone? Does Daniel know you are going to town?"

Hannah shrugged. "I don't think so. I didn't tell him I was, if that's what you are getting at."

"You can't go to town alone, Hannah." Opal poured herself a cup of tea.

"Why not?"

The housekeeper sat down at the table. "It isn't proper, that's why not. And with all the shenanigans going on around here, with the fences and cattle, I don't believe it's safe, either."

Confusion and anger warred in Hannah's chest. "I've gone to town alone many times in the past. Never have I been told it isn't proper." She waved her hand. "I'll be back before dark, so I won't be out when the rustlers come a-callin'."

"Hannah, Daniel isn't going to like this," Opal called after her.

She stopped. "Opal, I'm not going to do anything wrong. I'm going to the general store, and to the school to return Mr. Richards's books. There is nothing improper about either of those actions." Hannah opened the door and marched down the steps. She didn't like the idea of anyone telling her when and where she could go.

Opal followed. She stood at the door. "Hannah, please listen to me."

Hannah untied Brownie and then pulled herself up into the saddle. She looked to Opal. "I'm listening."

"I'm not sure what it was like where you came from, but Granite can be a rough town, especially on a Saturday morning. I'd feel better if you'd wait for one of the men to escort you." Opal's eyes pleaded with her to wait.

Hannah shook her head. It was broad daylight. What could possibly happen to her in town? "I'll be fine. I can take care of myself. I promise I'll be back soon, and I'll bring you your cinnamon." She turned Brownie toward town and hurried away before Opal could persuade her to wait.

The wind felt good on her warm cheeks as she rode off the Westland Ranch. Opal's concerns troubled her. Why did everyone think she needed a keeper? Did they really think that because she had a limp she couldn't take care of herself? It was the only explanation that she could latch on to, because she knew they didn't think her a child. At least she hoped they didn't. No, it was the limp. Hannah felt sure of it.

"Well, they are wrong. I can take care of myself." Hannah nudged Brownie in the ribs. Soon she and the brown mare were galloping into town.

Daniel stomped the mud from his boots before entering his mother's house. His stomach growled loudly. The rich smells of stew and fresh-baked bread tugged him into the dining room.

Opal came through the door carrying a pan of golden biscuits. A large pot sat in the center of the table.

He looked about for his mother. "Am I the first one here?" Daniel moved to his place at the table.

Opal set the pan of biscuits down and twisted her hands in her apron. A worried expression marred her normally smiling face. Something was wrong. "Something bothering you, Opal?"

For a brief moment, she looked as if she wasn't going to answer him. She twisted the apron even tighter before blurting out, "It's Hannah."

His heart picked up a beat. She'd missed breakfast this morning, but Opal had said she'd told Hannah she didn't need to collect the eggs on Saturday mornings. They'd all assumed she'd slept in. "What about Hannah?"

Opal looked down at her shoes. "Honestly, Daniel, I don't know if I should say anything. It really is none of my business, but I'm worried."

Bonnie entered the room, followed by Levi. "Something wrong with Hannah?" she asked, sliding into her chair.

"She's gone to town," Opal answered, still studying her shoes.

Daniel's gaze darted to his mother and Levi. "Who went with her?" he asked, reaching for a biscuit.

"She went alone."

He shot out of his chair. "Alone? Why?"

Opal's soulful brown eyes met his gaze. "She said she was going to the general store and to see the schoolteacher."

Daniel was almost to the door before he realized

he'd moved. He turned and asked, "How long has she been gone?"

"About an hour."

Levi stood. "Want me to come with you?"

Why had she run off to town alone? Had she decided to leave Daniel for the schoolteacher? Anger radiated through him. "No. I'll go get her."

As he rode to town, Daniel fumed. Didn't the woman know the kinds of danger a single woman could run into in Granite? Especially on a Saturday morning, after all the cowboys from the surrounding ranches had been corralling all night?

Probably not. As far as he knew, no one had told her. He should have mentioned it. Why hadn't Opal? It wasn't safe for a single woman to be on the streets of Granite on a Saturday morning.

A chill slithered down his spine. He pushed Tornado to get to town faster. His thoughts were focused on what could be happening even as he raced to find Hannah.

Then again, maybe she was leaving. Opal had said she was going to the general store, but what if she was really going to buy a ticket on the stagecoach out of town? Had she given up on him falling in love with her?

Daniel shook his head to rid himself of the thought. He didn't believe Hannah would just up and leave. She'd told him she'd wait six months to give them a chance. He believed she'd stay true to her word.

He entered town at a fast clip and had to slow Tornado down. Main Street was full of men coming and going. A few families were in town, probably doing their weekly shopping. Daniel didn't pay attention to any of them. His focus was on finding Hannah.

Opal had said she was going to the general store.

Daniel hurried there and tied the black stallion to the hitching post in front. He looked about for Brownie but didn't see the little mare.

Wilson Moore stood behind the counter. He looked up and smiled a greeting. "Howdy, Daniel. What brings you into town today?"

Daniel walked around several women until he reached the counter. "I'm looking for Miss Young. Have you seen her this morning?"

"Can't say that I have. Want me to ask Carolyn if she came in earlier?"

He nodded. "If you don't mind, I'd sure appreciate it."

"Not at all. Be right back." Wilson climbed the stairs to the living quarters above the store.

Daniel paced while he waited. A blue brooch caught his eye and he stared through the glass at it. If he wasn't so angry with Hannah right now, he'd buy it for her. Hadn't Jeb said the way to get a woman to fall in love with you was to buy her presents? The sound of feet on the stairs drew his gaze away from the jewelry.

"She's not been here this morning, Daniel," the shopkeeper said when he got within hearing distance.

"Thanks, Wilson. If she comes in, please tell her I'm looking for her, and to stay here until I come back." Daniel was already on his way out the door.

"Sure will. I hope you find her soon." Wilson went back to his work.

Daniel looked up and down Main Street. There was no sign of Brownie, and he was pretty sure Hannah would keep the little mare close. He decided to try the schoolhouse next.

Tornado snorted at the rough way Daniel turned him toward the school. "Sorry, ole boy."

His heart sank when he got to the school and didn't see Brownie. Where could she be? He realized the schoolmaster wouldn't be there on Saturday, either. The next question that slammed through his brain was where did the man live?

Daniel turned back toward the general store. Wilson could probably direct him to the schoolteacher's home. Daniel prayed she wasn't there. How would that look? His fiancée visiting with another man in his home? It wouldn't look good at all.

"Hey, boss," Tucker said, riding up to him on a brown gelding with a white strip down its nose.

"Tucker." Daniel nodded a greeting. He continued to scan Main Street for any sign of Hannah. "Have you seen Miss Young in town today?"

"I thought she might be the reason you're in town." Tucker's grin grew wider. "I told Sam and Miguel, 'There's the boss, and I bet you anything he's lookin' for Miss Young.'" He twisted in his saddle and nodded at the men standing a few feet away. "I was right, boys!" he called over his shoulder.

Daniel didn't have time for Tucker's silliness. "Tucker! Have you seen her or haven't you?"

"Oh, sorry, boss. Yeah, me and the boys saw her a little while ago." He continued grinning as if he were at the state fair and waiting for a prize.

Daniel wanted to knock the young man off his feet. Instead, he silently prayed for patience, then said, "Can you tell me where she went?"

"Sure can. She and a little boy went down that street right there, about twenty minutes ago." Tucker pointed down a side street between the hotel and the doctor's office.

"What little boy? Why did she go with him?" Daniel asked.

"Don't rightly know. I just saw the boy run up to her and say something. He pointed off that way and Hannah, I mean Miss Young, followed him." Tucker pushed his hat farther back on his head. "That's all I know."

"Thanks." Daniel nodded and turned Tornado down the side street.

"I have business to take care of, so I'll see you at the ranch, boss."

Daniel ignored Tucker and continued on. Why had Hannah gone off with a little boy? Was he one of the children she taught? Daniel doubted that, since all the kids who went to her school lived on the ranch.

He didn't know where the boy could have taken her, and prayed she hadn't fallen victim to some man's sinister scheme. Daniel wished now more than ever that someone had warned Hannah of the dangers of going to town alone.

His gaze searched each house and building he passed. Just when the street ran out and he was about to turn around, he heard her sweet laughter.

He released the pent-up air he'd been holding in his lungs. If she was laughing, Daniel felt sure she was all right. He followed the sound and soon spotted Brownie tied to a tree beside a small shed. The house beside it had seen better days and Daniel wondered who lived there. He halted the stallion and slid from his back.

He cautiously approached the shed. The little boy's back was to the door and Daniel couldn't see Hannah.

She giggled again and he squinted to find her in the shadows.

"Do you know which one you want, miss?" the boy asked.

Based on the sound of his voice and the build of his body, Daniel thought the boy was close to ten years old. He walked up to the door to get a better look.

"I think I'll take this one." Hannah stood, and he could see she held a squirming puppy in her hands.

"He's my favorite, too. I wish Ma would let me keep them, but she says she has enough mouths to feed without adding puppy mouths." The little boy bowed his head.

Daniel cleared his throat and both the boy and Hannah turned to face him. She had straw in her hair and a smudge of dirt on her cheek. What had the woman been doing? Rolling around in the hay?

"Look, Daniel, Steven gave me a puppy." Hannah held the little black-and-white dog up for his inspection. "Isn't she just the cutest thing you've ever seen? I think I'll call her Buttons."

Daniel couldn't decide if he wanted to strangle Hannah or hug her. She didn't seem to be aware of his emotions at all as she rubbed her nose in the soft fur of the little animal and laughed. "I just love the smell of puppies."

Did Hannah realize that when she liked something, she rubbed her nose against it? Daniel frowned at the thought. She'd done the same thing to Brownie that she was doing to the puppy now.

Steven wrinkled his own nose. "Really?"

Again she laughed. "Yes, and you know what smells even better than their sweet fur?"

The boy shook his head.

"Puppy breath!" Hannah stuck the puppy in Steven's face and reached out to tickle the little boy at the same time. All the pent-up anger melted away as Daniel watched her play with the child.

Now that he could see she was safe and happy, how could he be angry with her? Relief washed over him. Yes, he intended to speak with her about her behavior today, just not right now.

Chapter Twenty-Three

Hannah watched Daniel out of the corner of her eye. She sensed the moment he was no longer angry with her and inwardly sighed. She handed the puppy back to the little boy. "Would you mind holding on to Fred until my business in town is done? Then I'll come back and take him home with me."

Steven grinned. "All right." He cuddled the tiny dog close.

She walked over to Daniel. "I'm glad you decided to come to town." Hannah hooked her arm in his. "After I got here, I realized what Opal was trying to tell me. I'd decided to return to the ranch when Steven asked me if I'd like a puppy."

Daniel turned to face her. He plucked the straw from her hair. For the first time since she'd met him, he seemed speechless.

To fill the silence, Hannah continued, "I really hope I didn't worry you too much."

He wiped at something on her cheek with his thumb. She realized she must look a mess.

"Hannah, from now on promise me you will not

come to town without me or one of the other men. Mother doesn't even come to town alone." Daniel untied the horses, gathered their reins and began walking back toward Main Street.

"I promise." She tucked her arm in his once more.

Once she'd arrived in town, Hannah had seen the wisdom in Opal's advice to wait for one of the men. She'd been surprised to find the town full of cowboys who were either drunk or on their way there. When she'd come with Daniel the last time, she hadn't even noticed them. She knew she owed Opal an apology, and planned to give it as soon as she was on Westland soil again.

"What do you need to do before we head back?" he asked.

She matched him step for step. "I have to go to the general store. Opal needs cinnamon and I need sugar. After that, I'd like to return the books I borrowed from Mr. Richards."

Daniel nodded. "Do you have any idea where the schoolteacher lives?"

Hannah shook her head. "I thought I'd ask Carolyn at the store, but I never got that far."

"We could just leave the books at the store for him to pick up," Daniel suggested.

Regret filled her voice. "I suppose so, but I wanted to borrow a couple more from him. He has a wonderful collection."

"Doesn't the store sell books?" Daniel asked as he tied the horses to the hitching post in front.

Hannah laughed and pulled down the bag of books she'd borrowed from Jonah. "Yes."

Daniel captured her hand in his and tucked it again

into the crook of his arm. "Then while we're at the store, you can pick out new books to read. You don't have to borrow them from the schoolteacher."

As much as she wanted to do that, Hannah didn't want to spend any more of his money than she had to. "That's really nice of you, Daniel, but books are expensive," she protested.

He stepped up on the sidewalk. "Many things are expensive, but if what you are buying is something you will use or love, then it's worth the money." Daniel smiled and then leaned down and whispered in her ear, "You are going to be my bride, Hannah. Think of everything that you buy as a wedding present from me."

Hannah enjoyed the feel of his warm breath against her neck. She flushed when he pulled away. Daniel opened the door for her and escorted her inside.

"I see you found Miss Young," Wilson called from the counter.

Carolyn knelt beside a shelf with a stack of books and a large wooden crate beside her. "Hello, Hannah. I was just unloading a crate of books. Come see." She straightened her spine and groaned.

"Go on. Buy whatever you want." Daniel gave her a gentle push toward the shopkeeper.

Hannah set Jonah's bag of books on the floor beside Carolyn. "Would you like some help unloading them? I could unpack and hand them up to you."

Carolyn pushed herself up from the floor. "That would be great, Hannah. I'm not that big, but my back hurts almost all the time now. I do better standing." She rubbed the small of her back before moving aside.

After they'd changed places, Hannah grinned up at her. "I'm happy to help." She unwrapped each book from its brown paper, admired the cover and then passed it up to Carolyn, who placed it on the shelf.

From the corner of her eye she watched Daniel talk to Carolyn's husband. She couldn't make out what they were saying but saw Daniel point to something in a case.

"I heard that you and Daniel are getting married. Have you set the date yet?" Carolyn moved a few books around on the shelf to make room for the one Hannah had just handed up.

"No, but I'm thinking a Thanksgiving wedding might be nice." Hannah clamped her lips closed. Why had she told Carolyn that? She'd thought about it, but hadn't verbalized the idea to anyone, not even Daniel.

"Oh, that would be lovely. Wilson and I married a few days before Christmas." Carolyn smiled down on her. "I wish you had been here. It turned out so beautiful. I decided to have an outdoor wedding and it decided to snow."

Hannah shivered. "Wasn't that a bit cold?"

Carolyn looked at her husband and smiled. "Not when you are in love." She giggled. "I forgot all about the snow as we said our vows."

What would it be like to be so in love with a man that you didn't notice how cold you were? Hannah wanted that kind of love. She looked at Daniel again. He was a good man. She enjoyed spending time with him. His kisses were sweet. But was she in love with him?

He chose that moment to glance in her direction and smile. She felt the warmth of color enter her face at being caught gazing in his direction, and knew she had to be honest with herself. Maybe she loved Daniel a little, but not enough to forget that she needed him to love her, too.

She didn't want just a little piece of his heart. Hannah knew she wanted it all. She wanted—no, needed—to know that he would love her forever and never leave her, or force her to leave him. Regardless of what may or may not happen in their future, they would stick together. That was the kind of love she wanted.

Hannah handed Carolyn the last book and stood. She decided to change the subject, and hopefully take her own mind off love and marriage. "When is your baby due?"

Carolyn slipped the book into its slot. "Doc says he will be born in late August or the first of September." She patted her rounded stomach.

A smile pulled at Hannah's lips. "I take it you want a boy?"

"We both do," Carolyn answered as her cheeks turned a soft pink. She began gathering the paper and stuffing it back inside the wooden box.

Hannah helped her and then picked up the bag of books she'd laid down earlier. A part of her still wanted to go find the schoolteacher. "Does Mr. Richards come in very often?" she asked.

Carolyn picked up the box and started toward the counter. "About once a week. Why?"

Hannah followed, realizing she'd have to leave the bag with Carolyn. "I borrowed some books from him last time I was in town and need to return them. Only it's Saturday and he's not at the school. Would you mind giving them to him next time he drops in?" Hannah placed the bag on the counter.

Daniel came to stand beside her.

"No problem. I'll just put them with his mail." Carolyn took the books out of the sack and then handed the bag back to Hannah. "Speaking of mail, Daniel, I have a couple of letters for you." She turned around and pulled two envelopes from a slot on the wall behind her.

He took the letters from her hands and read the addresses. His gaze met Hannah's before he tucked them away. She couldn't help but wonder who they were from. Was he still getting letters from his mail-order bride ad? The one she'd answered?

"I'll be right back. There are a couple of books I want to get before we leave." Hannah walked over to the shelf.

"Take your time," Daniel said. He leaned a hip against the counter, pulled one of the envelopes out of his pocket and opened what looked like a letter.

Hannah didn't pay much attention to which books she chose; her mind was too occupied with the letter Daniel was reading. It really was none of her business, but she wanted to know if it was from another woman.

She felt a twinge of jealousy grip her and struggled to squash it. If the women writing the letters were more appealing to Daniel than she was, then so be it.

A month had passed since their trip into town. Daniel didn't know what to think of Hannah. She'd been quiet on their return to the ranch. Once they were home, she had gone about her business. He often found her riding on the range and would accompany her home. Gone was the woman who seemed to talk nonstop. In her place was a woman who waited for him to talk.

She seemed to be getting along well with his mother and Opal. Both women spoke highly of her when she wasn't around, but they, too, had noticed she'd become more reserved since she'd ridden to town alone and he'd gone to get her.

His thoughts went to the letter he'd gotten that day from the man he'd hired to find Hannah's father, Jacob Young. He'd written to inform him that Jacob had died of a fever several years earlier and asked if he wanted him to contact another member of the family. He'd written back, "Not at this time."

Daniel had also answered the lady who'd inquired about his mail-order bride ad. He told her he'd found a wife and thanked her for taking the time to write to him.

He didn't know how to break the news to Hannah, but figured someday an opportunity would present itself. Until then, Daniel planned on keeping the information to himself. What good would it do to tell her the man she called Father was dead?

Daniel prayed the Fourth of July celebrations would bring back the woman he'd begun to like and understand. He pulled the buckboard up in front of the house.

Opal, her two granddaughters, his mother and Hannah came out to meet him. All three women had their arms full. Opal had a basket of preserves she planned on entering into the canned-goods contest. His mother carried her newest prized quilt. And Hannah followed with three pie boxes. She had a book tucked under her arm.

The little girls scrambled up into the back of the wagon. Mary carried her favorite rag doll. Daisy held in her hands a few sheets of paper and what looked to be an oversize piece of charcoal.

Daniel focused on Hannah. She'd pulled her hair up and small strands escaped about her face. Her cheeks had a soft pink in them as if she was blushing, or had rushed to get ready. The dark blue dress with little white flowers she wore matched the color of her eyes. She smiled at him and then ducked her head.

His mother caught his attention. "Here, Daniel. Would you hold this while I climb up?"

He took the quilt and helped her onto the wagon bench. When she was seated he gave her back the quilt. Opal was next. She put her basket of preserves in the wagon and then he assisted her up, as well.

Hannah had already moved to the back and set her pies down there. The smell of cinnamon and freshly baked apples oozed from the boxes. Daniel saw Levi hurry to assist her into the bed of the wagon. His brother lifted her easily and sat her down so that her legs dangled over the edge.

"Hannah, are those pies for eating or judging?" Levi handed her the book she'd carried out.

She smiled at him. "Both."

"Then I'll have to make note of which ones are yours," Levi teased, before stepping away.

"Levi, would you mind driving this morning? I'd like to sit back here with my fiancée." Daniel didn't know where the word *fiancée* came from; he wanted to take it back as soon as it was out of his mouth.

Cole arrived at about the same time and grinned. He led both Tornado and Levi's horse.

Levi shook his head. "Sorry, Daniel, but I can't. I'm entering Snow in the races."

"You can tie him up beside Tornado," Daniel argued.

His brother grinned. "Yeah, I could, but I don't want to."

Cole shook his head at them. "I'll drive," he volunteered. "There is no way my horse could beat either of yours, so I'm leaving him at home." Cole handed each of them the reins to their horses and climbed up beside Bonnie.

Hannah seemed to be ignoring them all. She opened the book Levi had just returned to her and focused on its pages while Daniel tied Tornado to the wagon. He hopped up beside her and grinned. "What are you reading?" The light scents of honeysuckle and apple pie teased his nose.

Hannah's quiet voice floated to him like fall leaves on a breezy day. *"Sixteen Months at the Gold Diggings."*

He leaned closer to look at the pages. "It's about finding gold in California?"

"Yes. So far I've found it very interesting." She swiped at a wayward strand of hair on her cheek.

Levi rode up beside the wagon. "Daniel, what do you think your chances are of winning a race against Snow?"

He laughed. "If history repeats itself, I'd say pretty good."

"Last year doesn't count. Snow wasn't feeling too good. Were you, ole boy?" Levi patted his horse's neck.

Daniel turned to Hannah. "I wish you could have seen that race. Tornado took it by a full length. Poor ole Snow had to eat dust for a week."

"She'll be there to see Tornado eat dust this year, won't you, Hannah?" Levi grinned across at her.

She closed her book and looked at the two brothers. "If I'm not doing something else, I'll watch."

Daniel studied her profile as she returned to reading her book. What else would she have to do?

Chapter Twenty-Four

As soon as the wagon stopped at the temporary fair-grounds, right outside town, Hannah jumped down. She'd listened to Levi and Daniel go at each other all the way from the ranch and was sick of it. Granted, their words had often sounded playful, but there was that underlining of competition that set her teeth on edge.

If Bonnie or Opal had noticed, neither showed any signs. They'd chattered together like two old hens. Cole tossed back his opinions from time to time. The little girls had played and talked between themselves, so Hannah had reopened her book and pretended to ignore them all.

She watched as Cole and Daniel helped the other ladies down from the wagon. Then she picked up her pies and headed for the tent with the wooden sign that read Pie Eating Contest.

"Hello, Bertha. Here are the two pies I promised you."

The woman turned around to face her. "Well, hello, Hannah. Daniel. It's nice to see you two today."

Hannah hadn't realized Daniel had followed her. She

glanced over her shoulder at him. He'd pushed his hat back and was smiling like a schoolboy on the first day of school.

"It's nice to see you, too." Daniel took his hat off as he inspected the rows of pies that lined several tables. "What time is the contest?"

Bertha grinned. "Around three this afternoon. You going to give it a try this year?"

His rich laughter spilled out, much like a waterfall in spring. "No, ma'am. Too messy for me."

"You can set your pies over there, Hannah." Bertha pointed to a makeshift table to her right.

Hannah did as she was told. She kept the third pie and started out of the tent. "See you later, Bertha. I have to get this over to the Cooks Shack."

Daniel dropped his hat back on his head and followed her. "Bye, Bertha. Be sure and watch the horse races. I believe they start a little before noon."

When he caught up to her, Hannah asked, "Are you following me?"

"No, I'm going with you. If I was following you, I'd walk back there." He hooked a thumb over his shoulder.

She loved the attention, but wondered why he was suddenly showing it. For the past month he'd just about avoided her. True, they had meals together with the family, but other than that he'd used the excuse of having work to do to keep them far apart.

Hannah shook her head. "Oh, well, I beg your pardon, then." She smiled to show she was teasing him.

"That's better." He scanned her face with a teasing light in his eye. "Where are you going after you drop off this pie?"

"The cakewalk. I have the first hour of overseeing

the game." It felt good to have his total attention for a change. Hannah hadn't realized how much she'd missed it. Oh, she knew she missed not seeing him as much as she had before, but this feeling of pure joy that he was spending time with her felt nice.

"Then I'll join you."

Guilt nipped at her conscience. More than likely Daniel would enjoy spending time with the other ranchers instead of her. "You don't have to do that."

"Nope, I don't, but I want to. This is the first day I've had free in weeks and I want to spend it with you." He grabbed her hand and gave it a little squeeze.

Hannah looked into his face. His eyes shone with sincerity. Daniel really meant what he was saying; he wanted to spend the day with her. "All right. Let's drop off the pie and then head on over to the cakewalk. It should be a lot of fun watching everyone play and win."

They delivered the pie and walked to the gaming area. Hannah marveled that he still clung to her hand.

Families were dropping off small cakes, cookies, fresh breads and homemade candies for the game. Hannah's mouth watered at all the sweets that lined the table.

Mrs. Cree instructed, "Here are the slates for the numbers." She handed them to Hannah. "We have ten, so allow only eight people at a time to play. Do your best to make sure that everyone wins something before they walk away, all right?"

Hannah nodded. "Do they get to pick out their prize or am I responsible for that?" She looked to Daniel, who shrugged.

The older woman glanced at him. "Are you staying?" she demanded as she placed her hands on her rather rounded hips.

"I'm staying." He stood a little taller and pushed his hat back.

"Good, then you can help. No reason you can't, since you're just going to stand around and stare at Miss Young, anyways."

Hannah turned to hide the grin on her face. She listened while Mrs. Cree instructed Daniel on which treats to give out and in what order.

Daisy and Mary, Opal's granddaughters, stood on the edge of the woods with a group of older children. Hannah looked about for her friend. Did she know where the girls were? She probably did, since Opal watched them like a hawk watches mice.

"Now, Miss Young, do you need anything else before I head over to the sack races?"

Hannah pulled her attention from the children and nodded. "As a matter of fact, I do. I was wondering about the music. Who's going to play?"

"Mr. Richards will be along in a bit with his fiddle." Mrs. Cree waved the question away with her hand. "Is that all?"

"Yes, ma'am. Thank you." Hannah nodded. A line of people had gathered. She looked at Daniel. "I wonder when Mr. Richards will get here. I hate to make everyone wait for him."

Daniel's gaze was focused behind her. "Here he comes now." A frown marred her fiancé's handsome features. Did he not like the schoolteacher?

She turned to see Jonah Richards jogging across the grass. Today he wore a round hat on his head that he was holding down with one hand. The other hand was gripping a fiddle and bow.

"Sorry I'm late," he panted. "Where do you want me?"

Hannah laughed. "You're not that late. Mrs. Cree has a chair set up over there for you." She pointed to a wooden chair near the dessert table.

"I'd rather stand, if you don't mind." He walked to the chair and stood beside it. Jonah placed one boot on the seat and the fiddle under his chin.

"Not at all. Just let me know when you're ready to start." Hannah spread the slates in a large circle on the ground. Each one had a number printed on it.

Daniel moved to the dessert table and stood beside that. She heard Jonah plucking at the strings on his fiddle. "Ready!" he called.

Hannah moved to the front of the line and counted off eight people. When each found a number and was standing beside it, she nodded to Jonah to start playing.

He chose a lively tune and soon the players were walking around the circle and the game was under way. For the next hour, Hannah admitted people into the game, Daniel passed out the prizes and Jonah played his fiddle.

It was fun, but at the end of their shift, Hannah was pleased to see Carolyn and her husband show up to relieve them. Mr. Jones also came, bearing a harmonica to replace Jonah and his fiddle.

"How are you feeling?" Hannah asked Carolyn.

"Good," she whispered. "The baby has been moving around quite a bit today. I think he senses my excitement." She giggled and her hand touched her belly.

"I'm sure he does," Hannah agreed.

* * *

Daniel listened as the two women visited. He grinned at the way Carolyn lowered her voice, but because of her excitement didn't realize that it carried and he heard every word she said.

They wanted a boy. What would it be like to have a baby on the way? Would he want a boy, also? Or would he prefer a little girl who looked just like Hannah? Would Hannah's face light up with joy at the thought of bringing his child into the world?

Jonah Richards waved and walked away, but not before calling out, "I'll see you later, Hannah."

Did the schoolteacher like Hannah in a romantic way? Or did he just see them as friends? Daniel made a mental note to find out if the man was sweet on anyone else in town.

Hannah returned the wave but didn't seem to miss a beat in her discussion with Carolyn. Her sweet voice pulled him back into the conversation. "I think we're just going to look around now. Unless there is something Daniel would rather do." She turned to him with a smile.

All thoughts of Jonah Richards drifted from his mind. There were a lot of things he wanted to do, but Daniel had decided over breakfast to spend the whole day with Hannah. She'd seemed sad and he didn't like that expression on her face. He'd been so busy with the branding, fence mending and other duties on the ranch that he'd not made time to spend with her, and now he regretted it.

"Nothing I can think of." Daniel rocked on the heels of his boots with his hands in his pockets, trying to look relaxed and happy. He was rewarded with another charming smile.

"Well, I'll let you two go. I need to get to the dessert table. Wilson said my job is to simply stand and pass out the prizes." Carolyn looked to her husband, who had begun the next game. Mr. Jones started up a vigorous tone on the harmonica. "See you two later."

Hannah waved and then started back toward where most of the activities were taking place. Daniel fell into step with her.

"Where are we headed?" He snagged her hand as they walked. Pleased that she didn't pull away, he grinned at her.

"I'd like to see the quilts, but I know that would bore you to tears," she admitted in a soft tone. "So maybe we can go watch the sack races instead."

He stopped and pulled her around to face him. "Hannah, do whatever you want to today. I've been to dozens of these celebrations. This is your first here in Granite, so have fun and don't worry about me."

She reached up and gently stroked his cheek. "Thank you, Daniel. But I really don't want you to give up your enjoyment of the fair."

He covered her hand with his. "Good. Then let's go see the quilts."

She removed her hand from his face. "If you are sure…" Hannah left the rest of her sentence hanging.

He gently pulled her toward the tent that had been set up to display the women's quilts. "I'm sure." And he was. The hope of seeing the blankets had shone in her eyes, and Daniel knew he'd look at quilts all day if that was what would make Hannah happy.

She waited while he held the tent door open for her.

"I promise I won't stay long." The hint of honeysuckle tickled his nose as she went inside.

Daniel followed her. Quilts of all colors and designs filled the space. As they viewed them, he marveled at the tiny stitches that held each quilt together. His mother had been a part of the quilters' bee for years, but this was the first time Daniel had actually attended one of their shows. How many hours went into creating coverlets like this? He noted the different sizes and realized they would either take months or years to complete.

"There's Bonnie's quilt." Hannah pointed at the one his mother had been working on for what seemed like forever.

He'd never seen it hung before. His mother had held it in her lap the few times he'd seen her working on it. The blue-and-yellow star drew him like a mosquito to water. It really was beautiful. "Hannah, do you quilt?" He stood in front of his mother's work and studied the intricate stitches.

"Some. I'm not nearly as skilled with a needle as your mother," she answered, coming to stand by his side.

"I imagine you do just fine with a needle and thread."

Hannah stood staring up at the quilt. Her head was tilted slightly to the left and her gaze moved over the material as if she was trying to memorize each and every stitch that had gone into it. "My stitches are never that even and straight." She shook her head. "No, your mother is a master at quilting."

Daniel laughed. "I don't think it's a contest."

An older woman walking past huffed and rolled her eyes at him. She muttered, "Men," in exasperation.

A giggled escaped Hannah. "This is a competition, Daniel."

He felt heat on his neck. "Well, yes, but…" He watched amusement dance across her face. "Oh, never mind."

Hannah laced her arm into his. "I knew what you meant, and thank you." She gave his arm a little squeeze.

They moved through the tent, viewing the rest of the quilts, and then headed outside. The sun was bright overhead. "Are you hungry?" Daniel asked.

"A little, but I'd like to wait until the chili cook-off. Opal says that the men around here can sure cook chili." She grinned up at him. "But maybe a snack would be good."

Daniel looked down into her blue eyes. "What did you have in mind?" He knew she was up to something because a new light appeared there and laugh lines crinkled.

"A boiled egg."

"A boiled egg?" Daniel frowned. "Where are we going to find boiled eggs?"

Hannah began tugging on his arm. "This way."

He knew he was in trouble as soon as he saw the group of kids holding spoons and eggs. They were lined up to race from one point to another. "An egg race, Hannah?"

"Sure. You've done them before, haven't you?" she teased. Her eyes danced with merriment.

"Yes, but honey, those aren't boiled," he protested. "And besides, this is a kid's game."

"Yes they are." Hannah placed both hands on her hips. "Who says it's a kid's game?"

Daniel knew a dare when he heard one. "You're right. So you will play, too." He walked up to Mrs. Crandall, who was in charge, and said, "We need two spoons and two eggs."

The look on Hannah's face was worth making a fool of himself in front of the parents in Granite. He handed her a spoon, got in line and balanced his egg in his before placing the spoon handle between his teeth. Mrs. Crandall started the game.

From the corner of his eye, Daniel watched Hannah racing along beside him, trying to keep her egg in the spoon without touching it. She tilted her head to look at him and the egg slid off. The cracking sound it made when it hit the ground brought a smile to his face, and he lost his egg, too.

Shouts of encouragement met their ears as they both hurried back to the starting line to begin again. It took him three restarts, but Daniel finally crossed the finish line, seconds before Hannah. But not before several children.

Out of breath, he grinned at her.

She returned his smile and then swiped his egg from the spoon. "Thanks for breakfast, Daniel." Hannah began to peel it, which wasn't hard, since it was cracked in several places.

"Hey, isn't the winner supposed to get the spoils?" he teased.

"Not when they gloat." Hannah tossed the eggshells into a nearby trash can and took a big bite from the egg.

Two bright pink spots filled her apple cheeks and Hannah's eyes sparkled with merriment. Daniel knew he'd remember that expression on her face for the rest of his life. Her inner beauty shone through as well as her outer. Hannah Young could very easily be the one to capture his heart.

Chapter Twenty-Five

Hannah was tired. All day she and Daniel had laughed and played games at the fair. He'd entered the pie-eating contest at her urging, made a mess of it and lost to the mayor. Afterward he'd smeared cherry pie filling on her nose and whispered in her ear that if there wasn't a crowd he'd let her have a taste by kissing her.

Her heart rate had picked up a beat until he finished with, "But since there is a crowd, I guess you'll just have to do without my kiss for now."

She'd playfully slapped him on the arm, but deep down, Hannah knew she would have savored a kiss from him. Now she stood with Bonnie, waiting for the horse races to begin.

Hannah held her breath as Daniel, Levi and three other men brought their horses to the starting line. Tornado pranced around as if he knew he would win. Snow took large steps as if he were posing or stepping over cactus. The other men also had their horses parading about.

Daniel sat tall in the saddle. To Hannah he was the most handsome man there. She saw JoAnna Crawford staring at one of the other young men. The expression on her face said she was in love with him.

"I see JoAnna didn't wait for the leaves to fall off the trees before finding a replacement for Daniel," Bonnie said, moving closer to the fence that separated them from the riders.

"Can you blame her?" Hannah answered, happy that JoAnna had found someone she could love.

Bonnie shook her head and studied the young man. "No, I guess not. James McDougal is a fine catch, too."

The mayor indicated that the men should line up their horses. He held a pistol in one hand and a watch in the other. "Get set!" he called to the riders.

Hannah covered her ears when the gun went off. She watched as horses and men shot off. The dirt was flying so badly she really couldn't see much. "Do you think Daniel will win?" she asked.

Bonnie stood on her tiptoes. "The race?"

What else could she be talking about? Hannah wondered as she nodded.

Daniel's mother shook her head. "He doesn't care about winning the race."

"He doesn't?" She tried to see over the crowd that had gathered in front of her, but with her small stature, Hannah couldn't see anything.

Bonnie laughed. "No, he just wants to whip Levi."

More competitiveness between the brothers. Bonnie's voice sounded as if she was proud that her boys were competing again. What was it with the woman?

From the shouts, Hannah could tell that someone called Little Roy was winning. She shaded her eyes and looked up at Bonnie. Since no one was paying attention to them or their conversation, Hannah asked,

"Doesn't it bother you that those two are always at odds with each other?"

Bonnie turned around and looked at her. "You must think I'm an awful mother." She flung her braid over her shoulder.

"I didn't say that," Hannah answered in a calm voice. She felt as if a storm was about to burst and she was going to be in the eye of it.

As fast as the anger had built in Bonnie's eyes, it evaporated. "Hannah, you have to understand. Those boys have been competing all their lives. It's not done in malice—to them it's fun. Didn't you have siblings who you played games like this with?"

Hannah had not thought of her younger brother and sister since the day she'd told Daniel why she'd left her home forever. "No. I have a brother and sister, but they are younger than me."

"Well, surely with your teaching experience you've seen siblings compete with each other in their studies and the games they played." Bonnie turned back around and peered over the crowd. "Here they come, and Levi is in the lead!"

Hannah wanted to get excited about the race, but didn't feel any anticipation about knowing who was going to win. It no longer seemed important.

She'd missed so much of her brother's and sister's lives. What were they doing now? Simon would be twenty-four years old and Sarah twenty-two. Did Sarah look like their father or their mother? Everyone had said Hannah was the spittin' image of her father. Sadness enveloped her. Did Simon look like Pa, too?

"Well, I'll be dogged. James McDougal passed Levi up. Can you believe he won by a nose?" Bonnie turned to look at her. "Hannah? Are you all right? You are as white as a ghost."

"I'm fine. I think I'll go get a cool drink." Hannah hurried from the racing grounds. She pushed across the meadow, wishing for a quiet moment alone.

"Hannah? Have you seen Daisy or Mary?" Opal twisted her apron in her hands.

She shook her head. "Not since this morning. They were playing with a group of older kids."

"Thanks." Opal continued on toward where everyone was congratulating the riders. She called over her shoulder, "If you see them, please hang on to them and find me."

Hannah called back, "I will." She continued walking toward a booth where a young girl was selling lemonade.

Hannah recognized her as Betty Parker. Betty's family lived on the Westland Ranch, also. She had two brothers whom she walked to and from school with each day.

"Hello, Miss Young," Betty said, standing a little taller. "Would you like a glass of lemonade?"

"Yes, please." Hannah leaned against the table. She could hear shouts coming from the horse race, but her thoughts were on Daisy and Mary. Where could the little girls have wandered off to?

Betty handed Hannah her drink. "Is something bothering you, Miss Young?" she asked, taking the money Hannah passed her and putting it away.

Hannah nodded. "Opal, Opal Dean, just asked me if I'd seen her granddaughters. I noticed them playing earlier today with some older children, and I can't get them out of my thoughts."

"You don't think something's happened to them, do you?" Concern laced Betty's voice.

Hannah immediately wanted to reassure her. "Probably not. They might be down at the races. I'm sure Opal will find them." She took a sip of the sour drink.

"Mark! Luke!"

The sudden yell coming from Betty startled Hannah. She looked at the young girl in surprise as the two boys slid around the corner.

"What, Betty?" they asked in unison.

Hannah placed a trembling hand over her pounding heart. The boys, aged five and six, looked almost like twins. Their brown hair stood on end and their light blue eyes stared up at their sister.

Betty knelt down in front of them. "Have you two seen Daisy Brown or her sister, Mary?"

"Eellier," Luke, the five-year-old, answered.

Little Luke had several words he couldn't say very plainly. Hannah added *earlier* to her mental list of words to work with him on.

"Earlier?" Betty repeated. "When? Where?"

The boys looked down at their feet. Guilt seemed to weigh heavily on their young shoulders. Hannah wondered if she should step in or allow Betty to confront her brothers.

"Boys?" Betty's voice was firm.

"Daisy said she wanted to go look at Steven's puppy," Mark answered.

Betty's voice softened. "That doesn't sound so bad. Why didn't you want to tell me?" She laid her hand on the little boy's shoulder.

"'Cause that's not all they are doing." Mark rubbed his bare toe in the dirt.

She nodded. "Go on, you can tell me. You aren't in trouble, Mark."

Hannah admired Betty's patience with her brothers. Personally, she wanted to shake them and demand where the girls were, but knew Betty's wisdom in dealing with the boys calmly would get better results.

"They were going to the river with the big kids. I told Daisy her grandma wasn't going to like that," Mark answered.

Hannah turned to look off in that direction. Trees blocked her vision of the water and she could only think the worst. "How long have they been gone, boys?"

Mark shrugged. "I don't know. The big kids came back right before the races started."

"But you didn't see Daisy or Mary?" Betty asked.

Both boys shook their heads.

Hannah wanted to ask why they hadn't mentioned this sooner, but said, "I'll go tell Opal." She turned to the little boys; they stood with their heads bowed. "Thank you, boys, for telling us."

She hurried back the way she'd come. No longer was she worried about Daniel and Levi's relationship. Now all she cared about was finding those two little girls.

Disappointment filled Daniel when he realized Hannah was no longer at the races. Had she been disillusioned with him for losing to James? That seemed unlikely. He'd enjoyed the day with her. She'd teased him and played games all the while, never acting as if winning was her goal. So he doubted Hannah would be upset with him for losing.

Where was she? He searched the crowd for the top

of her head. Hannah was short; he might not be able to find her in the melee.

Daniel decided to go to higher ground and look down upon the crowd. Maybe he could spot her then. He climbed up on the judge's stand and searched.

He saw Opal rushing around like a chicken with her head cut off. Concern filled Daniel as he hurried down and headed in her direction, dodging many men and women who laughed and shouted as a new group of riders lined up to race.

The smells of fair foods, bodies and horses filled his nostrils as he jogged in her direction. "Opal!" he called when he saw her several feet away.

She turned toward him and the fear in her eyes sent a chill down his spine. Had something happened to Hannah? He knew his mother was with Levi because they'd said something about going to get a bite to eat before heading home.

"Oh, Daniel, have you seen Daisy or Mary? I can't find them anywhere and I'm starting to get scared." Opal wrung her hands.

Relief filled him momentarily. Then concern took its place. "No. When was the last time you saw them?"

A flush scored her cheeks. "Lunch. I was manning the pie-eating contest after that and the girls were playing quietly. I told them not to leave without me. Normally, they do just what I tell them to." Tears filled her eyes. "But when I came back to get them, they were gone, and I can't find them anywhere."

"We'll find them," Daniel promised. "I'll round up some of our men from the ranch and start looking. They can't have gone far." He turned to go get Tornado and find Cole, Tucker and Sam. He'd seen all three of them within the past half hour and knew they'd be watching the races.

"Opal!" Hannah's sweet voice stopped him.

Daniel spun back around and saw her running toward them. Her face appeared flushed and worry lined her eyes. Had she found the girls?

"I think Daisy and Mary are at the river." She held her side and panted for air.

Opal let out a little squeal of fear. "Why do you think that?"

Hannah stood there, trying to catch her breath. "The Parker boys said that they went down there after lunch."

Daniel looked deeply into her eyes and knew his reflected the same worries. What if they drowned? What if they got lost? So many what-if questions raced through his mind that he couldn't keep up with his thoughts.

His gaze moved to the sky. The sun would be setting in a few hours; they needed to find the children. "I'll go get the men and start a search party." He took a moment to lay his hand on the older woman's shoulder. "Don't worry, Opal. We'll find them." Daniel prayed it wasn't an empty promise.

Chapter Twenty-Six

The sun was beginning to sink in the west. Daniel ran his hand through his hair and down the back of his neck. He'd failed again. Daisy and Mary were nowhere to be found.

The sound of his men calling their names as they searched the river and riverbank drifted to him. He could tell some of the men had traveled a long way downstream, for their shouts were faint and distant.

God, where are they? Why aren't they answering our calls? Why would You let this happen? Daniel knew it wasn't his place to question the Lord, but he couldn't stop his thoughts.

Cole rode up beside him. In a low voice he said, "If they fell in the river, boss, there's no sign of them now."

The water's happy gurgling seemed to mock him. What was he going to tell Opal? He nodded to Cole and replaced his hat. "Have the men search one more time, then we'll head back to town." He looked to the woods that separated him from the grandmother who was waiting for him to keep his word.

He prayed that maybe the girls had headed home or

were in town playing, although he knew both scenarios were unlikely.

Shortly after rounding up enough men to search the river, he'd sent another set to search the town. Granite wasn't that big of a community, and already that search party had returned empty-handed. If the missing children were in town playing, they were well hidden.

In the distance he could hear women calling the little girls' names. Unlike his men's voices, theirs were loud and strong, almost as if they were standing a few feet away. And yet he knew they were calling from the fairgrounds.

Cole returned and shook his head. "No sign of them, boss."

Daniel sighed. He'd have to tell Opal that her granddaughters were still lost. With a heavy heart, he ordered, "Let's head back."

He felt the eyes of the other men on his back as he led the way. Did they see him as a failure? Or were they feeling like failures, also? Why did God allow men to feel this helpless? Was it a form of punishment for not being stronger for their families?

They entered the meadow and saw the women lined up and facing them. Daniel stopped Tornado and stared. Had the whole town come out to search for the little girls?

Hannah stood off to one side. She cupped her hands around her mouth, then nodded. In sync, the women cupped their hands around their own mouths and called, "Daisy! Mary!"

Then he noticed men lined up behind the women Once more Hannah cupped her hands around her mouth, nodded and yelled, "Daisy! Mary!" This time the area thundered as men's voices blended with the women's.

He didn't know what to think. Hannah waved to him and then pointed, indicating that she wanted him and his men to join the crowd of people yelling for the little girls. Chills ran down his arms at the magnitude of support the town was willing to provide to find two lost children.

Daniel dismounted and watched as his men followed his example. He located his mother and Opal standing on the side. Opal's shoulders shook and tears fell from her eyes. She looked older, more tired than when he'd left her.

Once more voices echoed, "Daisy! Mary!"

How long did Hannah plan on keeping this up? Wouldn't the little girls have answered by now if they heard them? Daniel moved to stand on the other side of Opal. He draped an arm around her shoulders and then looked to Hannah.

She raised her hands again, looked to the woods then instead of nodding, she broke into a run. His gaze swung to where she was heading.

From the woods came Daisy, holding Mary's free hand. Mary dragged a rag doll on the ground, as if she didn't have the strength to hold it in her small arms. Daisy clutched pages of paper in the hand that wasn't clinging tightly to her little sister's. Their hair was sticking up all over, with twigs in it. They seemed to be walking slowly, and from this distance he wasn't sure, but it looked as if they'd been crying.

Daniel heard Opal gasp and felt her tug away from him. He watched as she ran after Hannah. The crowd gave a shout of joy and men's hats filled the air. Then everyone was running toward the children and their grandmother.

Daniel continued to stand there, unsure what his feelings were. He knew without a shadow of a doubt that he was thrilled that the girls were safe and back in their grandmother's arms. But he also felt disappointed at himself, proud of Hannah and her quick thinking and angry with a God who could make him feel so helpless.

Hannah moved away from the girls and let their grandmother envelop them in her arms. Opal cried tears of happiness. Hannah backed even farther away as the whole town of Granite celebrated the children's safe return. Her eyes searched out Daniel.

He stood where they'd been calling out for the girls. She couldn't read his expression, but sensed his emotions were running high. When had she become so attuned to his feelings? Hannah ignored the question and walked to him.

When he didn't say anything, she noted, "They seem to be fine."

Daniel nodded.

"I'm sure the doctor will want to examine them, but then we can go home." Hannah didn't know why she'd said that. She simply felt that one of them needed to be talking.

Fear like none she'd ever felt before had entered her heart at all the possibilities of what could have happened to the girls. She'd suppressed those feelings, but now felt them rising up like an underwater spring breaking forth with the first spring thaw.

Daniel stepped forward and enfolded her in his arms. She felt him shaking and knew what he was going through. For the first time, Hannah didn't care what others might think. She held on to him and started sobbing with relief.

"Don't cry. You're right, they are fine." He echoed her earlier words against the top of her head.

She pulled away and smiled up at him. "Daniel, these are tears of joy, not sorrow. God brought them back to us."

He released her and stepped away. "You really believe that?"

Hannah stared at him. "You don't?"

Daniel shook his head. "I don't know what to think or believe anymore." He turned to leave.

She couldn't let him go. Not like this, not with him doubting God. Hannah grabbed his arm and walked with him. Where he was going didn't matter. She laid her head against his arm and held on tight as they walked to Tornado. The well-trained stallion stood where Daniel had left him.

Daniel grabbed the reins and led the horse as they continued walking. "Why would God allow them to get lost like that in the first place?" he demanded.

Hannah shrugged. "I don't know, Daniel. God is God. I can only speculate that maybe He wanted to bring the town together, or maybe to teach the girls to obey their elders. Or maybe He wanted me to make myself visible enough to help two little girls and not care what other people thought of how I walk. Only God knows why He does what He does."

Silence hung between them. Daniel continued to walk to where they'd left the wagon. He gently removed her arm from his and then tied Tornado to the side.

Hannah sat down on the wagon bed. "Are you angry

with God over Daisy and Mary, or over something or someone else, Daniel?" She held her breath, not sure that he'd answer her.

Daniel sat beside her. "I've been struggling with Gracie Joy's death for years. My sister was ten years old when she died. Today I realized there are only four years' difference between her and Daisy's ages. Hannah, that is too young to die!"

She nodded. "Yes, Gracie Joy was young when she died, but I have to believe that God knows what He's doing when He takes children from our lives."

Daniel turned sorrow-filled eyes upon her. "What was He doing when He took Gracie Joy?"

Daniel's pain begged to be soothed. Hannah wasn't sure she was the one with the answers. She'd never lost a sibling to death. Unable to look upon his sadness, she turned her attention to the other horses that stood beside wagons, waiting for their masters. She silently prayed. *Lord, please give me the words Daniel needs to hear.*

They sat in silence. The crickets began singing, horses stomped their feet to ward off flies and sounds of rejoicing and happiness rang out from the fairgrounds. Daniel stared off into space, as if some inner war raged inside him. Hannah listened for God's answer.

When it was obvious that God wasn't going to speak audibly to her, she took a deep breath and asked, "Daniel, didn't you tell me Gracie Joy had a limp like mine?"

He nodded and turned to look at her again. "It was similar. Only she was born with hers."

"Was she sick a lot?" Hannah wasn't sure where she was going with her questions but continued on anyway, still praying God would supply the right words.

Again, Daniel nodded.

"Did the doctor know what was wrong with her?" Hannah knew she was pressing.

His jaw hardened as he shook his head. "What are you getting at, Hannah?"

She captured her lower lip between her teeth. "Well, if the doctor didn't know why she was sick, we know God did. He knows everything. So maybe He took her so that she wouldn't suffer here." Hannah folded her hands in her lap.

Sadness enveloped her like a dark, thunderous cloud. She knew one conversation wasn't going to convince Daniel that God was merciful, and perhaps that was the reason He'd taken Gracie Joy to heaven early. Hannah could only pray that he'd listen to her and learn to lean on the Lord's faithfulness again.

Daniel tipped his head back and looked up into the night sky. Hannah followed his example and did the same. Thousands of stars shone down on them. She knew Daniel held a lot of hurt and bitterness in his heart. Would he ever give it all to the Lord? And if not, could she marry a man who didn't believe in God the way she did?

Chapter Twenty-Seven

The next morning, Hannah swung the empty egg basket as she walked to the ranch house alone. It wasn't quite light out, but she hadn't been able to sleep and had decided to get an early start on the chores. Her thoughts returned to the day before. The trip home had been quiet.

Both Daisy and Mary were fine. They'd gotten lost in the woods when the older kids had left them. Daisy had quietly told Opal that she'd wanted to draw a tree and that Mary had played house while she'd done so. When they'd decided to go back, neither could remember the way.

Opal had hugged Hannah later, saying the girls might still be lost if it hadn't been for her idea to call to them as a group. She'd assured Opal it hadn't been anything special, because deep down Hannah knew it had been God's plan. She didn't believe she would have considered it on her own.

That thought led to Daniel, not that her thoughts ever strayed from him long nowadays. He'd chosen to ride Tornado back instead of sitting with her on the bed of the wagon. Disappointment had been a bitter pill to swallow. She was sure the others must have thought they'd had an argument, since he'd remained silent the whole trip back.

They'd dropped her off at the school. Both Opal and Bonnie had said goodbye. The little girls had fallen asleep, and Levi had offered her a smile before they'd proceeded on home. Daniel hadn't said anything to her at all.

The sun began to peek over the horizon as Hannah opened the henhouse door. She stood back, for normally the chickens squawked and flapped their wings as they came out.

This morning, nothing happened.

Her first thought was that perhaps a fox had gotten into the henhouse, but there were no signs of blood or clumps of feathers. She looked about the empty house in confusion, noting that even the eggs were gone.

Jeb would have locked the hens up the night before, and even if he'd forgotten, they would have been in the yard. And there would still be fresh eggs to collect. So where were they?

The hair on the back of her neck stood on end. Hannah backed out of the henhouse and looked about. She walked back through the gate and studied the ground.

Horse tracks marred the dirt. The earth looked to be churned up, as if whoever rode the horses had left fast, kicking up clumps of soil as they left. Hannah felt fear climb up her spine and into her hairline.

The egg basket slipped from her cold fingers. She gathered her skirt and ran toward the house, her thoughts racing. What if whoever had been at the henhouse was still there? Were they watching her? Why would anyone steal all the chickens? What were the Westlands going to do for eggs? The last question was easy to answer: they'd either get more hens or go into town and buy eggs from the general store.

Daniel stepped around the barn just as she reached the corner. Hannah couldn't stop and ran right into him. He grabbed her arms to keep her from falling.

"Slow down, Hannah. What are you doing here? I was just on my way to come get you. What's wrong?" He continued to hold her until she became steady on her feet.

Hannah held on to his forearm. "Someone's taken all the chickens," she blurted.

"What!" He looked over her shoulder. "Are you sure?"

She released him and straightened. "Of course I'm sure. I was just there. If you don't believe me, go look for yourself."

Daniel handed Tornado's reins to Jeb, who had rushed out to join them. "I believe you. I'm just surprised." With long strides, he headed back the way she'd come.

Hannah trotted along behind him. "There are horse tracks in front of the gate and it looks like they left in a hurry."

Daniel knelt down and studied the tracks. "Yep, I'd say at least three horses."

She wanted to say, "I told you so," but didn't.

Jeb joined them again. "I closed them in last night, Daniel. I'm sure of it."

"No doubt about that, Jeb. Whoever took them did it under the cover of darkness. The chickens probably didn't even make much of a fuss." Daniel stood and pushed his hat back.

"Why do you think someone would steal the chickens?" Hannah picked up the empty egg basket. Chills popped up again on her arms as she realized she'd come out here alone. What if she had intercepted whoever had stolen them? Would they have taken her, too? Or done worse?

Daniel took her elbow and turned her toward the barn. "Let's get you into the house, and then I'll round up some men and see how far we can follow the tracks."

"I can walk by myself, Daniel. Go get your men. I'll tell Opal and Bonnie about the chickens."

She ignored the low growl that came from his throat.

"Hannah Young, you are too stubborn for your own good. Stay in the house with the other women." He turned away from her. "Jeb, make sure she makes it inside," he ordered, and then strode off ahead of them.

His ramrod-straight shoulders told Hannah how angry he was at her. She sighed and followed a little slower.

Jeb fell into step beside her. "Don't let his blustering get to ya. The boss is worried. When men worry, we grump at those around us."

Hannah felt a smile tug at her lips. Jeb was right. Daniel was worried about the chickens; why else would he have been so rude to her? "Thanks for the reminder."

When they got to the back door, Jeb held it open for her. "Miss Hannah, please stay in the house with the womenfolk until we get this figured out." Without waiting for her answer, he turned and jogged back to the barn.

Heat hit her in the face as she walked into the

kitchen. The smell of bacon filled the air. Opal stood by the stove, turning the meat in a skillet. Daisy sat at the table, drawing on a piece of paper with her charcoal, and Mary played with her doll under the table.

"Good morning, Opal, girls."

The older woman smiled. "You're here early this morning."

Hannah nodded. "Yes, I couldn't sleep. Where's Mrs. Westland?" She sat the egg basket down on the counter.

Opal looked up from the frying bacon and into the empty egg basket. Concern laced her face. "I think she's still upstairs."

"Daisy, would you be a dear and go ask Mrs. Westland if she'll come down for a few minutes?" Hannah asked. She walked over and washed her hands in the basin.

"Yes, Miss Young." Daisy slid from her seat. "I'll be right back, Grandma."

"That's all right, honey," she said, as Daisy rushed through the door. "And don't run!" Opal called as an afterthought.

A few seconds passed and then they heard the sound of Daisy's feet pounding up the stairs, proving she'd either not heard her grandmother or chose not to listen. Opal sighed. "That girl is going to get the best of me yet."

Hannah dried her hands. "What can I do to help this morning?"

Opal stared at her. "For starters, you can tell me what's going on around here. Where are the eggs?"

"I'll explain when Bonnie gets here." Hannah tilted her head toward Mary, who continued to play with her doll.

Opal nodded and returned to dishing up fried bacon. "Well, I suppose you can pull the biscuits from the oven and butter them for me while we wait, if you don't mind."

Hannah moved to the stove and reached for a pot holder. She pulled the fresh bread out and inhaled its yeasty aroma. Carefully, she opened each hot bun and stuffed butter inside.

She said a quick prayer for Daniel and the rest of the men's safety. Hannah wondered if they had caught up with the chicken thieves yet.

Her gaze moved to the door when Bonnie entered. As usual, Daniel's mother was dressed in a riding skirt and a pretty blouse. Her hair was pulled back into a braid and her wrinkle-free face shone.

"Good morning, Hannah. Daisy here says you want to see me." She patted the top of her head.

"I do." Hannah looked to Opal, who had stopped working on the bacon and stared openly at them. "This morning I went to check the henhouse for eggs, and all the chickens and their eggs are gone. The men have requested we stay inside until they find them."

Both women stared at her as if she had two horns and a tail. Bonnie was the first to recover. "The chickens are gone?"

Hannah nodded. She continued to butter the biscuits as if nothing was out of the ordinary. Thankfully, the little girls continued to play, unaware of the tension in the room.

"Grandma, can I go draw in the big eating room?" Daisy asked.

Opal looked to Bonnie, who nodded her consent. "Yes, dear, but don't touch anything."

"Can I go, too?" Mary asked, scrambling out from under the table.

"Yes, but you two be good in there," Opal answered. She returned to the bacon and finished dishing it up.

Hannah grinned as Daisy complained to her sister, "Why do you have to do everything I do?"

Mary shrugged. "'Cuz."

The door shut behind the children and Bonnie sighed. "I wonder who took the chickens. And when?" She eased into a chair. "Daniel and I had thought the raiding of cattle was over and that the rustlers had moved on. Now we have chicken thieves?" Her green eyes searched Hannah's.

"It looks that way." Hannah finished buttering the rolls.

"They must have done it while we were all at the fair. We should have left someone behind to watch the place." She shook her head. "I can't believe some no-good poacher took off with my hens!" Bonnie slapped the table hard.

Opal jumped, almost unsettling the platter of bacon in her hands. "I'm sure the boys will find them." She placed the food on the sideboard and wiped her trembling hands on her apron.

The sound of the front door opening and men's voices filling the dining room had the women scrambling. Bonnie charged out the kitchen door.

Hannah placed several biscuits on a separate serving dish and then grabbed the remaining rolls. Opal scooped up the bacon and a platter of pancakes Hannah hadn't noticed before. Hannah held the door open for her friend.

"Did you find the no-good thieves?" Bonnie demanded, with her hands planted firmly on her hips.

Daniel shook his head. "Nope. We lost their trail, too." He removed his hat and hung it on a nail beside the door. Then he walked to the table and sat down. "We'll keep looking after breakfast. I sent the men back to the cook shack. We'll regroup in a little bit."

Bonnie nodded. "I was hoping those thieves were long gone," she exclaimed. "And now they took my hens."

Levi went to the table and sat down, too. He winked at the little girl sitting in Hannah's seat.

Opal placed the platter of bacon and the pancakes on the table. "Come along, girls," she called to her granddaughters as she headed back to the kitchen.

Hannah followed her to see if there was anything more she could do before sitting down to eat with Daniel and his family. She watched the little girls hurry to the kitchen table. They normally didn't stay with their grandmother and didn't understand that she had to serve the Westlands first.

Opal's face revealed that she felt torn between her duty and her granddaughters.

"I'll fix the girls' plates, if you will take the coffee out," Hannah said, as if this was an everyday event.

Relief eased Opal's tense features. "Thank you, Hannah. You are turning out to be a really good friend."

Hannah laughed. "I try." She hurried to get the girls settled, aware that she was missing the conversation going on in the other room.

Opal returned a few minutes later and smiled. "I don't know if I could have done it without you this morning," she declared, pouring each of the girls a glass of fresh milk.

"Sure you could have, and by the way, you say that every morning." She grinned at Daisy and Mary. "I'm sure these two would have been good helpers."

Daisy sat up straighter in her chair. "I would have, but I don't think Mary would. She drops stuff."

"Would, too," her sister muttered.

Opal laughed. "Now, don't argue, girls. You both would have done fine." She placed a napkin in each of their laps.

Hannah now understood Bonnie's desire for grandchildren. It was obvious that Opal loved hers very much. The little girls were sweet and gave their grandmother unconditional love. Bonnie wanted that same kind of love, Hannah felt sure.

Opal gave each of the girls a kiss on her head and then looked up at Hannah. "You best get in there. They are waiting for you."

Chapter Twenty-Eight

Daniel tossed his napkin down on the table and pushed his chair back. "Hannah, I'll send Jeb over to walk you back to the schoolhouse. Since we're not sure what is going on, I'd appreciate it if you'd not wander the ranch alone today." He gave her what he hoped she interpreted as a stern look, the no-nonsense kind.

She gave him a pretty smile, but the blue in her eyes blazed hotter than a blacksmith's forge. "Tell him to give me a few minutes. I want to help Opal clean up before I leave." Hannah pushed away from the table and walked into the kitchen.

"Daniel, you have got to stop talking to her like that. She's not a child," his mother scolded.

"No, she's not. But when she's my wife she'll have to learn to do as I say. Might as well let her practice now." He knew he was being senseless, but he wasn't about to back down from his mother now. Besides, the fear of a cattle rustler or chicken thief getting hold of Hannah made him want to protect her, and for him to do so, she needed to stay in the house.

Bonnie gave an unladylike snort and pushed away from the table. "Yeah, just like I did your father."

Levi chuckled and walked to the door. He pulled his hat down and grinned. "Keep making her angry, big brother. My bride will be here any day now." He whistled happily as he walked out the door.

Daniel followed him onto the front porch. "Well, until she does, you still have to do what I say, too." He pulled himself up on the back of Tornado.

He felt pretty smug until Levi answered, "Not so, big brother. Up until today, I did it out of respect, and because you needed the help." He swung up onto Snow's saddle. The rigid way he held himself testified to the anger that was rising up in him, and then he added, "I'm done. You can run the ranch on your own from now on. But if my bride shows up before you and Hannah marry, you can kiss the Westland Ranch goodbye. I will have no ill feelings about taking it away from you." With that, Levi turned his horse toward town and rode away.

The curtain in his mother's bedroom window fluttered. Daniel saw her standing there and turned Tornado away from her accusing eyes. He hadn't meant to bully Hannah or annoy his brother with his arrogance. He'd spoken to both of them in anger and fear.

Under his watch, cows had been butchered and rustled, and now the hens had been stolen. He was angry that he couldn't find the men responsible. Daniel felt as if he couldn't protect his own family. He just wanted Hannah to be safe. The only way to keep her safe was to have her stay with other people. As for Levi, they'd bickered since they were kids. Daniel hadn't expected his brother to take this so seriously.

Now Levi was not going to help on the ranch, leaving him a man short. Daniel's gaze went back to his mother's window. He wanted to blame her for the rift between him and his brother, but knew that was unfair. She hadn't told him to act so prideful.

He rode Tornado to the barn and called for Jeb.

"You need something, boss?" Jeb came out of the barn. A piece of hay dangled between his teeth, much like a cigar.

Daniel tried to remember a time when the old man wasn't chewing on a piece of grass or hay. He shook his head at the silly thought. "I need someone to escort Miss Hannah back to the schoolhouse when she's ready. Would you mind doing that?"

"I reckon I can babysit for you."

Hannah would have a fit if she heard him say that. Daniel laughed. "I wouldn't say that too loudly, Jeb."

Jeb grinned up at him. "Say what?"

Daniel shook his head. "Nothin', I reckon." He enjoyed mimicking Jeb's turn of phrases.

"I'll get her home safe, Daniel. Don't you worry about that." Jeb ambled back into the barn.

Daniel turned Tornado toward the cook shack. More than likely he'd find most of his men still there. As he rode, his thoughts turned to his little brother. He'd have to apologize, and prayed Levi would accept it.

But not right now. Levi had looked mad enough to take on a bull when he'd ridden away. Daniel could only assume his brother was headed to town.

The question came to him. Would Levi ride into town and marry the first available girl? Worry ate at him. If Levi did, there was a good chance Daniel would lose the ranch. He didn't have time to dwell on the problem long, because Cole came galloping up to him.

When Cole galloped anywhere, it usually meant he was on his way to report more trouble. Daniel braced himself for the next round of bad news.

"Boss, we've found another butchered yearling in the west pasture." Cole's eyes said there was more bad news coming.

"And?"

"And it's a fresh kill. So fresh we can butcher it and save the meat." His gaze moved to the ranch house.

Daniel looked to the house, also. Hannah was coming out the kitchen door. He watched as Jeb walked to meet her. At least he knew she was safe, meaning he could focus on the poachers.

He felt Cole's eyes upon him. Daniel turned to look at his best friend. "Let's get busy."

Cole swung his horse around to ride alongside Tornado. "You're in love with her, aren't you?"

Was he in love with her? Daniel glanced over his shoulder and saw that Jeb had brought two horses from the barn: Brownie for Hannah and another mare for himself.

Hannah pulled herself into the saddle with ease. No longer was she the woman who'd been afraid to get too close to a horse when he'd first met her. Her skin had tanned over the past six weeks and she'd slimmed down. The riding skirts she now wore looked better on her than any dress a woman could wear.

His mouth went dry again at the thought that she could have stumbled on the poachers this morning. Who knew what they might have done to her? He cared about her deeply, but love?

Cole laughed. "If you have to think that hard on the question, then I'd say the answer is yes."

Daniel turned back around. His friend was right, but he didn't have time to dwell on feelings of love. And he definitely wouldn't confess it to her until after this business of poachers and rustlers was put to rest.

"Really, Jeb. I can make it from here." Hannah tried to convince the old man to return to the barn.

"Miss Hannah, my job is to get you back home safely, and that's what I'm a-doin'," he answered without looking at her.

She had to admire him for wanting to see his assignment through. "All right." Hannah followed Jeb's mare through the woods. She could point out that she'd walked to the ranch house in the dark this morning, but knew that wouldn't sway the old man to give her some solitude.

At least school wasn't starting for a couple hours, she told herself. She'd be able to settle down for a few minutes and reflect on her morning. Not that she really needed to.

She'd found the henhouse empty of chickens and eggs, told Daniel and gave the news to Opal and Bonnie. She'd listened as Daniel discussed with his mother what needed to be done to make the ranch more secure, and had been told by Daniel to not wander about the ranch alone.

Hannah knew he was thinking of her safety, but he needn't have talked to her like a child. She still fumed at the thought. The schoolhouse came into view; Hannah knew she needed to get her emotions under control before her students began arriving.

Jeb stopped on the edge of the woods. "I'll watch until you wave," he said.

She nodded. "I'll tie Brownie up, then wave good-bye."

"Fair enough." He moved the piece of hay from one side of his mouth to the other.

"Thank you for bringing me back." Hannah waited for his nod, then proceeded to the lean-to, which stood a good fifty feet from the schoolhouse. Brownie snorted when she tied her to the post.

Hannah left the saddle on. "I'll have one of the older boys unsaddle you in a little while." She patted the brown mare's rump and walked around to the front of the schoolhouse, where she waved to Jeb.

She watched as he left.

Was it her imagination or was she hearing chickens squawking? Hannah heard her puppy, Buttons, yelping inside the school.

She hurried up the front steps to let her out. It wasn't like her to forget to put Buttons in the pen Daniel had built for him in the back. Even now she would have sworn she'd done just that this morning, before leaving.

Hannah opened the door and feathers almost choked her as the air pulled them toward her. The roar of the dog barking and hens making a big ruckus filled her ears. What in the world was going on? She stepped inside and found the little black-and-white puppy chasing chickens.

They were everywhere! What were the chickens doing in the school? She made a grab for Buttons and slipped. Her feet flew out from under her and Hannah landed with a resounding thud on her back. She looked upward and saw frightened birds flapping about the room, trying to get away from the loud puppy.

"Buttons! Stop!" She tried to sit up.

Buttons ran over, licked her face and took off after another hen. His sharp yelps filled the air and caused her ears to ring. The angry and frightened chickens were making quite a fuss of their own.

"Buttons! Stop!" Hannah yelled again. She managed to stand up among the flying feathers and flapping wings. Her feet slipped in the goo that seemed to cover every inch of the floor.

The dog raced around her ankles. Hannah grabbed his wiggling body and hurried through the building to the backyard, where she promptly released the excited puppy in his enclosure.

She rushed back inside. The chickens were settling down, but still clucked and fussed. A few hopped and flapped their wings in aggravation.

Hannah groaned. Now that they had calmed down her other senses kicked in. The smell of poop and hot birds became overpowering. She covered her nose. What was she going to do with them? Why were they here? And how was she going to gather them all up?

The only pen she had was the one Buttons now occupied. She couldn't put the hens with him. But they couldn't stay in the schoolhouse; the children would be arriving soon. Hannah wanted to sit down and cry. She knew the mess had to be cleaned up and something done with the chickens.

She inhaled to calm her nerves and quickly wished she hadn't. She thought about closing the door and going to Jeb with her problem, but then remembered Daniel telling her not to wander about the ranch. Since the hens were in her house, that meant the poachers had been, too.

But why had they let Buttons inside?

Hannah didn't have the answers. She walked to her desk and sat down. The chickens now studied her as they moved about the room, making soft clucking sounds. Hannah was sure they were complaining about their new living quarters.

She laid her head on her desk and muttered, "Lord, what am I going to do now?"

Chapter Twenty-Nine

Daniel looked up at the bright sun, which was straight overhead. They'd worked all morning cleaning up the butchered calf. He'd given most of the meat to the men and taken the rest up to the big house.

He and Cole had tried to track the poachers but had lost their trail along the river. All morning he'd thought of Hannah and knew he owed her an apology for his rude behavior. Tornado pulled at the bit, wanting to go faster. Daniel held him at a steady walk.

What was he going to say to Hannah? Should he confess he loved her? Tell her that he'd been praying over the words she'd said the night before? Explain that it would take time for him to understand his new feelings toward her and God? He leaned against the saddle.

The sound of children's laugher could be heard as he got closer to the school. Assuming they were at recess, Daniel was shocked when he saw them walking in a straight line, holding a chicken, with some holding two.

Hannah was leading them. She held four hens upside down by their feet, two in each hand. Where had she gotten the hens? He stopped Tornado and watched as they passed, seemingly unaware of him and the horse.

Daniel could hear the hens clucking now. He spotted Opal's granddaughters in the line. Daisy cuddled a hen close and stroked its head. Mary walked beside a ten-year-old boy who held a hen in each hand, the same way Hannah carried hers.

"Stay in line, children. You older ones make sure the younger pupils are keeping up. Once we get these chickens put away, we'll start on reading."

Groans filled the air. "Can't we have a break, Miss Young?" one of the children asked.

"No, we cannot. All we have done today is chase these poor hens around. We need to get some school-work done." She glanced in his direction, raised one chicken-filled hand and gave a sort of wave.

So she had known he was there. He called to her, "Miss Young, what, may I ask, are you doing?"

Hannah stopped walking. The children stopped, too. "Why, can't you tell, Mr. Westland? We're taking your hens home," she called back.

"I see that. But how did you get them?"

"Someone was gracious enough to leave them in the school for me to find." Hannah began walking again. "Come along, children." Her students followed her like baby ducks.

Daniel felt the hair on his arms and neck stand on end. Was she saying someone had broken into the school and left the chickens inside? What if she'd been there?

He fell in line after the last child. When they got to the henhouse, Hannah put her chickens inside and then instructed the children to do the same. She supervised, and assisted them if they needed help. The kids seemed to be having fun as they laughed and watched the chickens reacquaint themselves with their home.

"You've all done such a wonderful job, why don't we go to the house and see if Miss Opal has any cookies we can have?" Daniel suggested.

Though his question drew a loud, excited response from the little ones, Hannah frowned. "I don't know if Opal made cookies today, Mr. Westland."

The children all became quiet at this new information. He grinned at them, then answered, "I was just up at the house and the smell of sugar cookies tells me she did."

Once more the children shouted happily. "My grandma makes the best cookies," Daisy yelled above the cries and laughter.

Hannah laughed, too. "Well, thank you, Mr. Westland. I do believe we'll take you up on your kind offer." She lined the children up again, from youngest to oldest, and marched them toward the ranch house.

Daniel couldn't help but admire the way she worked with the kids. After they each received a cookie, Hannah took them out to a tall oak tree and had them sit down in the cool grass to enjoy their snack. When everyone seemed content, he pulled Hannah to the side.

"I'm sorry for the way I spoke to you this morning, Hannah. I was worried about the chickens and the men who had taken them, and I came across as bossy. I'm sorry." He laid a hand on her shoulder and looked deep into her eyes.

She smiled up at him. "Thank you."

He gently squeezed her shoulder and then dropped his arm, tucking both hands in his back pockets. "The chickens were in the school when you got there?" He hoped he sounded casual.

"Yes, and so was Buttons. I know I put her in her pen this morning, but someone let her into the house with the chickens." She watched the children eat and play. "But, I can't figure out why."

"I can. They probably thought he'd accidently kill one, and then once she tasted the blood she would kill the others." Daniel felt sick to his stomach at the thought of what Hannah would have found if Buttons had done that.

"Oh, that's horrible." She shook her head in disgust.

Daniel nodded. "I agree, but whoever is doing these things isn't nice."

Hannah turned her attention back to him. Her blue eyes searched his face. "What else happened?"

How did she know something else had happened? Was he that easy to read? Or did she just have a sixth sense about these things? "Someone killed a calf in the west pasture."

"Oh, Daniel, I'm so sorry." Hannah glanced at the children again.

Now was the time to make his suggestion. "Hannah, I think you should move here with Mother, or come live with me."

Her head snapped back around. "What? Why?"

He pulled his hands from his pockets and pushed his hat back. "I'm worried about you living alone. Those men were in the schoolhouse today." Daniel wanted to just tell her she didn't have a choice, but he expected she'd come to that conclusion on her own.

"No. I won't give them the satisfaction."

That wasn't what he expected. Why couldn't she be

sensible and do as he asked? He studied her profile as she watched the children. Her lips had thinned and her jaw was set. In this mood, he doubted he could talk her into moving. Daniel knew when he was whipped. "Please, think about it."

The children were getting restless. Hannah looked at him. "I'll think about moving in with your mother. You and I will have to be married before I move in with you."

"That's all I can ask." He knew that Hannah was never going to be alone at the school again. If she didn't move to his mother's, then he'd guard her every night and put a guard on her every day. Now that he'd found her, Daniel couldn't let someone take her from him.

Hannah spent the rest of the afternoon thinking about Daniel's request. The thought that someone had been in her living space gave her the willies.

But she also enjoyed her freedom. She and Bonnie had become friends, but Hannah couldn't forget that Daniel's mother was the reason she was living in the schoolhouse to start with.

She wasn't surprised after school when Bonnie rode up on her horse. Moments later, she entered the building.

"Good afternoon, Bonnie. What brings you out here?" Hannah had learned that Daniel's mother was a straightforward person who appreciated the same characteristic in others.

Bonnie came forward and sat in one of the front desks. "Two reasons. One, to say thank you for bringing the hens home, and two, because I want to invite you to move into the ranch house."

Hannah asked the question that burned in her mind. "Did Daniel put you up to asking me?"

"No. As soon as I heard what happened this morning I knew it wasn't safe for you to live alone here. I know I wasn't the most sociable person when you first came, and I'm sorry about that. I really would like it if you'd move into the house." Bonnie ran her finger over one of the grooves in the wood of the desk.

Hannah knew how hard it was for this woman to ask, and she was grateful for the invitation. "I'll think about it, but honestly, I'd rather stay here and face my fears."

"Do you realize how much alike you and I are?" Bonnie asked, looking her in the eye.

Hannah laughed. "I suppose we are a little."

"A little, nothing. You know your own mind and don't back down until you're good and ready. I'm the same way." Bonnie stood to leave. "But Hannah, I've often regretted not using common sense in some of my decisions. Please don't make the same mistakes I have." With those words, she walked out the door.

What had she meant? Did Bonnie think Hannah was acting foolishly by staying? Maybe she was. Was she being prideful in thinking she could take care of herself? All her life she'd done things on her own. Why did this have to be any different?

Memories of being held hostage with her friends Rebecca and Eliza sent a fresh chill down her spine. Even then she'd tried to be brave and strong. Until today, she'd not let those memories frighten her. She'd put on a brave front for her friends and believed that God would keep her safe.

For the first time in a long time, Hannah was scared.

She silently prayed, *Lord, I have to be strong. I will continue to lean on You and believe that You will keep me safe.*

Daniel rode into town with a heavy heart. Hannah still refused to move out of the schoolhouse, and Levi hadn't been home in three days. Daniel's job today was to find his brother, apologize and see if he would return to the ranch.

Why did everyone in his life have to be so stubborn? His mother's anger at the rift between him and Levi caused her to stubbornly refuse to talk to him about anything other than the basic workings of the ranch. Levi's stubbornness kept him in town, when he should be home, working. And Hannah's determination to prove she could take care of herself had Daniel's gut in knots.

He'd already stopped at the hotel, looking for Levi, and been told to check at the new boardinghouse on Elm Street. Daniel mounted Tornado, all the while wondering when the boardinghouse had opened.

From the looks of Elm Street, several businesses had popped up over the past week or so. He scanned each sign as he passed it: Bob's Mercantile. A Sewing Room. The Bakery.

He stopped in front of the next business, a three-story house with a wooden sign on the front lawn that proclaimed Beth's Boarding House and Restaurant. He recognized the simple scroll design around the name as Levi's handiwork.

Tornado's saddle creaked as Daniel stepped out of it. He tied the stallion to the hitching post and walked up to the boardinghouse and restaurant. A bell dinged over his head as he entered.

The fresh smells of baking breads and pastries filled his nostrils. A large wooden counter rested against the back wall, with another of Levi's signs hanging behind it that read Registration Desk. To his right was a stairway that he assumed led up to the rooms for rent, and to his left a door opened to a dining area filled with tables and chairs.

Daniel walked to the dining room door. A long glass counter rested just inside, with fresh baked cakes, cookies and pies temptingly displayed. His mouth watered and his stomach rumbled.

"I see you've found me," Levi said from behind him.

He turned to look at his brother. "It would appear so. I'm hungry. How about lunch?"

Levi nodded. "Sounds good. Beth makes the best meat loaf in town."

Daniel followed him to a table beside the window. A young woman hurried over and offered them coffee. She poured it into their cups and asked what they'd like to order.

"We'll have the meat loaf special, Beth," Levi answered for the both of them.

Daniel smiled up at her. "I'd like a slice of pie, also."

"I'll be back with your food in a few minutes." She left their table and headed for the kitchen.

"She seems awful young to be running a business," Daniel observed as he watched her leave.

Levi laughed. "Beth's a little older than you'd think."

"Single?"

"Widowed." He blew on his coffee.

Daniel did the same. "Interested?"

"Nope, just a friend."

"You make friends fast. I don't recall her living here." Daniel sipped at the hot, strong brew.

Levi set his cup down. "You didn't come to town to talk about Beth Winters. What are you here for, Daniel?"

The moment he'd been dreading had arrived. "I came to apologize and ask you to return to the ranch." He swallowed hard. "I need you."

A smile brightened Levi's face. "Yes, you do."

"This is serious, Levi. After you left, Cole found a butchered calf in the west pasture. And every day more and more of our cattle are disappearing." Frustrated, Daniel ran his hand over his neck. "Also, someone broke into the schoolhouse and put the chickens inside. Hannah wasn't there, but she could have been."

Levi sobered. "That is serious. I've been asking around and we seem to be the only ranch getting hit. Why do you think that is?" He raised an eyebrow, as if to tell Daniel he must have made an enemy.

An older couple entered the restaurant and took a seat several tables over from them. Beth returned with their food and silverware. After serving them she headed to the new customers' table.

Daniel said a quick prayer over their food before answering. "It would appear to be an inside job. The bandits seem to know where we are at all times." He picked up his fork and started to eat.

Levi dipped his fork into his mashed potatoes. "That's what I thought, too. As soon as I hit town Monday morning, I put the word out that I was through with the Westland Ranch. I've been doing odd jobs about town and listening to the men, but haven't heard anything that will help us."

Daniel studied his brother as they ate. "So that's why you left? Not because I made you mad."

"No, you made me mad, but on the ride to town I got to thinking about the poachers and the rustlers. I'm sure the two are connected, but like I said, if anyone knows anything about it they aren't talking."

They continued their meal in silence. Beth brought them each a slice of apple pie and fresh coffee.

Daniel took a generous bite of his pie and sighed. "The food here really is good. I think this is going to be my new favorite place to eat."

Levi laughed and finished his dessert. "I'm glad you like it. When you're done, we'll go upstairs and I'll show you my room. You might want to stay here sometime, too."

Daniel finished his pie and coffee and then nodded at Levi. "Ready." He looked about for a place to pay for the meal.

"Don't worry about the bill. I'll cover it." Levi pushed away from the table and led the way up three flights of stairs.

"They rent out the attic here?" Daniel asked, stepping over the threshold of Levi's room. He shut the door behind them. When he turned around, he realized it was more of a suite than just a bedroom.

Levi grinned over his shoulder. "Nope, these are my private quarters. I own the boardinghouse and restaurant."

An hour later, Daniel was heading back to the ranch. He was impressed that Levi had bought a couple houses in town and turned them into businesses. Over the past few months, while Daniel had been worrying about the ranch, his brother had been starting businesses in town.

According to Levi, he owned Beth's Boarding House and Restaurant and Bob's Mercantile. Daniel's little brother didn't want anyone to know that he was the owner, so he had helped a few people down on their luck make it look as if they owned the property. He paid them a salary and gave them room and board. Only the bank, himself and now Daniel knew what Levi had been up to.

For a brief moment, Daniel had thought his little brother had given up the notion of owning the ranch. But as Levi said, that wouldn't matter to their mother. Another reason he hadn't advertised that he'd been buying property in town was because she would have a fit if she knew. Bonnie Westland might get so angry she'd sell the ranch. Neither of them wanted that.

Levi assured Daniel that when his mail-order bride arrived, he'd be getting married. But for the life of him, Daniel couldn't understand why. Levi seemed content in town. Was his brother really going to marry just to inherit the ranch?

Daniel frowned as he mentally went over their discussion. Levi had assured him that if he won, Daniel would always have a home on the Westland Ranch.

He didn't want just a home. Daniel wanted ownership of the ranch, and he wanted to marry Hannah.

Chapter Thirty

Hannah tossed the dishwater out the back door and sighed. Two weeks had passed since Daniel had apologized. He'd made a point of spending each evening with her, and Hannah knew she'd fallen deeply in love with him. The truth was she'd loved him for a long time, but was just now accepting the truth of it herself.

Over the past two weeks she'd prayed and reasoned with the Lord to not let it be true. But when it came down to it, Hannah realized that whether Daniel ever loved her or not, she'd always have the Lord's love.

Daniel was handsome, good with children, a hard worker and a good kisser. What more could she ask for? She knew he'd be a kind husband and father.

Yes, if he showed up tonight, Hannah planned on telling him of her love and asking if he would mind having a Thanksgiving wedding. She smiled at the thought.

She'd started to turn from the open doorway when she saw Daniel and Tornado burst through the tree line on the other side of the stream. The stallion continued across it at a fast pace. Daniel's face was set with determination.

He slid to a halt by her back door. "Hannah, I need you to go to the house and see if Levi is still here. If he is, tell him to gather up the boys and meet me at the canyon on the back side of the ranch."

"The one you took me to a while ago?" she asked, reaching to grab her shawl off the nail beside the door.

Tornado stomped his hooves and Daniel tightened his grip on the reins. "Yes. Tell him I think I've found where the rustlers have the cattle corralled. I can't take them on by myself—there are too many of them. I'm going back to watch them. If they leave I want to see which direction they go."

Dread entered her heart that he'd found them and now planned to spy on them on his own. "I'll go, but why don't you wait for Levi and the other men?"

"I don't have time to wait. They could be rounding the cattle up now, about to leave. Just hurry. I don't want to lose those cows or the men who stole them." With that, Daniel spun Tornado around and splashed across the stream once more.

Hannah prayed that Levi and the men hadn't already headed to town. She knew Friday nights were when they all went and spent their hard-earned money. If worse came to worst, she and Bonnie could back Daniel up. They might not be men, but both of them were good with a gun.

Deciding she didn't have time to saddle Brownie, Hannah took off at a run through the wooded area. Halfway there, she was wishing she had taken the time to get her horse. When she got within sight of the house, she ran toward the barn and yelled, "Jeb!"

The old man came to the door. He didn't look well.

His face was pale and he coughed hard. "What's wrong?" He wiped his hand across his mouth.

"Have you seen Levi?" She stopped and held her aching side.

Jeb nodded. "Yep, he and Mrs. Westland headed to town about two hours ago."

Hannah groaned. Just as she'd feared. "What about the rest of the men?"

"Gone, too. What's got you all riled up?" Jeb began coughing again and couldn't seem to stop.

Hannah knew he'd be no help to Daniel. With all the coughing he was doing, the rustlers would know they were being spied on in no time. It was up to her. She'd send him for Levi and then go help Daniel. "Jeb, do you feel up to going after Levi and the men?"

"I ain't goin' no place till you tell me what's goin' on around here." Jeb coughed again.

"Daniel has the rustlers spotted down in the canyon. He needs Levi and the men to come help him bring them in. I need you to go get them. Please."

He jerked his hat off and slapped it against his leg. "Why didn't you just say so, instead of hem hawin' around? I'll go get Bessie and get down there and help him." Jeb rushed back inside the barn.

Hannah ran after him. "No! You'll give him away with all that coughing you're doing. He's not going to do anything but watch them until you and the ranch hands get back. Please, go get them."

Jeb continued saddling his horse. "And if I go get the men, what are you gonna do?" He cinched the strap and then looked at her suspiciously.

She didn't dare tell him that she intended to help Daniel. The old man would fuss and waste more time. "Pray. So please hurry." Hannah planned on praying a lot.

He walked the horse out to the yard and then mounted. "We'll be back as quick as we can. You stay here." Jeb didn't hang around to see if she'd follow his orders.

Hannah waited until he was out of sight, and then ran back to the schoolhouse. A stitch in her side pulled as she rounded the corner and entered the lean-to, where Brownie was stabled. Hannah hadn't lied to Jeb. She prayed for Daniel's safety while she saddled the mare. She led her to the back door, tied her reins to the porch and hurried inside.

She jerked on a dark blue top and a matching riding skirt. Hannah took a deep breath and then purposely made her way to the suitcase under her bed. She pulled out the gun she'd never told anyone on the Westland Ranch about.

Her father had given it to her years ago and taught her how to fire it, if need be. Hannah prayed she wouldn't need to use it. She tucked the gun into the waistband of her skirt and then went back to Brownie.

It took another thirty minutes for her to get to the base of the canyon. Hannah's heart pounded in her ears as she worried that Daniel might have already been discovered. She nudged Brownie up the steep incline, praying she wasn't making too much noise and that any guards wouldn't hear her.

Twilight was gathering when she reached the rim of the canyon. Unsure where Daniel might be, she scanned the area. Hannah spotted Tornado and dismounted, leaving Brownie tied to a tree. Gravel scraped Hannah's palms as she crawled to the edge and looked down on the campsite.

They were camped beside the stream that she and Daniel had visited not so very long ago. She counted nineteen men in various stages of drunkenness, but thankfully, she didn't see Daniel in their midst. Hannah wondered where the guards were posted. So far she hadn't seen any, but that didn't mean they weren't there. Her gaze scanned the other ridge and the caves it concealed. Nothing. Where were they?

Daniel crept up behind Hannah. He quickly reached over and pressed a hand across her mouth, preventing her from crying out. She struggled for a moment until her eyes grew wide with recognition.

"Take it easy, Hannah," he whispered. "If we are discovered now, we're as good as dead."

Hannah nodded. Her whole body seemed to shake, but he didn't have time to comfort her right now. Daniel released her and returned his focus to the men below. Until she'd shown up, he'd been keeping his gaze on Ben Wilder. He spotted Ben standing beside the fire now.

"Where are the guards?" Hannah hissed.

Daniel frowned at her. "Below us."

She seemed unaware of the danger they were in. Didn't the woman know there was a time to talk and a time to be silent? He wanted to wring her neck for showing up here, and without the other men.

He placed a finger over his mouth to indicate silence. Daniel had questions of his own, but now wasn't the time to ask them. Such as where were the ranch hands? What did she think she was doing here? And was the woman crazy?

He shifted his focus back to the group below. Ben still stood by the fire. Then he did the unexpected: he turned slowly and stared in their direction. Ben couldn't possibly have seen or heard them, but he seemed to know they were there, just the same. "Get down," Daniel rasped.

Instead of doing as she was told, Hannah raised her head and whispered, "Uh-oh, I think he saw us. I can pretend I'm alone. I'll go down there and you go get help."

"Oh, no, you won't." Daniel pushed her head down and returned his attention to Ben. The rustler sniffed the air like a wolf after prey before taking a step in their direction.

Hannah scrambled to her feet before Daniel could drag her down. When he made to grab her, she jerked her leg from his grasp, kicking him upside the head while doing so.

Blackness pooled around his brain and enveloped him in inky darkness. His last thoughts were, *When I get my hands on that woman, I'm going to kill her, if Ben Wilder doesn't do it first.*

A few seconds, possibly minutes later, he awoke and raised his aching head. Hannah was almost to the bottom of the hill. Her boots slipped and slid, announcing to the world she was there.

Daniel struggled to focus his eyes and gather his wits. When he did, he realized that she'd left a gun lying on the ground beside him. She was headed into the lion's den unarmed.

Did she think he needed the added gun to protect himself? Hadn't she noticed he had a rifle? A rifle that wouldn't help either of them at this distance.

He watched, helpless, as Ben walked forward to meet her. She held up her hands. Every instinct Daniel possessed urged him to go after her, but he didn't dare move. He had no alternative at the moment but to trust Hannah with his life and her own. Whatever her plan, it was inadequate, but he didn't have a better one at the moment.

Daniel couldn't read Ben's expression from this distance, but could tell by the way he held himself that he didn't believe whatever she was telling him. Hannah talked fast, and Daniel would have given the Westland Ranch to know what she was saying, but all he could make out was the nervous tone of her voice. Her actual words were just beyond the bounds of his hearing.

He watched like a man trapped in a bad dream as Hannah allowed herself to be ushered into the den of thieves. She didn't as much as glance in his direction. Hannah was acting as if she were alone, to save his sorry hide.

Careful not to move too quickly and risk drawing attention to his hiding place, Daniel wiped the blood from the side of his head, trying to think what to do next. He couldn't leave her there alone, as she'd suggested he do. Daniel continued to watch the scene below, praying he'd think of a way to get her out of there.

One of the rustlers rose shakily to his feet, approached Hannah and spoke to her. Ben's pistol flew into his hand as if it had wings. He shot the man, then waved the gun around and looked at the other rustlers. It seemed as if he was daring one of them to do the same as their companion. Daniel wished he could understand what Ben was saying to the men around him, but his voice was too low.

No one moved, including Hannah. She stood bravely, watching the scene about her. The woman had spunk, and when this was all over, Daniel planned on revealing to her all that was in his heart.

But for now, he did what he could, and that was pray for Hannah's safety, that they'd get out of this alive. If they did, he'd tell her that he loved her, and ask her to forgive him for not confessing his love sooner.

Lord, please keep Hannah safe. I love her so much, and now know that I can't protect her myself. But I trust that You can.

Metal scraped against metal as a gun cocked behind him, putting an end to the silent prayer. Before he could draw his weapon, roll over and fire, Daniel felt the cold barrel press against the nape of his neck.

The bandit snarled, "So the little lady didn't ride into the canyon alone, after all. You think the boss will be angry with her for lying to him, or happy that she brought a Westland with her?"

Hannah watched in horror as Daniel stumbled into camp. A trickle of blood ran from his temple and down the side of his face. The guard behind him grinned over his captive's shoulder. She ignored the bandit. "You're hurt," she said, and took a step toward Daniel.

Ben caught her around the waist and jerked her back against his dirty chest. The smell of sweat and other body odors gagged her. "Hold up there, little lady." His whiskey-tainted breath turned her stomach.

Daniel actually smiled like a crazy man touched in the head. What was wrong with him? Didn't he know they might both be dead by morning if they didn't think of something quick? "Tell me, Ben, when did you start taking women prisoners?"

The rustler tightened his grip on Hannah. "When they started walking into my camp. This one's mighty pretty, don't ya think?"

She watched the green in Daniel's eyes turn into a blazing fire. His jaw tightened, but he held his smile. "Yep, you're holding the woman I love just a little too close, Ben. I suggest you let her go now."

The rustler tossed his head back and laughed. The sound was cold and malicious in Hannah's ears. "Aw, now, ain't that just about the sweetest thing you've ever heard, boys? He loves her."

Everyone laughed except Hannah and Daniel. Hearing him say he loved her *was* the sweetest thing Hannah had ever experienced. She just prayed he'd be able to say it to her again. "I love you, too, Daniel. I have for a long time."

Ben jerked hard on her midsection, cutting off her air. "Naw, I'm keepin' this one for myself."

Daniel growled deep in his throat. His fist knotted and he took a step forward. "Tell me, Ben, when did you first come up with the plan to become a rustler? Was it before or after I hired you as a horse trainer?"

The outlaw pointed his gun at Daniel's gut and snarled. "Do you really think yours was the first ranch I stole cattle from? Don't flatter yourself, Westland. I've been rustling cattle since I was a pup."

"You still look like a pup to me, Ben. Only now you smell like a wet dog who's been fed too many bones from its master's table." Daniel laughed as if he'd just told the funniest joke.

Hannah was shocked when Ben's men joined in the

laughter. Some slapped their knees and others simply hee-hawed.

Rage boiled in Ben, and he howled. He tossed Hannah to the side as if she were a wet rag and spun around, aiming his gun at the men. "Keep laughing and I'll put a hole in all of you, even if I have to hunt you down to do it."

It wasn't an idle threat. They'd already seen him gun down one of their own. They all became as still as tombstones, even those who were half-drunk.

She couldn't believe Daniel would continue to taunt Ben, but he did. All humor had left his face. Now only anger showed there. "Aw, what's the matter, Ben? Did I hit a nerve?"

The rustler turned toward him again, much like an angered bear. He pulled back the hammer on his gun and grinned evilly. "I'm going to enjoy killing you, Westland."

"You're nothing but a thieving coward, Ben," Daniel taunted in a quiet voice. "Without that gun in your hand, you'd be just another man. And not much of one at that."

Hannah knew he was trying to buy them time, but did he have to get himself killed in the process? The look in Ben's cold eyes said he'd shoot him in a heartbeat. She scrambled to her feet. "Daniel, don't do this."

He ignored her. Hannah decided to try to scare Ben into leaving. She hurried to his side. "Ben, stop this while you still can. There's a posse on its way. Run before they get here," she pleaded.

He, too, ignored her. "Cade! Come take this gun. I'm going to kill me a Westland with my own bare hands." Ben kept his gaze locked with Daniel's.

Daniel began rolling up his sleeves. He looked calm

and in control. Hannah shook with fear for him. Even if he beat Ben, what was to stop one of the other men from killing him? Several had their guns drawn and pointed at him.

One of the bandits moved from the crowd and walked over to stand beside Ben, reaching out his hand to take the gun. As Ben handed it over, he ordered, "Cade, if anyone tries to interfere, shoot him—" he glanced in Hannah's direction "—or her."

"All right, boss." Cade took the weapon, stepped back to where he could see all the men and trained his gun on Hannah.

"Please, stop." Hannah grabbed Ben's arm.

A chilling shriek of rage erupted from the rustler just before he backhanded her hard across the face. Blood spewed from her nose. She stumbled backward, arms flailing, and then fell.

Daniel bellowed like a mother bear out to protect her cub and lunged for Ben. Both men went down with the impact and rolled on the ground, Ben fueled by whiskey and rage, Daniel by anger, sheer desperation and the will to survive.

"Daniel, no!" Hannah screamed. She clutched the bridge of her nose to stop the flow of blood. *Dear Lord, please send help. I know he loves me and I can't lose him. Not now.*

The sound of men and horses echoed in the canyon and the rustlers scattered, running for their own mounts. But the battle between Daniel and Ben intensified, growing fiercer with every blow and every grunt of pain.

Hannah heard shouts in the gathering darkness and gunshots all around them, but she couldn't take her eyes off the two men fighting in front of her.

They rolled close to the fire, then away, and suddenly Daniel was on top of Ben. His fist continued to pound into the rustler until the man stopped moving. Only then did Daniel seem to realize the fight was over.

He looked up and saw Hannah, then stood and stumbled toward her. He wrenched her into his arms, crushing her against his chest, and she wanted to melt into him. Then the sobs began.

Hannah clutched Daniel's shirt and felt him press her head into his shoulder, all the while murmuring soft words of love to her. If they weren't in such an ugly place she would have assured him again of her love for him also, but all she could do was cry. Tears and blood soaked into his shirt, but neither seemed to notice.

The posse, led by Levi, poured into the camp. Hannah wasn't ready to face anyone else at this time. She buried her face deeper into Daniel's shoulder.

Levi jumped from his horse and walked slowly toward them. "Are either of you hurt?" The concern in his voice touched Hannah's heart.

Daniel answered, "No, we're going to be fine now. I'm glad you showed up when you did." He hugged Hannah tighter, if that was possible.

"Me, too. We got twenty-one of them. They hardly put up a fight. Truth be told, I think most of them are too drunk to know they've been captured." Levi's gaze landed on Ben. "Is he dead?"

Daniel wiped blood off Hannah's lip. "No, but he will wish he was tomorrow." Daniel stroked her hair and then kissed the top of her head. "I need to get you home."

Levi nodded, just as Jeb stepped out of the darkness. "Boss, a bunch of us figure on taking the prisoners to town, where they can spend the night in jail," the old man said. "That all right with you?" A cough racked his body.

"I'd appreciate it if you'd see Hannah and me home, just in case someone got away and plans on jumping us from behind." Hannah knew Daniel wanted Jeb with them only because the old man was sick. If he followed them back to the ranch, he'd be in bed before the posse even made it to town. She looked up at Daniel and touched his cheek. His heart was in his eyes when he looked back at her.

Jeb puffed his chest out a little. "Be my pleasure to be yer rear guard, son."

The two men shared what looked to Hannah like a nod of respect. She laid her head back on Daniel's shoulder. Weariness enveloped her.

Someone had rounded up Brownie and Tornado and led them into camp. Daniel hoisted her into the stallion's saddle before climbing up behind her. He reached around her and took the reins. Adam, one of the ranch hands, took charge of the little mare.

Hannah relaxed and leaned her head against Daniel's shoulder. His strong arms about her, and the gentle rocking of the horse, seemed to wrap her in peace. This was where she always wanted to be.

"Daniel, I'd like to have a Thanksgiving wedding. Would that be all right with you?" she murmured.

He kissed the top of her head. "No. I love you more than I can say, and I would like to get married tomorrow morning."

Hannah sat up a little straighter in his arms. "Tomorrow is too soon. I don't have time to—"

His laughter cut off any further words she was about

to utter. "I was teasing, Hannah. I do love you more than anything in the world, including this ranch. So if you want a Thanksgiving wedding, that is fine with me."

"Daniel, before we can get married, I have to ask you something." She didn't want to, but Hannah knew she had to ask him this.

"Sure, honey. What would you like to know?"

Hannah snuggled into him, praying she'd be able to continue to do so after he answered her question. "Do you remember what we talked about at the July Fourth fair?"

"Uh-huh."

"Do you still feel the same way?"

The soft sound of the horse's hooves hitting the hard soil filled the silence between them. She felt Daniel's arms tighten around her. "No. A wise woman once told me that 'God is God.'"

Hannah looked to the heavens and enjoyed the sight of the stars as they twinkled above. She thought she knew where Daniel was going, but didn't say anything, she simply listened as he continued.

"It took me a while to understand what she meant, but I've been in constant prayer about it and believe she was saying that I have to give everything to Him. I can't control what happens to people, but I can trust God to do what is right." Daniel kissed the top of her head again.

Hannah smiled. He had found his way back to trusting the Lord. "I'm glad."

He hugged her and nuzzled the side of her neck. "So am I."

After several quiet moments he asked, "What about you?"

"What about me?" Hannah yawned.

"Are you really ready to get married? Or are you postponing until Thanksgiving just to make sure I really love you?" Weariness echoed in his soft questions.

Hannah sat up and leaned back enough to look him in the eyes. "I've never told you why I wanted you to hear you say the words that you love me, and that was wrong." She swallowed and then continued. "Daniel, when I was about sixteen a man named Thomas asked me to marry him. I assumed he loved me and I thought I loved him, too, but then on the day of our wedding, in front of all our friends and his family, he told me he couldn't go through with the wedding and that it was because he knew deep down he didn't love me." She paused.

Daniel opened his mouth to say something, but Hannah stopped him by resting her fingers across his lips. "I know now that I didn't love him. Tonight when I saw you fighting with Ben, I realized what true love is. It's not wanting the one you love to get hurt. It's putting your life before theirs. Tonight when you came into camp, you didn't have to say you loved me. I saw it in your eyes and it was as if I was looking into your soul. You love me. I know it and you know it. That's all I've ever wanted." She continued to search his eyes, and when he didn't say anything, Hannah pressed on. "I love you, Daniel. I have for a long time, and if you really want to get married tomorrow, I'm willing."

He removed her fingers from his lips and shook his head. "No. I believe you. I want you to have the perfect wedding, Hannah. It will be the one I want you to remember and I want it to be the last one you'll ever

have. I love you enough to wait for when you're ready."
Daniel leaned forward and kissed her forehead.

Hannah raised her head so that their lips connected.
Her mouth was sore from the slap Ben had administrated, but she relished the feel of Daniel's lips on hers.
At last she knew that she'd found the love she'd been
searching for so long.

Epilogue

Hannah tossed the bouquet over her shoulder with laughter. The sounds of squeals had her turning around to see who had captured it. Her eyes locked with Jo-Anna's as the young woman clung to the flowers. Hannah smiled.

Everyone knew JoAnna and James McDougal were planning a spring wedding. Once she'd learned that James had been in love with her since they were children, she'd quickly lost interest in Daniel and fallen for him. For that blessing, Hannah was thankful.

She turned her eyes back to her groom. Daniel was the handsomest man there. He wore black trousers, a green shirt and black boots. The green in the shirt brought out the color of his eyes—eyes that seemed focused only on her this day. Her day. Her wedding day.

The minister announced, "You may now kiss your bride."

Daniel reached out and snagged her around the waist. He whispered in her ear, "Congratulations. You are now Mrs. Daniel Westland."

Hannah giggled and nuzzled his face with hers.

"Those are the most beautiful words I think I've ever heard," she whispered back.

His deep green eyes gazed into hers before he claimed her lips. She accepted the soft kiss and felt her heart leap at the knowledge that this man truly loved her. To Hannah's way of thinking, the kiss didn't last long enough.

The guests all shouted with joy as they parted. Friends and family rushed forward to congratulate the happy couple. Hannah looked at Daniel, who still seemed to only have eyes for her.

After everyone had eaten and the wedding gifts were opened, they said their goodbyes and headed to the wagon that awaited their departure. After all these months, Hannah was headed to her new home.

Daniel gently helped her up onto the seat and then hurried to the other side to climb aboard.

Levi handed Hannah's bag to Daniel and shook his hand. Since the brothers seemed at a loss for words, Hannah leaned in front of Daniel and kissed Levi on the cheek. "Thank you for remembering my bags." She smiled at him.

Levi dipped his head forward and grinned before stepping away from the wagon. Daniel nodded at his brother and then clicked his tongue and the horses moved forward.

Hannah scooted closer to him and leaned her head on his shoulder. One strong arm snaked about her waist and pulled her close.

"I never thought this day would arrive after our run-in with Ben and his gang. I'm so glad it is over and you are now Mrs. Daniel Westland." Daniel gave her waist a gentle squeeze. "I love you, Hannah."

At home in his arms, Hannah lifted her face close to his for a kiss. A mischievous twinkle entered his eyes and he grinned. Daniel leaned down and rubbed his nose against hers. She giggled and said, "And I love you."

* * * * *

Dear Reader,

Hello, and thank you for picking up Hannah and Daniel's story. I've never lived on a ranch, but have lived on a small farm. I love horses, cows and chickens. If you haven't guessed, I'm a country girl at heart, much like Hannah. Today I prefer reading about life on the farm, rather than living it. Getting up before dawn to feed livestock, having to help the animals get out of the mud and grunge, isn't something I enjoy as much anymore. But I do admire our hardworking men and women who live on ranches and farms. So whether you are a country girl/boy or not, I hope you enjoyed reading how Hannah and Daniel overcame their fears as they lived their lives on the ranch.

Feel free to visit me on my website and blog, www.rhondagibson.net. My email address is rhondagibson65@hotmail.com. I'd love to hear your thoughts on Hannah and Daniel's story.

Warmly,

Rhonda Gibson

Questions for Discussion

1. When Hannah learns that Daniel didn't get her letters stating she wanted to marry only for love, she decides to stay and wait for Daniel to fall in love with her. Would you have stayed if you were her? Why or why not?

2. Daniel fears having children because of the hardships of ranch life and his sister's death. Do you think his reaction is normal?

3. Some people might think Hannah was being unreasonable in her demand for unconditional love. If you had been Daniel, would you have sent her back? Explain your answer.

4. Daniel's love of the ranch has him doing things he'd never normally do, such as sending for a mail-order bride. Have you ever wanted something so badly that you would do anything to get it? Or to keep it? If so, what?

5. Hannah grew up thinking her father turned her away because she was no longer perfect and couldn't help on the farm. Have you ever felt as if someone you loved turned against you because of something that happened in your life? How did you overcome that?

6. Hannah was afraid Daniel would be like her father and leave her or send her away if she didn't

prove to him she could be a rancher's wife. Is there something in your life that you feel would disappoint someone else and cause that person not to love you? If so, have you taken it to the Lord and asked Him to help you?

7. Daniel had to learn to trust God with those he loves. Was there a time when you were afraid to trust God with a problem or person in your life?

8. Hannah doesn't understand how Bonnie can make her two sons compete for the ranch. Have you even met someone who did this? Or seen a situation that you thought was wrong but later realized was all right for the people involved? Did it change the way you thought about that person? Or the situation?

9. Daniel feels he has to catch the rustlers before he can tell Hannah that he loves her. How do you feel about that? Should he have waited? Why or why not?

10. Did this book fit your idea of what life was like on a Texas ranch in the 1800s? Why or why not?

REQUEST YOUR FREE BOOKS!

2 FREE INSPIRATIONAL NOVELS
PLUS 2
FREE
MYSTERY GIFTS

Love Inspired
HISTORICAL
INSPIRATIONAL HISTORICAL ROMANCE

YES! Please send me 2 FREE Love Inspired® Historical novels and my 2 FREE mystery gifts (gifts are worth about $10). After receiving them, if I don't wish to receive any more books, I can return the shipping statement marked "cancel." If I don't cancel, I will receive 4 brand-new novels every month and be billed just $4.74 per book in the U.S. or $5.24 per book in Canada. That's a saving of at least 21% off the cover price. It's quite a bargain! Shipping and handling is just 50¢ per book in the U.S. and 75¢ per book in Canada.* I understand that accepting the 2 free books and gifts places me under no obligation to buy anything. I can always return a shipment and cancel at any time. Even if I never buy another book, the two free books and gifts are mine to keep forever.

102/302 IDN F5CN

Name   (PLEASE PRINT)

Address   Apt. #

City   State/Prov.   Zip/Postal Code

Signature (if under 18, a parent or guardian must sign)

Mail to the **Harlequin® Reader Service:**
IN U.S.A.: P.O. Box 1867, Buffalo, NY 14240-1867
IN CANADA: P.O. Box 609, Fort Erie, Ontario L2A 5X3

Want to try two free books from another series?
Call 1-800-873-8635 or visit www.ReaderService.com.

* Terms and prices subject to change without notice. Prices do not include applicable taxes. Sales tax applicable in N.Y. Canadian residents will be charged applicable taxes. Offer not valid in Quebec. This offer is limited to one order per household. Not valid for current subscribers to Love Inspired Historical books. All orders subject to credit approval. Credit or debit balances in a customer's account(s) may be offset by any other outstanding balance owed by or to the customer. Please allow 4 to 6 weeks for delivery. Offer available while quantities last.

Your Privacy—The Harlequin® Reader Service is committed to protecting your privacy. Our Privacy Policy is available online at www.ReaderService.com or upon request from the Harlequin Reader Service.

We make a portion of our mailing list available to reputable third parties that offer products we believe may interest you. If you prefer that we not exchange your name with third parties, or if you wish to clarify or modify your communication preferences, please visit us at www.ReaderService.com/consumerschoice or write to us at Harlequin Reader Service Preference Service, P.O. Box 9062, Buffalo, NY 14269. Include your complete name and address.

LIH13R

Reclaiming the Runaway Bride

Seven years and two broken engagements haven't erased
Garrett Mitchell from Molly Scott's mind. Her employer insists
Molly and Garrett belong together. To appease the well-meaning
matchmaker, the pair agrees to a pretend courtship. But too late,
Molly finds herself falling for a man who might never trust her.

Garrett is a prominent Denver attorney now, not the naive
seventeen-year-old who always felt second-best. Surely the string of
suitors Molly's left behind only proves her fickleness. Does Garrett
dare believe that she has only ever been waiting for him? The third
engagement could be the charm, for his first—and only—love.

Charity
HOUSE

Finally a Bride

by

RENEE RYAN

*Available November 2013 wherever
Love Inspired Historical books are sold.*

Find us on Facebook at
www.Facebook.com/LoveInspiredBooks

www.Harlequin.com

LIH82987

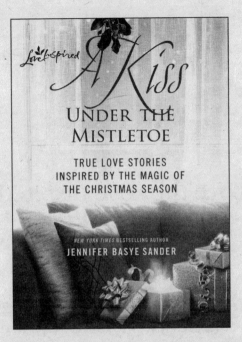

Christmas has a way of reminding us of what really matters—and what could be more important than our loved ones? From husbands and wives to boyfriends and girlfriends to long-lost loves, the real-life romances in this book are surrounded by the joy and blessings of the Christmas season.

Featuring stories by favorite Love Inspired authors, this collection will warm your heart and soothe your soul through the long winter. *A Kiss Under the Mistletoe* beautifully celebrates the way love and faith can transform a cold day in December into the most magical day of the year.

On sale October 29!

Love the Love Inspired
book you just read?

Your opinion matters.

**Review this book on your favorite
book site, review site, blog or your own
social media properties and share your
opinion with other readers!**